DISTANT TRAIN

Middle East Literature in Translation

Michael Beard *and* Adnan Haydar, *Series Editors*

Other titles in Middle East Literature in Translation

IBRAHIM ABDEL MEGID

DISTANT TRAIN

A NOVEL

Translated from the Arabic by Hosam M. Aboul-Ela

 SYRACUSE UNIVERSITY PRESS

English translation copyright © 2007 by Syracuse University Press
Syracuse, New York 13244–5160
All Rights Reserved

First Edition 2007
07 08 09 10 11 12   6 5 4 3 2 1

Originally published in Arabic as *Al Masafaat* (Cairo: Dar al-Mustaqbal al-Arabi, 1983).

The paper used in this publication meets the minimum requirements of
American Nation Standard for Information Sciences — Permanence of
Paper for Printed Library Materials, ANSI Z39.48–1984∞™

For a listing of books published and distributed by Syracuse University
Press, visit our Web site at SyracuseUniversityPress.syr.edu

ISBN-13: 978-0-8156-0859-2
ISBN-10: 0-8156-0859-4

Library of Congress Cataloging-in-Publication Data
'Abd al-Majid, Ibrahim.
[Masafat. English]
Distant train : a novel / Ibrahim Abdel Megid ; translated from the Arabic by Hosam M. Aboul-Ela.
p. cm. — (Middle East literature in translation)
ISBN-13: 978–0–8156–0859–2 (hardcover : alk. paper)
ISBN-10: 0–8156–0859–4 (hardcover : alk. paper)
I. Aboul-Ela, Hosam M. II. Title.
PJ7804.M323M3713 2007
892.7'36 — dc22   2006101394

Manufactured in the United States of America

Contents

IBRAHIM ABDEL MEGID is one of the premier novelists of his generation in Egypt. He was born and raised in the literary city of Alexandria, where the majority of his works are set. After receiving a bachelor's degree in philosophy from the University of Alexandria, he turned to the writing of fiction and immediately won attention for his experimental approach to the novel. *Distant Train*, based on memories of following his father during his shifts as a railroad engineer, stands out among these early novels. His more recent output includes award-winning novels such as *The Other Place*, winner of the inaugural Naguib Mahfouz Medal for Literature, and *No One Sleeps in Alexandria*, winner of the Cairo International Book Fair special award for best novel of the year. His novels have been translated into many languages. He currently divides his time between Alexandria and the working-class neighborhood known as Imbaba in Cairo. Megid continues to write essays for the Egyptian press, as well as fiction.

HOSAM M. ABOUL-ELA is a critic and translator who grew up in Texas and currently teaches at the University of Houston. He has published essays on topics as diverse as Naguib Mahfouz, the Egyptian media, Latin American intellectuals, and William Faulkner. His previous translation is the novel *Voices* by Soleiman Fayyad.

Translator's Acknowledgments

While working on the initial draft of this translation, I worked closely with Ibrahim Abdel Megid. His help was invaluable, as was the support of Hisham Kassem during this initial phase. I would also like to express my appreciation to my colleagues at Syracuse University Press, Mary Selden Evans, Michael Beard, and an anonymous reviewer, for their professionalism and their very helpful suggestions. Finally, I extend a special thanks to Hani Hanafy, whose help with some of the particularly elusive Arabic passages was generously offered with care and brilliance.

DISTANT TRAIN

PART ONE

Celebration

THE CHILDREN

While the fading autumn sun cruised toward the horizon, the young boys headed home from in front of the twenty houses—or, to be more precise, from in front of the tin shacks that formed the entrance to each of the twenty houses. As they had been doing throughout that summer, they left their marbles and spinning tops, unable to stay outdoors any later.

That summer they had not stayed out under the moonlight or enjoyed the glow that spread glistening over the lake in front of them. The moonglow bounced over and around stalks of cattails and made them look like shining spears. The children did not see the moonlight as it lay down across the wide empty earth in front of the coops and off to their left, exposing its resilient face and offering them comfort and reassurance. As it moved, it glided to their right toward the expansive desert, until it became invisible upon reaching the horizon. The darkness played a game of fright and intimidation with their young hearts, which yearned for that moonlight. Under its glow they would chase each other to the train station behind the twenty houses. Without the light the train station seemed like a ghost, the switch house like the sea's surface on a cloud-filled night: black, menacing. The same was true of the light poles mounted all along the railway stretching from east to west, or the thick telephone polls. Both without moonlight were like demons and evil spirits.

They were not used to seeing anything at night without the moon's glow. But this past summer the children didn't play their usual games. They did not go hedgehog hunting under the railways or fish for the beautiful freshwater bass. The boys' wet dreams, their adolescent bucking and spinning under their sheets, stopped. The nocturnal jinn of the sea did not visit. The birds did not fly in from the west. The bird traps were not even set.

All that was left were perpetual marbles and tops until nightfall. In the game of marbles they hovered over a small patch of dirt unaware of the rest of the earth or sky around them. They let their tops collide and spin on the ground at first. Then one of the boys would raise it up to the palm of his hand through a sensitive movement of his middle and index fingers. The top spun on his palm and his gaze locked onto it until his eyes spun with it, his head spun with it, time itself spun until everyone was shocked that summer had gone without ever really coming. And they asked one another when the train would come and "calm their fears," as the adults put it.

The sun did not set; it just fell in the west and died. Darkness dropped like lead over the landscape. The moon sunk into the pit of the lake's waters. Each mother spontaneously told her child, "Go to sleep at sundown, or the lake water will empty out on us and flood up to our doorways."

Then one night, as the children were just starting to retreat indoors, something strange happened. They found their mothers coming out to join them.

LAILA AND SUAD

The women had decided to celebrate. The night in which the train would return after a full year's absence was no ordinary night. Suad's face beamed happiness and anticipation. Her eyes could have conquered the world. Meanwhile, Laila's face was a solemn half-moon. The sun stopped at the western horizon, fuming with rage, angry at its perpetual motion, or perhaps, at its daily servitude to this small patch of earth. But Suad's face was lit up with joy because the moon was rising shyly from behind the waters of the lake to turn back the outermost waves of darkness in Laila's countenance.

Suad stopped in the open space in front of the shacks. She let go of Laila's hand and looked around her. There she lost herself. Drunk with the moment, she began to rock her hips. A forgotten joy crept into Laila's expression also as her eyes laughed off two tears, tears whose secret no one could have known. Suad let out an ululation as though she were greeting a bride at a wedding. The cattails shook with her shouts. A young plover called back. A flock of ducks bolted from its hiding place. A few bass jumped out over the waves, and seagulls began to hover in the empty sky filling the crushing void around the plover.

Then the other women began to gather. Tambourines appeared. Then drums. Then clapping . . . shouting . . . laughter. A circle formed, one that hadn't been seen for over a year. They sat on the ground in a huge ring with small children sitting between their legs and older ones sitting next to them.

Suad always started and ended things. She stood in the middle of that ring which included all the local women, excepting the wife of the local inspector, and the old mother of Gaber and Zeinab. The women were not surprised by the absence of the inspector's wife. They knew her husband was strict. They also understood that Gaber's mother had not come because of her missing son, who had gone out that morning and never returned. Zeinab skipped the gathering out of concern for her husband, Hamed, who also had not returned with the others at the end of his work shift.

Suad stood out and her wide eyes sparkled. She spun around like an ecstatic gazelle. Old Sheikh Masoud had failed to convince her to bring the short twirling ends of her cloak down to her ankles. So he had given up. They ended at the knees, exposing two supple calves with the whispered moonlight bouncing off her flesh at every movement; while her round heels and bare feet slipped free from her slippers and leapt forth like temptation and fire.

Suad smiled and showed the seagulls a bright row of teeth. She threw her hair back and ran her thumbs along the collar of her wide cloak around the base of her long neck supporting her round face and rested above cleavage that barely held her two exuberant, inviting breasts.

"It's as though she hasn't had to suffer through the summer."

"As though she weren't bothered when the train didn't come."

"She laughs all day and night."

"She goes to meet Fareed on the roof."

"Her husband defies death."

"Why are you stopping, Suad?"

"She's crying from happiness."

"We play the drum to keep her moving."

Laila shot her an uncertain glance as she sat down. Suad's hips shook again. Her white hood fell to her shoulders, then continued gently all the way to the ground. Her hair came loose and spilled down over the sides of her face, onto her shoulders, her back, almost to her feet. Her face looked like the sun settling in the middle of the lake waters on a brutally dark night.

Her cleavage fell open more and her white arms flew out to her side wildly. Finally, the sun disappeared completely, as the moon began climbing in a distant and feeble ascent over the lake waters toward the heavens. Only pale light from a lamp in front of the Inspector's house dissipated the darkness of the night.

Suad flew back up like a butterfly. The rhythm section regrouped. Its rhythms strengthened. When hands clapped alongside the beating of tambourine and drum, Suad spun around with strength, and sweat beaded on her face. Her pale blue undershirt began to appear at the collar of her cloak and the bottom of the cloak spun with her circles.

A chant arose, "Laila. Laila. Laila."

Shyness overtook Laila. Her mother sitting next to her smiled. It was her first time to smile since the train stopped coming. Suad came to Laila and tried to lift her up. A small boy stepped out from the circle and walked over to the lake to urinate. The lake water was not going to rise to his doorstep as his mother had threatened. Nor would a female jinn escape from it as his father suggested. Another boy left the circle to go back to his house and look for his old bird traps. Tomorrow he would try to catch a swallow. They were such stupid birds. He just whistled to draw them over to him. When he had set his traps in a large circle, he used birdcalls to lure his prey. He woke up at dawn and went to dig mud from the side of the lake to harvest a few of those earthworms birds cannot seem to resist. A third child walked away to attend to his old fishing pole. He was smiling and his eyes had brightened as he imagined the awesome, sad jumping of the colored fish while he clung to his tackle to wrench it from the water.

Meanwhile, envy was eating at the hearts of all the women. Even Laila's mother remembered her youth and became jealous. Suad and Laila's hands came together, and the crowd whispered,

"It's as though they were sisters."

But Suad's eyes were black, and Laila's were blue. Suad's face was round, but the form of Laila's was angular. Suad's hair was black, Laila's almost like amber. Laila's cloak was longer than Suad's. Secretly, she would have loved to wear a short cloak but did not dare. The day she had gone to the city with her mother, her eyes nearly popped out as they darted here and there behind the city women who floated around them like butterflies. She gaped at their swift, trembling legs, their burning eyes, their uncovered heads, their half-visible breasts. Laila read a sign that had caught her attention—she still remembered her old reading lessons—"Manstalker" it announced over a full-bodied woman with chest and legs exposed, who reclined and pushed out her breasts in loud invitation over the name of the cinema. Laila felt a burning within her chest cavity and a shudder through her flesh. She felt her thighs sticking together. She laughed. What had she been afraid of?

The women let fly a long, loud ululation, as the two dancers parted, and Suad fell next to the seated women, throbbing with exhausted laughter. She felt drops of sweat descend her body through her breasts toward her legs, joining at her belly and burning her navel, and burning her under her armpits. "Damn the both of us, Sheikh Masoud," she shouted, and laughed heartily, but the women couldn't understand the secret of her laughter as they watched Laila fall despondently.

Tomorrow, she would be jumping between the freight cars of the train and climbing atop them. Probing their salvage goods like a packrat. The soldiers would throw her out. She knew that Fareed would hate her for doing this. Could he really hate her?

He had just had a long talk with her the night before. He vowed to meet her that night before the dawn call to prayer sounded, and she promised to give herself to him then. She knew then that he really wanted her, and she wasn't afraid. He would soon be hers and hers alone—one way or another. But he wouldn't have her if she wasn't pure and clean-shaven from head to toe. But how? The train would come tomorrow, then one sorrow would pass, and a new one would begin.

The men appeared, coming out from behind the houses, having just finished their evening prayers. The women scattered dragging their children behind them. Suad grabbed Laila's hand, and the two went to the lake together. They sat by its bank and dangled their feet in the cool water. They each raised their cloak to mid-thigh. The pale light of the moon spilled down over their legs and made them glow.

"How do fish make love?" Suad asked.

But Laila seemed not to hear her. She had uprooted the stalk of a cattail and was now dragging it across the water. She was asking herself if it could be true that Suad loved Fareed also. Why hadn't he told her so the night before?

ZEIDAN

Neama, Zeidan's wife, slipped out of the circle of women during the celebration to go home and slaughter a rooster. When Zeidan got back from evening prayers he smiled and muttered something to himself. An hour later the four of them, Neama, Zeidan, their son Mustafa, and their daughter Ahlam, had crowded around their low brass table.

Neama placed their gas lamp beside the low table. She wanted them to see the cooked bird clearly. Zeidan thought to himself, "The table's nice and wide, but there's only one small bird on it, ambushed by eight hands, forty fingers, and over a hundred teeth," and lines appeared all over his dark, leathery face.

Zeidan was always saying, "Cholera was trying to take all of Egypt; smallpox concentrated on our settlement and won." Then he'd laugh darkly and mutter to himself.

He looked at his son's delicate face, which resembled Neama's. He laughed and muttered. Then he looked at the daughter's homely face, which resembled his own, and again he laughed and muttered.

When his wife scowled at him, he laughed and muttered. She said, "You're a man with no spirit," but he just laughed and muttered. When the train stopped coming and she picked more fights, he laughed and muttered. Once, she abandoned him, walking out with the two children clinging to her cloak and crying. He tried to grab her arm to stop her, but she brazenly pushed him down on his back at the front door of their shack, even though he was twice her weight. The women and men all laughed at him, as he cried like one of the children, "Don't leave me, Neama." But that night she was back, repelling his advances, and he thought back on what happened and laughed and muttered.

Neama said, "Tonight, our meal is blessed by the train."

Zeidan muttered. He reached out to tear the bird into four pieces. She started to reach for it at the same time, then he pulled back muttering.

"Did you see the army train?" she asked.

He shook his head, but she didn't understand what he meant.

"Why was there one train headed west, and another east?"

He didn't answer.

"Did you see the soldiers and weaponry on both the trains?"

He didn't answer.

"You never know anything."

"I'm hungry. Besides, you're always obsessed with the trains. We won't die without them."

He noticed then that she had saved him the biggest portion of the bird. She told him softly, "Eat it, Zeidan, to your health."

"I don't know what that young fellow Gaber's always thinking about," he said. "He's depressed these days, more than I've ever seen him."

She didn't answer him. She wasn't interested.

"He's always with Zeinab's husband, Hamed. They whisper to each other, and if anyone approaches them, they split up or stop talking," he said.

"It's really none of our business."

"Yesterday, I overheard them cursing Sheikh Masoud. Today they didn't show up."

"Eat, Zeidan. Don't get involved."

She said it irritably. But Zeidan had lost much of his appetite since he had sat down. He felt that he was missing something, and he had to figure out what it was. He asked himself what the secret of his constant imperturbability was. Then he said, "Anyway, it's good that the train will be here tomorrow. We're in terrible shape."

Wasn't all the havoc the result of the train's not coming? Zeidan had been trying to fish all summer without success. He had traversed the entire lake, near and far. One time he had felt a big fish pulling at his tackle, he had raised up, gathered all his strength, and focused all his energy in bringing the fish in. For a moment he felt such a joy enliven his body that he didn't realize that the fish failed to buckle when the cool breeze over the waves hit it for the first time. It landed on the riverbank without twisting its body or flipping itself. He went to pick it up and found it dead. He realized that the putrid smell that had suddenly filled the sea breeze was emanating from the dead fish. He turned and staggered away. He clutched his stomach as it surged toward his throat. Then he sat down and began vomiting violently.

That day he had used only the best bait: delicate, serpentine worms dug from the mud at the edge of the lake, worms with the glistening, coffee-colored skin that sparkled beneath the water and drew fish up from the darkest depths. He stopped fishing at his usual times, afternoons on workdays and mornings on his days off. He spent most of the rest of the summer wandering off on late afternoon walks among the fig orchards in the desert, never leaving until he was chased off by the caretakers. He whiled away other walks going through abandoned government orchards, transfixed by the tall windmills. He stood underneath them staring upward for long periods of time. The windmills circled before him, and he turned with them until he buckled to the ground from dizziness, chanting,

Turn, turn, O windmills,
Send the train to cure our ills.

He understood what it meant now. Our ills. All of them . . . thmm . . . thmm . . . thmmm.

"Zeidan, what is this 'them'? Aren't you going to eat?" Neama asked, surprised, and he suddenly started to pick at the breast. He bit off a piece, chewed it, found it bitter, spit it back out. He stood up and went over to the wooden couch and sat down. Neama had finished feeding the children and sent them to sleep in the entryway so she and Zeidan could be alone that night.

She brought in the large, metal cone-shaped fowarika stove, which burned wood, from in front of their hut, stepping deftly back inside as its heat seared her face. She set it down in the middle of the room and went out to the washroom. She rinsed her hands and feet, and rubbed her hair with fresh water and cheap perfume. Then she stepped back into the dark doorway and stood over her two children sleeping on mats on the ground.

Tomorrow she would be hopping all around the train. The policemen would have to chase her from car to car, until she gave them a small bribe to leave her alone. . . . No, that wouldn't happen. Arfeh would protect her so she could explore the insides of the train cars. Would she find anything in the caboose? The policemen stored coins there. She heard Mustafa asking for a drink. He had not fallen asleep yet. She filled a jar, handed it to him, and thought to herself, "If only he looked more like his father, and she looked more like me."

Mustafa gazed at her over the edge of the jar as he drank. He handed the jar back to her. She wiped off his mouth with the edge of her robe and kissed him. She covered him and began to cry. Did Mustafa understand? And if he didn't understand, why did he hate the mere presence of Arfeh?

He came up behind her suddenly as she slipped into the caboose. He locked the door before she could get out. The other door was already locked. He had prepared everything. He told her she couldn't escape from the window. She faced him like a cornered tigress. She would have given anything for a piece of steel to plunge into his head. He advanced toward her. He cocked his gun. "I'll scream," she said. "I'll kill you," he answered, "It's within my rights. You're a bunch of thieves." "It's a salvage train," she told him. "The law is the law," he answered. She tried pleading with him once, then stopped and muttered to herself, "So what?" She leaned toward him so suddenly that he thought for a moment it was a trick. He stepped back and told her to strip first. He found her acquiescent. She lifted off her dress over her shoulders; she was wearing nothing underneath it. He told her he had seen nothing like her the whole train trip. She laughed sarcastically. He began cooing at her about her firm lips, her round ass, her statuesque thighs, her provocative breasts. He told her she had unusual body control, and he promised her the whole of the next train. She stepped down from the caboose straightening her hair. She found Mustafa beneath the steps crying. The train never came after that. Arfeh settled in the area and became Zeidan's friend.

Mustafa had finally fallen asleep when Zeidan came out to wash his hands. He realized that he did so even though he had not eaten. When he came back into the room she had already gone ahead of him and thrown herself on the bed, completely naked and clean-shaven from toe to crotch. Zeidan didn't bother to strip before he climbed next to her. For some reason, he didn't feel the passion he normally felt as he ran his hands up inside her. He turned his back to her.

"Zeidan."

He didn't answer. She started to lift off his garment and she turned over him.

"Zeidan. It's a special night. Tomorrow the train comes."

His eyes were fixed on the ceiling.

"Zeidan? What's wrong?"

It was starting to rain outside. She trembled. Finally, he covered her with a wool blanket, then looked into her face gravely and said, "Leave me alone, Neama. I'm not myself. . . . And the train won't come."

ABDULLAH

That night they would celebrate tomorrow's arrival of the train. Twenty houses collected together, touching each other, virtually piled on top of each other. Anyone looking from a distance would say that some wonderful bond united them, and that a single intruder might tip the delicate balance. An outsider there would either cry or go insane. Twenty houses beyond the outskirts of the city completely surrounded by the lake waters on one side and the desert on the other. Train after train passed somewhere in the distance, but the one that they waited for was all they cared about.

They had gathered that night to meet it. Rain began to pour down. The night dragged on, and the gathering of the women continued for hours. Their bedrooms held the vague hopes of those sleeping in them but were also unsettled by an ominous wind.

That night the flame of the fowarika stove flickered like a point of communion between dreams and hopes. It crackled in a tin cone made of steel

with thick, low sides and a wide foundation. There were two round han-
dles attached to the cone made of heavy strips of tin. They divided it into
two halves; the walls of the lower half were perforated. The upper half
where the wood and fuel were placed had a lining made of yellow clay
brought from the lake's bank.

The light, portable fowarika stove had been pulled out that night from
under the straw that covered it all summer. It appeared in front of the
house with the tongues of its flames opposing the night's soft breezes. Its
smoke curled up into thick waves, dispersing in front of one house, col-
lecting in front of another, then dispersing all together. Its flames buckled,
then sparkled with spots of red. It was carried out by the women's hands,
with their long, pointed fingers, or the square hands of the men, with their
wide palms and cracked skin. Railroad workers always have cracked skin
from the heavy grease that invades their pores. They stood on wide feet
with bulging veins, swollen bones, and large, raw toes from the heavy shoes
they wore. They were always black and the toes always curled back toward
the foot over the dirt and sand caked beneath them. Mounted on the feet
were two thin legs covered with coils of thick hair. The trunk of the legs
was like a plank of wood, the wrinkled skin in back of it shaking comically
with every movement. Black, woolen long underpants hung down just
over the knee, held up by a thick drawstring. Above the waist, a brown or
black vest embroidered with white vertical stripes covered a bright yellow
or tan long sleeved shirt. By the middle of the night the fire's embers were
fading at Abdullah's house as he asked himself, "Why don't we just marry
the rabbits?"

Abdullah didn't sleep until the embers had all died. It never occurred
to him to throw water on them when he became sleepy or to dump the
ashes outside. He just sat there and fought off sleep until the fire went out
ever since his friends died ten years ago. He stood and yawned his usual
yawn. He went outside to wash at the rain barrel then came back in to pray
the morning prayer. The thin needles of a winterlike breeze pricked his
face. He stood facing his five sleeping roommates. The second time he

bent to the ground he couldn't rise up again, and he broke off his prayer with a plea for mercy. He turned. He could hear neither whispering, nor breathing. His knees began to tremble and he asked God to protect him from temptation. He turned to the East, wanting to resume his prayer, but he couldn't. So he turned back again. They were really dead. The deaths were explained later as the result of asphyxiation from the embers that had been smoldering all night in the fowarika. From that day he hadn't slept until the embers of the stove had completely died out. Then, when the night had also died out, he took the fowarika out to the haystack, listening to the sound of water drops on the roof. He came back in to find his wife still patching holes in a large basket from rope.

"You've made three baskets. Isn't that enough?"

"It's the return we've yearned for, after a long absence, Abdullah."

He looked at the two little ones sleeping motionlessly on their cots. He thought about the four others sleeping in the courtyard. The question hopped back, "Why don't we marry the rabbits?" Then he let his head drop with a heavy sadness.

"Don't worry, my son."

"But my boy's ill, Sheikh Masoud. My only son . . . and I'm over fifty."

And he heard Gaber's mother say,

O distant train
O distant train
Your return is our salvation
Your absence, tribulation.

It had been a month since the train had inexplicably stopped coming. No one knew why, just as no one knew the secret of when it might come back. Sheikh Masoud had taken him to the small mosque they had built behind the houses where the workers gathered. Each man had a story to tell about his wife and how she had miscarried—particularly when carrying a male. They insisted they were healthy, but he sensed health dissipating. He prayed with them. When he leaned forward, a tear fell on the mat and slipped between a green braid and a yellow braid.

Abdullah looked up at his wife's broad face. The tattoo on her forehead was a large circle with decorated edges. There was a small round tattoo on her chin, and a little green spot on her nose atop a bulging mole.

He asked, "Are you taking Samira along?"

"Maybe. She didn't say anything to me today. During the celebration she acted worried, even though the rest of us were dancing and clapping."

"If we just could have asked about his family, woman, or even where his village is!" he said.

She didn't answer right away.

"I'm telling the truth, Abdullah. Mursi said he was plucked from a tree. He said he works as a traveling guard on the trains, and that the train is his home, his family and his tribe."

She laughed.

"Why are you laughing?"

"I'm crying and laughing at the same time. He used to come every week with the train. Surely, he'll show up tomorrow with many gifts for Samira."

"I want to ask you about the women, and the men who guard the train," he said.

She looked at him in amazement and said, "No one has come near us. That story of Neama and Arfeh is a big lie."

"What about the others?"

"If you must know, I think Suad's the one. She doesn't go out to meet the train, but everyone knows what she does with the inspector's son on the rooftops."

He looked down as he said, "Don't take Samira with you tomorrow."

He didn't really know why he had said it. He groped at his neck and found it gaunt and shriveling. Then he added,

"Do you understand my pain and suffering?"

"You're killing yourself," she said. "Only God is omnipotent."

He walked along the rails that lead to infinity, carrying a bar over his shoulder from which hung a basket containing a hammer, pegs, and a French railroad switch. He stopped and wrapped his arm around the bar to shift the unbalanced basket, then continued along the rails. He always walked from east to west in the mornings looking for damage in the rail line. Small things he could fix himself. Large ones he marked with chalk, then he would tell the workers or the inspector about them when he came in at the end of the day, so that they could find the chalk mark and fix it the next day. The sun was always behind him as he walked. When he returned in the evenings, the sun was still behind him. It seemed to concentrate on the nape of his neck both coming and going. He would have loved to be able to see the sun just once. He knew that it moved from east to west, as he did, but was he so much faster that it could never pass him? If only he could grab it, rip its heart out, and know what sort of fire made it. No doubt Musi, Samira's long-lost fiancé could catch the sun. He traveled by train. He could smash into the sun or pass right by it. For twenty years the sun had been chasing him. For twenty years he'd asked, why does the sun circle and come back? Why doesn't it die like we do, and be replaced by another sun that could possibly come from a different direction? How he had tried when he had started out in the morning to turn back right away, but he found his feet betraying him! They refused to turn back around. They had become used to one course only over twenty years. They continued until that point in time when the sun was in the West, so it would remain behind them.

"Watch out for these soldiers, woman. Tomorrow they'll be vicious."

She didn't answer. She could hear a choking sound coming from the front. She got up and headed toward it. Then he heard her awakening their daughter: "Samira, Samira."

She grabbed her and shook until Samira ("the Beautiful," as her mother called her . . . as she even called herself) sat up. She was terrified. Her mother gave her a glass of water. She took a sip and her mother recited over her the verses, "Say: Lord of the people, Prince of people, God of the people; Lord save us from the treachery of the terrible tempter, who tempts our hearts from heaven and hearth." She rubbed her daughter's head as she spoke. Then Samira at her mother's urging laid on her right side and fell asleep. Her mother covered her with the old sheet and went back to her bed. Her husband had climbed into the bed so she climbed up as well and met him in the middle of the bed. They both could hear the heavy sprinkling outside, and they said together, "Water's running down the walls."

They got up, went out, moved the beds of the two daughters away from the walls, covered them tightly, then went back to bed.

"I thought for a second I was losing my sight," Abdullah said. "But I think it's just the weak bulb. Why don't you buy a double-strength one?"

His wife's answer stuck to her lips. The bulb was double-strength. She turned to her right and he turned to his left. They pulled their rough woolen blanket over themselves. He put his arm around her waist and pulled her toward him. As he pulled her closer she stretched herself down under his garment and began to tug at his shorts. He reached toward her. Then she suddenly said, "What's this story of a train full of Europeans passing every day?"

He didn't answer.

"Today they were saying they'd seen a foreigner kissing a woman in a passing window."

"The boy's calling you, woman."

"The boy's calling you, Abdullah."

The night ended up not so wintry. The two of them went through their motions and parted as they were about to drown in sweat. They went through the motions, then parted. She turned her back to him and cried burning tears. He turned his back silently. He stared straight ahead at the lines of leaking water on the walls. The streaks formed a vague image be-fore his eyes that seemed at times like sun rays, and at times like a train; at times a girl surrounded by dozens of hands, at times like a man walking alone behind the rail lines in the desert. His heart began to pound vio-lently. He wished Sheikh Masoud would finally call out for the dawn prayer. He wanted the Sheikh to keep calling them to prayer forever. It was as though, knowing something mysterious, he was scared like a small child asking, "Why do I try to catch the wind?"

ALI

Laila was just returning at that same time when Ali began to ask himself, "Why does she always go out just before dawn. Where is she going? Why did she leave tonight and last night even earlier than usual? Why did she come back so late?" He never thought of asking his sister before; nor would he ask her now, but he'd felt for a long time that something was wrong. Her predawn departures awakened him without her realizing it. At first, he himself didn't understand what had awakened him as the dawn drew near. But this time, like yesterday, he woke up well before dawn, and sensed her departure even earlier than usual. It would not be long until he heard Sheikh Masoud's thin, hoarse call to prayer:

> *Gather, O faithful, for the prayer*
> *Gather, O faithful, for salvation . . .*

His father never got up for dawn prayer. He was always snoring loudly, and his snoring always filled the house then forced its way outside. That could have been why he had awakened. When he finally heard the call to prayer, his father's snoring ended. A heavy silence settled in the room, so thick he could smell it on the old furniture. The mother turned over and the bed buckled under her weight. She smacked her lips and snorted a few times, then silence fell again over the room. Meanwhile, the lines on the wall in front of Ali formed many images, and Laila pressed her back up against him. Their narrow bed did not allow for a reasonable space between them. He curled up in a ball with his knees pressed against his chest without moving away from the wall. His knees always touched it. He could hardly believe his father wrapped a wool cover over his legs every night to protect him from the cold seeping through the old walls. He would not need such things once he had grown. Neither the wall nor anything else would be able to hurt him.

They had forced him to sleep early in the summer. He still remembered last summer, when he would stay up late near the one lamp in front of the inspector's house preparing his fish hooks for the morning and bird traps for the afternoon. In the evening he would bravely stride to the edge of the lake and get out the worms and put them in a can with the same piece of black clay until morning. He went back to the house and washed then went back to his friends to play games and trade jokes.

His little sister turned on the couch. Laila got out of bed to hold her, but she wouldn't go back to sleep. Every night Laila was the one to get out of bed, never the father or mother. He learned to wait for his sister's distress and Laila's trips to take care of her. At that moment he flipped over, then flipped back and felt content that he had made himself more comfortable.

Laila climbed back into bed and lay motionless on her back. Her eyes fixed on the ceiling. He wondered what she was thinking. Now she was about to do it again. He heard her muttering something, but he couldn't make it out. Always, after she got out of bed and thought for a long time, she reached out and pulled him toward her. He let himself go into her arms like a corpse. He bit his lower lip and closed his eyes so he couldn't see the wall. He put his hands between his legs and felt a sharp pang. She did not even realize that he had grown. At the beginning of the previous summer, the days had sparkled and Ali had seized the opportunity, when the house emptied, to sleep by himself on his stomach. The coarse smell emanating from his shorts no longer bothered him. At the start of the summer he had not believed all the talk of the train and the trouble it had caused. But later he believed it, and he still had a vague apprehension about the things that had been said. The train stopped coming and the fish died. Why? He couldn't find anyone who would talk about it. The rooster died. Why? The hedgehogs left. Why? He couldn't ask anyone, and Laila didn't even realize he had grown. No one knew that summer they were cursing was his summer. Now, Laila, after coming in from outside, didn't pull him to her. Was she happy the train would be coming in the morning? He hated the train. He hated its guards. He hated the women and what they were willing to do. And the men and their complicity. Still, he would go with his sister and stick close to her. He would jump from car to car like a tomcat. Crouch atop one like a hedgehog. The same hedgehog he hadn't been able to trap all summer. He couldn't forget he had bought a flashlight to help in finding them before his playmates did. There was always a hedgehog under one of the rail switches—under the strip of steel stretched between the two rail lines or between two adjoining strips of steel themselves. He was surprised that the hedgehogs weren't afraid of being crushed by an oncoming train, but when one of the boys asked him this very question he found himself answering confidently.

"The rail switches touch the ground, stupid. Before they can be switched, a person has to come and switch them. The hedgehog senses them coming and runs away."

He pleased himself with the way he had figured this out, even though he had just been asking himself the same thing. He had come to know the answer without realizing it. He began to feel proud. The rail switches that he had found the hedgehogs between were all done by hand. Never had he found one under one of the switches that could be moved from the switch house. With these switches he would always find them beneath the planks joining the two rails. When the switch took place, the planks moved above the hedgehogs without bothering them. But hand switches needed hands to switch them, he told himself, and rail workers feet wore heavy, worn shoes plastered with grease, and the men lumbered when they walked like his father.

• • •

Ali knew he was set apart from the others. He was only twelve, yet he was already tall, taller than them all. And he was stronger than all the others as well. In spite of his father keeping him out of school, he was bright. His father was deeply religious, although he never went to the mosque for the dawn prayer. He spent most of the evening reading the Quran and chanting. He would pick one of God's ninety-nine names to chant over and over. His father's chants often scared the mother. She said that one night a huge angel crashed through their roof and spread his enormous wings over his father, and Ali, sleeping near him, screamed loudly. Ali neither remembered seeing the enormous angel nor screaming, but his mother insisted he had seen the angel and that had caused him to scream, which he would not normally be likely to do since he was not one for screaming and sadness. He even remained stoic when his father was depressed by "the poverty and humiliation of life" as he called it. He only saddened when he saw Laila depressed. When he noticed her tears he had to restrain his own. But tonight she was not depressed. She lay still next to him while he himself curled up in a ball.

He flickered the flashlight over the rail switch quickly from afar, and the hedgehog sensed the light. He turned it off, moved away from the rail, and turned in a large circle like a hyena. Of course, he had never seen a hyena, but his father had told him they ran in circles; and he believed both this and his father's explanation that bones in their necks caused them to make these wide circles. He walked on tips toes. He was barefoot, so he always had to wash his feet before going to bed. His father's feet were always clean, since he always washed them before prayer, but he himself didn't conduct the pre-prayer ablutions. Once he had washed himself than gone to the mosque to pray, but the wooden sandals he put on after washing cut into his feet as he walked. So he took off the sandals and walked barefoot to the entrance to the mosque where Sheikh Masoud was calling the faithful to pray. When he saw Ali barefoot, the Sheikh cut off the call to prayer and cursed at him. Ali could not forget hearing the Sheikh say, "*Gather, O faithful, for the prayer, Ga . . .* —get out of here, little bastard, son of a bitch —*Gather, O faithful, for salvation.*" He had run back to the house in tears. "No more of Sheikh Masoud and his alley cat of a wife for us. Stay and pray here, boy," his mother said. But in fact, he neither prayed nor washed for prayer after that.

At the beginning of this past summer when the days had sparkled, he wanted suddenly to see the fabled alley cat as he had never seen her. He dreamed about her. He suckled at her tits in his sleep and cried on her breast. She rocked him back and forth. He spent the whole summer waiting for the winter, since Suad was unable to sleep during winter by herself in her house. Most nights, Sheikh Masoud left her by herself in the house and went to spend the night in prayer at the mosque. Then Suad came over to meet Laila and escape her loneliness. This winter, as in the past, the two of them let Ali come along with them. Laila at the time still stammered, and he himself still cowered like a hedgehog before elders. His father's back was frayed like a hedgehog's. He said that to himself when he looked at the back of his father's vest.

After the hyena's circle was completed he found himself standing over the hedgehog. He stretched out his small hand without grabbing it. The hedgehog's quills extended. When he put his hand right over the hedgehog's back, and the breath trapped in his chest was about to explode, and the sharp stones under him were cutting into his feet, finally, he grabbed at the hedgehog who curled into a ball with quills extended. He picked it up carefully with both hands. He laughed and remained unfazed by the hedgehog's howl. He ran frantically to Uncle Abdel Nur, superintendent of the switch house.

Abdel Nur was a dark-skinned man who enjoyed buying hedgehogs and (according to the adults) eating them. He gave Ali one or two piasters, depending on how big it was. He left the switch house and went to look at the empty train station. No trains came at night, but the previous summer they had celebrated night trains too. At least that's what he had heard the adults saying. They said that some carried soldiers and others Europeans. He snuck out once and saw a train with passengers with red faces—both men and women. He tried to get closer, then disappeared behind the station manager's office to get a good look. But he could hear what they were saying though he couldn't understand it. So it was true. They were in fact foreigners! . . . In one of the windows he saw a man with a huge mouth laughing, and behind another, a naked woman, her breasts hanging out over the top of the glass. Another night he snuck out to see the foreigners. Instead he found a large black train crammed with soldiers and their equipment. That time he heard nothing.

Now he could not understand his sister's stammering. At first, he had thought it was the sound of light drops of rain on the roof. But the rain thickened and Laila turned around, and he drew back. She kissed him, tenderly on the shoulder, then she turned around again and with her back to him, slept. He told himself he shouldn't have to shrink himself more. He unfolded his body; but he heard her tell herself, "What I thought was all wrong. God will keep him for me. I am the only one who read his papers. I will understand."

He didn't understand a bit of what he heard. His surprise grew. Who was Laila talking about? Thunder pealed, winds shook the walls, and the light of the lightning bolt came down through the small glass window and filled the room. But the thunder kept right on pealing as though the heavens were stacking on top of one another over the earth. Ali thought of the smallest hedgehog he had ever stalked—so small that Abdel Nur refused to pay him. That was two years ago. After he let it go, it didn't run anymore; it just curled up with its quills extended, tucking away its long mouth and the rest of its face until it became a prickly ball. How badly had he wanted to take it back to his house that night and leave it there! Hedgehogs ate insects, his mother always said. But his father hated the sight of them and always said their mouth (although longer) resembled that of a mouse and thus disgusted him. So he threw them out. But Ali remained fascinated by the cowardly little animal that preferred to curl up in a ball rather than run. He was fascinated by Uncle Abdel Nur's habit of buying them and eating them. But his amazement peaked when he asked Uncle Abdel Nur flat out what he wanted with them, and he answered that he bought them because they ate insects and that insects had become unbearable throughout the area, and he wanted to get rid of them all. At that point the cowardly hedgehog finally revived and uncurled itself to run away. It looked hilarious jumping around the walls of the sleeping inspector's office and atop the platform where Ali left it.

Ali began to remember other things. He wasn't sure why, but he kept remembering a lot of talk about Hamed and Gaber's disappearing. He had a vague feeling that the next morning would bring a different type of day. He shrunk himself even more trying to make himself the size of a hedgehog.

SHEIKH MASOUD

As the night approached its end and the sky began to appear above the horizon thanks to a frenetic thunderstorm somewhere in the distance, hope began to dissipate in many of the houses. They all felt the warmth from the flicker of the fowarika stove fading and the piercing cold spreading through their rooms as though it were a conquering enemy. Bodies spun around each other and longings were repressed again. The lake waters seemed to recede as the desert winds rolled in and reminded everyone of their sins. The children screamed from an ominous dread. Um Gaber called upon her Lord, "Lift your curse from your faithful servants," then began repeating the words incessantly as she cried burning tears for her son who had still not returned since going out the previous morning. Zeinab got up and held her three children as she cried for Hamed, who also had not come home last night. She thought about Gaber coming to their house last night and mumbling a few words to Hamed that she hadn't been able to hear. She remembered how frightened she was by the knocking at the door. She grabbed Hamed's arm without knowing why and said to him, full of sadness, "Why did you do it, Hamed?" as though she knew it all. Zeidan rose up to rush to the bathroom. Um Samira shouted a plea, sworn by the lightning, the thunder, the earthquakes, and the birds sailing through the sky for Mursi to come back to her daughter, and Samira's warm tears burst forth once again. Laila turned around to pull Ali close to her with all her strength, and for the first time he became frightened and shrank into a ball smaller than that smallest of hedgehogs. As for Abdullah, he had pleaded with God that He stop the sun from beating down upon him, that He bless him with a son, and that his prayers be received in heaven at the awesome pearly gates. "My Lord," he said, "I have no sin for you to hold against me." Neama prayed that Arfeh die and that Mustafa forget. Suad became startled and jumped out of bed. She tripped over a coffee table at which her husband read the Quran, and she fell and bumped her forehead. Blood trickled as she raised the flames in the kerosene lamps, and she cried to herself, "Where are you, Sheikh Masoud?" She begged God to protect him as she stumbled around the room tense and trembling. "God preserve him; I have no father nor mother nor son," she said. She realized she had awakened from a beautiful dream in which young Ali had been with her. They all realized that the community was besieged.

But the spears of cold had been turned back in the small mosque in the middle of the twenty houses. Warmth filled the place until it became small around the figure of Sheikh Masoud.

"Fire be cold and peace upon the believers." He chanted: "May the flame warm the hearts of your servants with the faith." He rose after closing the book with his right hand. So familiar with ways of the other world, God also knows the secrets of this world. He put the book in an old purse and hung it on the wall. Then he prepared to call for the dawn prayer.

He turned around in the small mosque, a bent-over sheikh with a dangling white beard. His narrow eyes struggled against the heaviness of sleep. Mud will block the roads, Sheikh Masoud. You're not accustomed to doing the dawn call to prayer in the mosque. You've always called as you strolled among the houses, repeating the call several times. The thin strips of daylight strengthened as you cried out. That was such a summer, but where could this summer be hiding? This wintriness has a fierce taste to it. Winter has appeared early as though it wanted to assault the other seasons. And this night was thick; its veils would not lift before light from the east. Back when your spirit had traversed the height of heights, you could not be held down. You ascended the towers. You surpassed purgatory. You arrived at the divine. You ate fire and weren't burned. You didn't bleed. Your saliva was milk and honey. You saw neither the lake nor the houses, the earth nor sky, nor the fisherman you once saw every afternoon looking like a lonely sparrow floating in the distance near the center of the lake in a narrow boat. No movement of fishing boats coming in and out of the lake's marsh, casting their nets or readying their wire baskets, both of which they might leave until morning. No train station, and what have you seen more of in your life than train stations. No switch house in the pale light. The cosmos has become light upon light. Blinding. Fixating on a dazzling void. You are flooded with light. You capture the secret of secrets. You crumble in tears your face covered in dirt. You implore your guardian: "O bestower of blessings, take me on Gabriel's wings. I love you, my master." But your master Khidr argues with you and drives you out. You ask him where matters will finally end. He yells, "Shut up." You in turn yell, "You neighbors of mine, shut up. Hamed, my son, don't give up on God's grace. Cursed Arfeh, are you fooled by your own blond moustache, light hair, and green eyes? Keep your hands off Zeidan, only I am still with you, and God sees you always. Leave the children; do not frighten them. Spirits haunt the lake, Sheikh Masoud! Stop corrupting youthful minds. Don't make them like us. What is our sin, Sheikh? Bastards. You're all bastards. Shame on you, Sheikh."

· · ·

But the train no longer comes. The birds have stayed away. The fish have died. Signs of the end times, Sheikh Masoud. He almost brought up the golden sea bass that had jumped out of the lake last time he went fishing: how this golden sea bass had spoken, and how it danced as it spoke. How it had confided in him that the days would spin in a vicious cycle. Birds would turn to beasts. Beasts would turn rotten. Rails will twist and cry out in space, as they see new trains that don't run on the ground, ridden by men with red faces. Soldiers with evil in their eyes, excessively huge. Their leader will become a tyrant. God will abandon them for a while. The golden sea bass said these things as it danced. Then it said salvation was a narrow window, and it cried a big, crystal tear that looked like mercury. It floated on the face of the lake; then the golden sea bass dove underwater. Its tear spread and covered the lake. Night fell, and an army of repugnant bats came out of the marsh looking for faces to latch onto. They were surrounded by a swarm of black quails with long thin wings and they filled the air with shrill piercing shrieks.

Their eyes had mocked him since Suad's arrival. They had a grudge against him for marrying a girl so much younger than he. Their eyes continued to lust after his beautiful wife, who had filled his nights with warmth and pleasure and whose sleek body emanated a timeless, devious odor. She would lie between his arms like a sheet of velvet, twisting inside his embrace. She gave him a drink of pure nectar from a sparrow's tongue.

How many times, when he was on top of her, could he feel their eyes around the bed. Under the bed. Even as the warmth between her thighs flowed through him all the way to his head, as he shook in a crazed pleasure—and he, an old sheik—he felt their eyes on them. But fate is difficult. He had gone through religious training and learned Islamic law. The years had passed. He had matured through youth, middle age, and old age. He had lived bitter and powerful experiences, only to end up living among the heathens. They had killed him this past summer. He had tried to oppose them to no avail.

"We've become destitute, master."

"We're hungry."

"Is there some rotten germ that entered us without our realizing it?"

"We are humans, master."

"Believers in the faith."

"Our women are left naked."

"The ground's swallowing our feet."

"The rails have pierced our hands."

"The sun has seared our eyes."

"Women have eaten our bodies."

"Children pick at our livers."

He screamed, "Call upon God. Remember Him so He'll remember you. You must say this, you, my servants, who cannot control your appetites. You sons of bitches must not give up on God's mercy."

Then they screamed, "Their appetites are swallowing us."

He looked and saw blood trickling from Um Gaber's eyes. He knew she had made charms for the women in order that the train would come back. He told himself she is a godforsaken woman and nothing more.

Neama came to him complaining about her husband's loss of appetite, and he told her, "The heart knows what, at times, the eyes cannot see. Go back to your husband."

She looked at him in shock. His eyes horrified her. She stood once she realized what he was saying and took two steps to go out. Then she stopped and turned, crying from feelings of betrayal. And she said, "Are you throwing me out Sheikh Masoud, although I'm like your daughter?"

Unable to control himself, he screamed, "Can't you understand, you whore? You know good and well what God thinks of you."

She bowed her head and said, "God forgive you, Sheikh." Then she went out, leaving him with the feeling that she was laughing at him, and he cursed the times they lived in.

Zeinab came to him complaining about Hamed and how he got up every night in the middle of the night and left for who knows where. Then he would return at dawn or later.

He asked her, "How do you explain it, young lady?"

She said, "I'm afraid he's stricken with something. They say that people have begun to sleepwalk since the train has stopped coming."

He laughed and she went on, "I dreamed that the train snatched him away. It made me more scared about his walks."

He patted her shoulder to console her and said, "When Hamed gets up, get up with him and ask where he's going."

She left confused. Was this what she had come to hear? He knew she was thinking that to herself. He wished he could approach Hamed and settle the matter, but he knew it was no use. He saw him wasting away little by little every day. His strength was leaving him. The sheikh fired a rebuking glance at him, and Hamed just looked away into outer space until a whole day had gone by without him speaking to anyone.

Sheikh Masoud wanted badly to go home. He would not even do the dawn call to prayer, for what he really needed was to go to Suad. No doubt she was scared. But rain had gathered mounds of mire outside. A deluge threatened the mosque. Strong thunder pealed, and rain flowed freely. He asked himself whether the golden sea bass was real or a dream. What was this train that it could cause all this misfortune? They say it dates back to the time of Ismail Pasha, but he couldn't believe it. The golden sea bass said the blacksmith who had made the train also made the cross that crucified Christ. The train used to come every Friday and tomorrow was Friday. But Christ wasn't really crucified. Was the train the blacksmith's revenge after the deception of the crucifixion was discovered? Or was it the revenge of the Jews? He picked up some mats and stacked them on top of each other. He opened an old box and took some covers out of it. He started to make himself a bed to sleep through the remaining time. He asked God's pardon for not performing the call to prayer for the first time since he arrived at the houses, as sleep began to overtake his frail body.

He remembered dozens of scurrilous books he had read. Not so much religious books, as superstitious and fantastic tales. He thought also of all his close friends who had passed on to the land of the dead. He had no desire though to think about the world of the jinn. Of the living he had come to care only for Suad, daughter of the prince of Mecca, whom Ibn Arabi had fallen in love with. If only he had lived in the days of the prophet, been a sword bearer in the army of Hussein. Instead, he lived in the age of the golden sea bass that talked. He began to hiccup a little then coughed forcefully. What would he have for dinner? An aged piece of cheese and a cup of goat's milk. A drink of milk was the finest drink of all. He wished the golden sea bass had said that. Instead, he went on about a sun chased by men who cannot catch it, or a wide desert with men twisting inside it, or fires that water wouldn't squelch, or a city made of glass.

"Listen to my final words to you all. You know nothing of suffering and patience. Go to the inspector. Why are you all so dependent on the train?"

No one answered. The next day he heard the children sing: "The inspector is supposed to be so busy! Inspecting what? He doesn't give a damn."

"The train is salvage," he told them.

"So what. It's stopped coming."

"What exactly do you want?" he asked.

"We want to know what is wrong and what is being done about it."

He knew the attitude of these bastards. The years had taught him. Was it possible that sons of fornication could fill an entire twenty houses?

In recent days they asked him about the significance of the trains filled with Europeans, and their kisses from behind the windows. God's judgment upon them. They asked about the armies passing in every direction. Complaints multiplied about a lack of provisions. Disruption of menstrual cycles. Deaths of roosters. Um Samira put her head between his hands and cried and begged the sheikh for a charm to bring her daughter's fiancé back from roaming like some strange bird. He told her she should wait for him for a year and if he did not return, marry someone else. With broken spirit she said, "But we are traditional people, Sheikh Masoud."

He said, "The world is unforgiving, change is inevitable, and God forgives all sins. Besides, you have no other recourse."

She left and he knew she would not listen to what he had said. He told himself, "Uh huh, from the jackals." He remembered he had left the lamp lit and he got up to turn it down. He felt thirsty. At home when he felt thirsty, Suad brought a fresh, pure drink. He would sleep thirsty this night. He put out the gas lamp and went back to go to sleep. After he had pulled his covers over him, Suad's two lips sneaked under his bedding, and he smiled in welcome. He saw a tear on her cheek. An asp danced around her, and he called for God's protection. "My Lord," he cried, "don't I deserve a boy to protect my small angel? My Lord, why have your sons become evil?" When the light of dawn finally arrived, exhausted from its long journey in the heavy darkness, Sheikh Masoud was sleeping soundly. When he had fallen asleep blackness itself entered the mosque and filled it. It came to him with eyes bulging, tears streaking, and fists tightened. At the same moment, Sheikh Masoud remembered he had told Zeidan of the golden sea bass. He thought to himself, "Why did I choose Zeidan out of everyone? Woe unto us both." Then he fixed his eyes fearlessly on the advancing blackness. After he had fallen into a sleep so deep that no one could have foretold it, the advancing blackness left the mosque and closed the door. The night ended and the morning began. With the morning, they all knew how the night had ended and how the day of the train's return had begun.

PART TWO

Metamorphoses

SUAD

A year passed, more or less. Here years are marked by the rain, and rain had been falling for days. Tonight, finally, the cosmos had settled into a portentous silence. Beginning that morning, people's hearts had heaved with foreboding, exactly as in the previous year. The night was motionless, as sleep overtook most of the homes.

This night Suad was trying not to break her routine from the past year. She was still waiting for God to send her someone. Everything seemed to be letting her down, even her body. She talked this way every night when she spoke to her husband. She still had a beautiful body, and she would try to get him to stare at it in the mirror with her. She asked him if he saw the breasts that he liked to cling to like a small child. They had not changed; they were still nubile and curved like a jug, with a firm nipple, protruding like a little bully blocking the path of small children. She asked him if he would touch her lips, which were always full and sensuous. They were always like that, and they caused everyone to jump to unfair conclusions about her. He was the only one who understood her. He had called her a flame of passion that could not be extinguished, and she couldn't even control herself. A flame of passion, who still had a sleek, flat stomach, whose hips were still round. There she was, completely naked, the way he had always enjoyed her. But now he did not give her a second glance.

Every night Suad used to take off her clothes and roll over on to him, but now there was no longer anyone in bed to roll onto, and he himself no doubt knew it. Everyone knew it. Their fear of her grew. But she practiced the rituals of love with him only. That was the way she was and the way she would be whether he liked it or not.

He wanted her to be that way. He had never tried to teach her a single verse of the Quranic verses he carried with him in his heart. He always said to her, "If the Quran came down on a mountain, it could crush it. The Quran is not everyone's burden. The world is divided into those who bear the Quran, and those who bear the burden of their sins." She didn't doubt for a second that he spoke truthfully. But her eyes grew weary as she wondered why her husband condemned her. Her eyelids grew more drowsy. It was not the languor that he liked; it was rather a deep-seated and sorrowful languor. Since he died—and no one knew how he had died or what made him fall into that ultimate deep sleep one night—she got up before dawn every morning and begged the heavens to relieve the parched earth, to return things to normal. She prayed as her husband had done. Perhaps the suffering she had begun to endure would bring about some repose in the near future. She asked herself where the still young, strong Gaber had gone. Why did she do to him what she had done? Where had that sad young Hamed gone? And why had she done to him what she had? The former had left an old mother, the latter, a wife, Zeinab, and three children. It was exactly like her husband who had abandoned her. How she loved them despite what had happened! But she knew which one was for her. The boy who still hadn't slept with her, who had not come with his sister any of the nights of the previous winter. Those sad nights were not suitable for youngsters. What's more, she still had not shaken off her sadness, so she spent her time begging her husband's forgiveness or talking to him.

You're harsh with me, my master. I know things that you don't. It was the despair. The despair. Do you know anything about that, my good master? Despair glowed from the eyes of Hamed and Gaber. It was in their gait.

They had no refuge. Ask God to pardon them. You're closer than we are to God right now. Your words are heard. Your offerings ascend with the call to prayer. You know my heart's big, yet God has sent no one to save me. At dawn I feel as if the gates of heaven have burst open. All this past winter, the one you didn't survive, it rained on me as I stood by myself. Every morning at dawn, my clothes and my body were soaked. I take off my head-scarf and shudder. I see the distant lights over the bridge, and then I ask is there really such a thing as humanity? I remember seeing them walking like spirits in the daylight and praying for them. I see the lights of the train station. I watch the station with its slumbering superintendent and I re-member the train. I call for its return, for the sake of Samira the beauty, whose heart is hung on the traveler who lives above its cars. I see the dis-tant lights of the city like stars in the heavens. I ask what afflicts them. What sort of fire do they sleep on, and what sort of despair do they awaken to? I wish that I knew, or that they would tell me. I only saw them once with you. Still, I pray for them, and I'm reminded that the stars in the heavens in the winter don't attend to us, or even look our way. I fall sad after seeing the moon that the dark clouds obscure and cause to fade before the morn-ing light. I take off my wet clothes. I cough. But I'm still strong. I look at my shivering body and I lie down to sleep. Nothing comes to me.

Throughout that past summer Suad ranted. She saw many visions of spec-tacular lands. She saw her derelict father. She began remembering his old tales, like the tale of the jinn that haunted them and made her mother jeal-ous. She saw her father traversing the lands of salt and mud, or joining forces with men made of wind and smoke. The poor, pitiable man. Since he had become a beggar, she and her mother were also made beggars. She watched her mother walk barefoot along the railroad tracks from town to town. The tracks stretched into the distance toward far away settlements, and on the banks of canals or the borders of the villages, she searched for a man whose name she no longer remembered. She remembered only that he was her husband. Meanwhile, Suad clung to her hand and gently reminded her of her father's name, only to be cursed by her and called a liar. Finally, they met Sheikh Masoud on the platform of a desolate train station. Every night she thought about that first meeting as though it were still happening, and she talked to her master:

Do you remember? There were the rail tracks and faraway lands and sleepy train stations. My mother and I were sleeping on the wood bench on the old platform made up of square tile, until you came one night to cover us with your own blanket, then took us the next morning to a shop that sold tea and mashed fava beans. It was a shop like the ones that we bought our things from or like the ones that we see when we are going to buy fish because the men are not fishing. These days, ever since the train stopped coming, we go to that place to buy our fish, because here the fishermen have stopped fishing. Zeinab has started to sell fish there with a woman named Um Haneya. Zeinab is full of stories about Haneya and her mother. She says they feel sorry for her. When she went to the bridge in order to look for work after Hamed abandoned her and their money ran out, Haneya looked into her eyes and said that she knew her. But Zeinab never said how Haneya had known her. She went to work now and left old Um Gaber to sit and wait with the children. Zeinab stopped being sad. Neither did she turn happy. She had become like the Quranic verses hanging on her walls, immutable and remote.

Don't you remember, Sheikh Masoud, when you fed us tea and fava beans at that shop? Remember how you looked at me? One look stole my heart, and you such a grave, old man. You took my mother and me to the marriage officer. You married me and brought me here, and you left my mother there. Why did you do that? Where is she now? You had given her that blanket. You told her we would come back and visit her. But we never went back. My mother had no fixed place. We had gone from place to place looking for our destitute father and his jinn. Then suddenly, I no longer heard anything about my mother, but I seem to have seen her face a million times this year, white and radiant. She kept appearing to me as a corpse in spite of her bright radiance. But I loved you so much, our life

seemed to overshadow everything else around me. We ended up tied together by an unbreakable bond. I loved you so much and stayed faithful in
life and death, even if I wasn't always in control of impulses.

Suad had the same dream over and over during the past few days, and
it had disturbed her greatly. She saw herself riding a creature toward
heaven. The creature was Alborak, upon which the prophet had ascended
and about which Sheikh Masoud had talked to her many times. But she
had not known what it looked like. All he had told her was that it was something between a horse and a camel. She had descended on the creature in
the middle of a beautiful land with clusters of lemon trees and blooming
flowers, but it was ruled by a dictator. He raped any woman that passed by.
When he came toward her she escaped, but she heard a woman screaming
from where she had left him. When she looked behind her as she ran, she
saw that it was Laila underneath him screaming.

Do you remember Laila, my master? You used to say she was the best
friend I could have even though you had never spoken to one another. You
used to say that there was a bittersweet pain in her expression that was beyond human comprehension.

Once Suad escaped from the huge gate of the city, she rode a train. It was
a train full of white people who began passing her around among themselves. One grabbed her right breast, another her left, and a third her
crotch. She shuddered as she pulled herself out of the crowd. Again she
turned around while running away and saw Laila lying prone in the middle of them. Suad screamed at her to escape, but she did not respond.

She's sad, my master. There is Fareed, the apple of her eye, who died.
You used to tell me he was cultured and kept to himself. That one time
when you saw his eyes for a moment as he raised his eyeglasses, you noted
his fiery intelligence. You told me that you thought him modest, although
he never spoke to people and in spite of his lying and proud father. Laila
kept loving him although he didn't speak. They tried to say I was his lover.

But you told me that you believed no one because you knew that I was a flame of passion that no one else could control. When I told Laila the truth, the truth that everyone knew, that Fareed did not speak to me, just as he did not speak to the others, she cried on my breast. Plea for forgiveness on my behalf if I ever made a mistake or lied to someone. You are closer to God than we are. His ears surround you and listen to you now. I beg Fareed's forgiveness as well if death has come because of me. I still remember the time he asked you, "Doesn't this place remind you of anything?" and you didn't answer. Then he asked you, "What does it mean that we're between the lake waters and the desert and the railroad, and the trains come and go, but for some reason we've picked out the one filled with salvage?" Then he told you, "Can you imagine that the desert and its sun have made a deal with the lake and its thick, fetid waters. What fire and flood will they bring?" He added, "I won't tell anyone of this, my Uncle." You admitted to me you didn't understand him. But still you were happy because he had addressed you as "Uncle." You asked me if I knew what he was talking about, and I told you knowledge can sometimes drive one mad. One day you asked me to tell all the latest news of the men and women. You knew that every house opened up to me out of fear and that I always walked out leaving bickering and envy behind. You told me, "Don't ever imagine that I'll be jealous. I know what you're made of and I believe in you. Our Lord, Khidr, told me to leave you as you please since you were a flame of passion that no one could approach."

I am yours as promised. I never imagined I'd be the cause of so much suffering to Hamed, Gaber, and Fareed.

When Suad's tears began to drip to her feet, she decided to turn away from the mirror and climb into bed with her husband. She kissed him and told him that the story had started on that morning after the night that they began to say, "The train will come tomorrow." That same night she had danced like tongues of fire. Laila joined her in the dance; and the two washed their legs in the lake water, until the young boy, Ali, came by to es-

cort his sister back to their house. At that moment, Suad had noticed him
approaching manhood. She had not said anything to him at the time, nor
would she say anything now, but she was watching him grow up before her,
and noticing in his eyes a new restlessness, sullenness, and intelligence.

It had all started that night and that following morning, in which they
had found Sheikh Masoud dead and alone in the mosque. Mud had been
stuffed in his mouth and black marks streaked across his face, and thus far,
no one had any idea how his mouth had become stuffed with mud. Who
had put it there and why? They had forbidden her to see his body as it lay
shrouded under a white sheet. She had wanted to attend the cleaning of
the body. In fact, she had wanted to wash him herself . . . and then sleep
with him and purify him. But they had told her that the washing of a man
was men's work. She slapped her cheeks with grief before remembering
that he told her Islam forbids such displays. She grieved for him louder
and with more passion than even the hired mourners that come and wail
at funerals. She had forgotten that he had said such grief was a torment
that the dead soul would not bear. Now, she felt that everything had let her
down. Even the rain that had emptied her tensions whenever she climbed
up on the roof, now could not penetrate her. And neither the train nor the
disappeared returned.

There were more trains filled with strangers. An evening several days
ago, they saw them fishing in pursuit of the beautiful fresh water fish. They
fired at flocks of geese. Baskets of fish came out of the lakes and baskets of
geese fell from the skies. But when the villagers went out they caught nothing. Fish still came out of the lake dead and rotting, and the swan just
floated up into the clouds.

The morning of the next day the strangers disappeared. They boarded
their train and left. No one knew where they had come from, or where they
were going, but their eyes spoke a treachery and an evil. When the men
went to ask the station inspector about them, he would not say anything.
Finally, he complained that they had awakened him abruptly, disturbing
the sleep he had slept almost constantly over the past years. A few of them

had dragged him from his office then gone in with some women. They told him to make them tea. After they came out, he walked back in and found the teacups tossed in the corner and some underwear hanging from the cabinets. He could not figure out exactly what had happened, but he said to himself, "One day, I'll tell the whole story from the beginning."

The military trains multiplied, but they no longer inspired fear. Some over the last few days had come back filled with wounded. No one came out to meet them anymore except for Ali. He had come to Suad and Laila two days ago to tell them that he had climbed the train and seen the wounded soldiers, who were actually happy to see him. They told him, "Don't be surprised, Ali. We know who you are. Tell all the children that we're on our way back from the four corners of the world. We've fought in the land of the blacks and of the whites, of the red and of the yellow. We've waged war against every religion, creed, government, and all peoples, until we've come to hate them all indiscriminately now that we've forgotten why it was we set out to fight in the first place."

Ali memorized their whole statement. A soldier asked if he could repeat it back in front of them and he did. Then he repeated it again before Suad and Laila, and by the time he recited it to the other children, he could sing it as a song. Even so, he slapped his forehead and asked himself why it was that he could not figure out what the words meant. He asked Suad and Laila if they understood, but neither of them could understand anything. They kissed each other. When Suad kissed him she noticed his cheek was warm. The boy trembled, but Suad shook even more.

Suad climbed up onto the bed. She told her husband that she wanted him to drink now from her pure milk, but then she related to him a summary of what had happened the past few days.

They had found Arfeh, the guard, sitting on a chair at the station after Fareed's death. An ax split his head into two halves and stuck between them. Blood streamed over the hanging halves of his head and all over his clothes. They all said with a dark laugh that they had found him planted in his seat like the village Omda.

Meanwhile, the inspector had left as soon as Fareed died. They had seen him tearing at his uniform and crying, as he howled, "The government killed my son." No one was shocked by what he said. They were surprised, though, when he piled all his furniture onto a small cart to be moved. There was a bed, a couch, a broken desk, a mat, and a chair with three legs. Everyone said he had blown all his money on opium. The cart moved down the street, dragged by a sickly mule and driven by a halfwit coachman, as the inspector ran behind them dragging his wife with the wandering eyes.

The last thing that had happened was the appearance of a huge foreigner that evening. He had a blond pencil-line moustache and spoke as though he were in charge: "Do not despair. The train will come tomorrow, Friday. It will bring everything with it as well . . . including Mursi, Samira's fiancé." As he said these things, he smiled eerily. Everyone was amazed that he could tell the future, except for Laila who told him, "You're a liar. Fareed said the train wasn't coming back." Then young Ali stood up and said, "You're a liar," and began leading the other children in chanting, "There is the liar!" They chased the foreigner away, chanting all the while and throwing stones until he made it back to the station where a transport car was awaiting him. Even so, before long the women were repeating to one another that the men had learned of the train's coming.

Suad could not tell her husband any more. She said maybe tomorrow I can speak to him again. Her conversations with him were always during prayer. Finally, she said aloud, "Let me tell you about my uncanny intuition, as you always called it. If God does not send someone for me from above this year, he will send someone next year because God cannot delay more than two years. Isn't that right, my fair master? Isn't it right, Sheikh Masoud?"

She turned to embrace her dead husband. She buried her face in the pillow over his own face.

ZEIDAN

The night gave way to a pure daylight and a sky bereft of clouds other than scattered white wisps, which dispersed timidly in the remote distance. A light breeze fell over the houses and the huts whose walls were drenched from the rain that had lasted all through the night, and the cattails swayed over the lake. A flock of black birds rose over the water and surrounded a group of white ones. All the people came out of their homes stronger than they were the night before.

In front of the houses, an old rain-soaked wooden cart was being pulled back and forth behind a wandering mule driven by a young, strong driver, who exchanged morning greetings with everyone.

Carefree children came out and chased each other. Several women blubbered with laughter, although no one knew why. Then, everyone walked out and stood before the houses, gathered around the cart, waiting or watching.

Neama walked out dark and dejected without speaking to anyone. She motioned to the cart driver who came toward her and went into her house. Then the two of them began moving her old furniture. Abdullah and his wife came over to help and then Suad joined in. No one said a word, and they all moved without noticing Zeidan's presence inside the house.

He was sitting wanly in a corner. After all the furniture had been moved and the cart had been filled, Neama stood with the two children waiting for him to come out. No one realized that Zeidan had spent the night in the house. All they knew was that he had been seen meandering about the lake and the desert.

The driver said to Neama, "Let's go."

And she answered, "The man will be coming in just a minute."

Abdullah looked at her and said, "Zeidan is inside?"

She nodded yes, and he walked back to the house. When he saw Zeidan sitting in the corner, he could not believe that he hadn't noticed him as he was moving the furniture.

Zeidan's eyes were glassy and distant. His face was pale and half-covered by coarse stubble. Abdullah reached out to help him up, but Zeidan sat motionless. Abdullah came closer and said, "Get up, Zeidan."

Zeidan neither answered him nor moved.

When Abdullah took his arm sympathetically, Zeidan twisted in fear. "Zeidan! Get up for God's sake!"

He finally came out holding Zeidan's hand. The whole village stood and stared at him in sorrow. Zeidan walked through them in silence, and a silence had fallen over the crowd as well. While no one could have known what they were thinking at that moment, it was clear from their faces that they were frightened.

When Zeidan arrived at the cart, he looked back for a moment then stared at his wife and children. Then he looked back at all the other children and broke into a gallop. Some of the children ran after him throwing rocks. Tears streamed down Neama's cheeks. They were thick, warm, salty tears, making their way with sobs across her cheeks. Suad, fighting away grief and pain, told her, "Look after your children, Neama."

She kissed her, as did Abdullah's wife. Then Neama kissed the back of Abdullah's hand.

As the cart pulled away, everyone stood frozen. They were all watching it. A small, dilapidated cart cutting through the enormous cosmos, the ample morning, the clean heavens, and the tranquil lake. The cattails swayed, the black birds climbed into the sky and a flock of white birds cut through the middle of them, while water left over from last night's rain trickled through the gutters and kept the earth moist. The rain-soaked walls showed their cracks.

The cosmos was stunning at that moment like a mere small child with supple bones and flesh and clear eyes. The cart carried with it a certain beauty from a distance, as though it were a dream or some other type of vision. No one knew where it was headed. In spite of living together so many years, and being tied together in so many different ways, the villagers knew nothing of each other's origins.

They all followed the cart as it disappeared. They were not thinking about Zeidan at that moment. He was plodding toward the fig orchards. When he made it to the edge of the grove, he found the first tree barren and the wet ground around them covered with leaves. He felt that the vast morning was his and that he was alone in the universe. He dropped down and slept beneath a short, naked tree. When he woke up, his countenance was gloomy. No one understood why his head was inclined. What load was weighing him down? What anxieties pressed on him? He made his way toward the deserted government farm. He stopped under the mill where a mange-covered dog was twisting. He thought that he couldn't watch the mill turn anymore as his heart thumped.

Noon broke by the time he got up to leave the mill and walk back to the lake. What did Zeidan believe he was doing on these peregrinations? No one knew. Zeidan didn't even know why he went back to the lake. When he was halfway back, he rested against the guardrails of the railway bridge that crossed the irrigation canal. He sat with a guard whom he knew, an old man who had once been a rail worker who helped build the railroads. As he sat and watched Zeidan, he saw someone more senile than he was. He made Zeidan a cup of tea and gave it to him with a piece of bread. Zeidan began to wolf down the bread with his two hands as though he were blind and destitute.

"What are you thinking, Zeidan?"

He did not answer.

"Are you still subjecting yourselves to constant torment? Why have you tied your whole lives to the train?"

Zeidan said nothing.

"My son, this is a new time. Haven't you seen the trains that come through here? Haven't you seen the trains full of foreigners, my son? It's exactly like the old days, when I was your age, and I was working on the railway. The trains of the Allied Forces used to pass through during the War. Ah! The world spins and spins, my son, then goes right back to where it started."

"They say that a huge bull is carrying this whole world on one of his horns," Zeidan said. "When he tires, he puts it on the other horn. When the exchange happens, the earth quakes. But the world is not quaking these days. These days, the bull is passing it back to the first horn."

The old man laughed. He was happy that Zeidan had finally said something, although he made no sense.

"My son," he answered, "your mind is the only capital you possess. There are neither horns nor bulls. No one understands this world."

The old man thought for a moment, and then smiled as though a lamp had lit up over his head.

"Who would have believed that everything would return to the way it started? God save us! Even our beginnings were nothing like this really. In any case, you all are in the wrong."

"She has cheated on me. She has killed me."

The old man gave him a pat on the back.

"She's only a woman. Maybe she didn't really cheat on you. You've been listening to people's idle chatter. Okay, I know all the homes here and what people inside them say. The police used to come. They sat with me and talked. Go back to her, Zeidan."

"I can't. I'm possessed."

"What?"

"Possessed."

"By what?"

"By a jinni. What else possesses men?"

The man smiled as Zeidan continued: "I used to fish every day in the late afternoon, as you know. But once the train stopped, the fish started to come out of the lake dead. At the beginning of last winter I had gotten tired of people's talk. I said something then that no one understood. When I first began to say that the train would not come, they made fun of me. Arfeh was coming to my house everyday. But then Sheikh Masoud died. Then Fareed. Then Arfeh." He paused. "Then I decided to fish at night. I said to myself, 'maybe the night fish will still be alive.' Maybe the golden sea bass will explain to me how everyone had died. This golden sea bass is a secret; Sheikh Masoud had told only me about it. But I ended up not doing any fishing. I started to talk to the sea, until I had talked for so long that I got up to shit. Suddenly, something pulled me down toward the water. I went under, and I saw under the water a red castle with a beautiful jinni in it.

She rinsed me with blue water and dressed me in yellow clothes. She asked me to come into her mouth since, as a jinni, she had no vagina. I entered her and listened to her breathing through her nose, then she disappeared. I came out of the water in my yellow clothes, but when I walked back to the village they called me crazy. Ever since that day, I'm a fugitive. Only yesterday did I go back home because when I had descended into the lake I hadn't found anything. The jinni had left. I'm waiting now for her to send me a message and let me know her new home, and until that message comes I'll search for her through the whole wide world."

"Drink your tea, my son."

The old man could think of nothing else to say. Zeidan began to sip at the tea as the old man got up to flip the rail switch. He noticed signal lights in the distance, indicating an approaching train.

When he came back, there was no sign of Zeidan. He stopped for a moment and pondered. He turned around and looked up at the sky. He said to himself, "I used to do this twice a day. Now I do it every thirty minutes. So many trains. Old armies, new armies. Old wounded and new. Foreigners overrun us in every new age. Only You are merciful. Only Your face is eternal. Nothing remains but Your grace. Everyone is possessed in these troubled times."

And for some reason it stuck in his mind that Zeidan was barefoot.

ALI

He did not enjoy the sight of watching Zeidan's family moving. When the inspector's family had moved during the middle of the last summer, Laila had spent the night next to him crying. He knew that she would not cry tonight though. Lately, she had taken to sitting by herself and flipping through old tattered papers.

While he had no idea what these papers were, he had thought of stealing them several times, but she was careful to keep them always under her galabeya pressed against her breasts. All he knew was that they were papers

that Fareed had given her, and ever since they had found Fareed's murdered corpse on the tracks, Laila had been reading them; and whenever
she was left alone by herself she would cry. He had spent many long nights
listening to her say to herself, "They killed him. They say he was electro-
cuted . . . and that a live wire fell on him. But they're liars . . . liars."

When he had gone out to watch the inspector and his family move, he
remembered that he had left Laila alone at home crying. He left the crowd
and walked to the bridge. A dark girl stopped him and grabbed at his
throat.

"What are you doing here?"

"Whatever I want to do!"

He tried to walk away from her.

"You're from over there."

"Yes."

She had pointed toward their houses. As she spoke, she tried to pull
him toward a shack made of reeds.

"Tell me before I kill you. Where has Hamed gone?"

"No one knows." He was amazed that she would ask him about
Hamed. How did she know him? He remembered hearing Suad tell Laila
that Zeinab had complained to Sheikh Masoud about Hamed going out at
night and not coming home.

"Go back to your mother then."

Then she slapped his face. His small body became inflamed. He
jumped up and slapped at her with a strength he did not know he had,
until she fell at his feet. She erupted in a powerful scream, alerting her
mother who came with a huge stick. He burst into a sprint in front of her,
then stopped a short distance away and looked back. He picked up stones
and threw them until they flew all around the mother and daughter, who
began wailing at the top of their lungs. Several men then came toward
them, and Ali had to flee.

Today he had no desire to go to the bridge. He walked aimlessly
through an empty lot toward the train station. It was deserted. No trains.

No passengers waiting. The inspector, as usual, was sleeping when Ali peeked through the window of his office.

The sun was pale. Yesterday's rains had soaked the benches and awnings. Light, gray clouds began to scatter themselves over the station. A mass of sparrows began gathering on the rusty rails.

He looked into the switch house where he saw a man with a white face. This certainly was not Uncle Abdel Nur, with his dark skin and long gray whiskers. Uncle Abdel Nur took the night shift.

"Ali, my son, my grandfather was on the border patrol and always worked at night; my father was also a village night watchman. Even my mother working as a midwife ended up going out at night only because that's when the village women gave birth . . . and that's why I came out black."

Ali laughed. That was Abdel Nur's answer to Ali's question, "Why is your skin black but your moustache white?"

That was four years ago. The children at the time had all burst out laughing. But Uncle Abdel Nur, rather than getting angry, added, "That's the story of my black skin. Your father will tell you about my white moustache."

But Ali never bothered to ask his father. He just stared at the white whiskers. He stared at Sheikh Masoud's red face and found he also had a white moustache. He thought about asking the Sheikh, since he had the status of the prophet, but he never did. He ended up dismissing the question from his thoughts, just as he had dismissed the hedgehogs from his games. These things became old and tired to him, like the rust that started to cover his flashlight.

The white-faced switch house operator signaled to him to climb up. Ali was surprised to realize that he didn't know the daytime switch house worker. Why had he failed to go beyond his friendship with Old Uncle Abdel Nur? He climbed up overtaken by a sense of his ignorance. He looked at the faded and cracked wooden stairs with splinters sticking out in every direction, drops of muddy water hanging from their edges, and nail heads covered with dark rust sticking from each side. The iron rail felt cold and rough under his palm. He lifted his hand and found it covered with rust. When he brushed his hands together instead of disappearing, the rust spread like henna.

He went into the switch house. The man before him was young and his moustache was also white. He smiled. He asked Ali, "Can you buy me something from near the bridge? I know it's quite a distance, but if you can do it, I'll take care of you when you come back."

Ali nodded yes. He decided without telling the man that he wouldn't take any payment. The man started looking for his money in the pockets of the uniform hanging on the wall. Ali started to consider the nearby switch attached to the two rows of track. What would happen if he decided to turn the switch on an impulse? They said that it would make the trains run off the tracks. Why didn't the man make them run off their tracks and crash? Once his father had explained it to him. "The switch is heavy. Force is needed to move it. One mistake could end the life of the switch house man." Ali had been absentmindedly playing with one of the switches. Now, as the switch house man was immersed in searching for money, he gathered all his strength and pulled the switch backward.

Since his run-in with the woman and her daughter at the bridge last winter, he had known that he had become strong, but he didn't realize that he would be able to move the switch by himself. What really surprised him was how fast the switch had yielded to him. His face lit up with pleasure, as the man came running toward him screaming and kicked him with all his strength, while he cursed Ali's family. He grabbed Ali with one arm and grabbed the switch with the other. He tried to move the switch with one hand, but he could not, so he let Ali go and pulled the switch back with both his hands. Ali jumped out the door then hopped down the steps in wide leaps. All the man could do was go to the window and yell out threats and curses while Ali stood on the platform and laughed. He signaled to the man to come down to him, if he could. But the switch house man gathered himself. He invoked God and cursed Satan. He clapped his hands together and stepped away from the window. Ali climbed down from the platform.

Ali didn't know why, but he felt like throwing another glance at the sleeping station inspector. When he looked at him through the window he found him snoring loudly. He smiled and walked away. He gathered up a handful of dirt then turned around. He threw the ball of dirt between the two bars and onto the sleeping station inspector. He waited a while for the inspector to awaken, but when he realized that he wasn't going to, he walked away, full of wonder, not only at the sleepy inspector, but also at himself and what he had done that day.

Walking between the two rails of the track, he felt so light that he thought he might begin to fly through space. He started to fling stones at the distant horizon. He scrutinized the distance each stone traveled and found every successive stone to have gone further. His arm became sore, but he still flung stones.

What would happen if he threw a stone that never landed? What if the stone kept swimming through the air? Where might it land, or who might it strike in the end?

He wished he could do just that: send a stone flying from place to place, through station after station, and everywhere it flew, the whole world would point to it and say, "It's Ali's stone, still flying through space." The years would pass, and the stone would keep flying, and children would ask their fathers about the stone that had sped past that afternoon and where it had come from and who it had come from, and the father's would say it was Ali's stone which he threw ten years ago. He would be ten years older then. As the years kept passing, children would ask their fathers again about the stone that had flown by that day. Where had it come from? Who had it come from? The fathers would answer that it was Ali's stone that he threw over twenty years ago in some distant land. By then, he would have grown more than twenty years. As the years continued to pass, the children would ask their fathers about the stone that had sped past that afternoon and where it had come from and who it had come from, and the father's would say it was Ali's stone, the one he had thrown fifty years ago! Until finally the stone would return after completing its cycle.

But then his heart fell. He felt that the stone would return to his orbit and fall back at his feet, and the people would say, "It's your stone, Ali. It's come back to you." Then he would go on, the years would pass, the children would grow up, and they would forget the stone that swam through space.

The radiant colors of the hoopoe sparkled in his eyes. It was standing on one of the rails nearby, its crest raised haughtily and its breast thrown forward, surveying the world as though for the first time. Ali wanted to throw a rock, but just then it spread its wings, dazzling him with its brilliant whites, graded shades of brown, and shiny, jet black streaks. Ali felt a euphoria at the sight of the colors. The bird faced the rock fearlessly as Ali aimed it to fly over its head. It stood there motionless and stared at him. Ali came near it, but still it did not move. It occurred to Ali then that he could reach out and grab it, but when he bent over it, the hoopoe flew away and set itself down on a far-off rail.

They each stood staring at one another. Ali finally smiled and headed back to his house. Zeidan's family would have moved by now, and the people would have gone back to their houses.

Ali recalled what was being said yesterday about today's arrival of the train; and how no one seemed to have prepared to go out to meet it. He had heard one man say, "They always say that it will come on Friday. If they said some other day, it would come." He didn't understand, and this bothered him. They seemed to have forgotten. But Ali knew that if it came back, they would come out to it, and he also would come out. He could not let Laila go by herself. Maybe this time he could stop her. He was not sure, but they had become preoccupied with other things . . . perhaps by fear as well. He himself was only afraid when he saw Laila crying, but his parents still kept him from going out at night to hunt for hedgehogs. His father had smashed his traps and his fishing tackle. He had forbidden him to do any hunting or fishing. "Just play," he told him. But Ali didn't play.

None of the children played last summer. Not even with the marbles and tops that they had played with the previous summer. No one got them out that year. The last time they had brought out their things, they had found that none of the boys could bang one marble into another. They could not make the spinning tops stand. They would only spin a little bit before collapsing on their sides. There was nothing left for him to do but go out and stare at the trains filled with foreigners or soldiers. The trains with foreigners were many; those with soldiers became few. One of the children said that the trains with foreigners were really only one train that went back and forth, so that it seemed like many. The other children had beaten this child for saying it, but Ali thought to himself that it could be true. The soldiers, on the other hand always seemed wounded. Yesterday, he had seen Abdullah chasing a fox that was stalking their chickens that had caused a stir. But the fox had been too swift for the old man. His daughter, Samira, had begun sleepwalking according to the talk among the people. Her mother had told them all how she tied her daughter's feet to the bedpost, so that if she tried to get up she would trip and fall, and the mother would get up and give her something to drink and recite Quran and invoke God. Now he could see Samira standing at the wooden rail at the end of the two tracks that the train ran over. She was sitting on one of the tracks, mesmerized by all the little stones before her. She was flicking small pebbles calmly under the haze-covered sun reflected off the glitter at the edges of her headscarf. He walked toward her. As he came nearer, he felt himself a man approaching a small child.

"What are you doing here alone, Samira?"

She smiled. Her eyes brimmed with tears. They were vague and honey-brown, like the eyes of the fox. She began to run them back and forth over his face and the rest of his body. Then she wiped off a tear with a finger of her left hand. She said in gentle amazement, "You've grown up, Ali."

This annoyed him.

"Are you still waiting for the train? It's almost noon."

He pointed to the sun peaking in the heavens and said, "If it was coming at all, it would have come earlier."

Samira stood up. She looked at her two palms, which were covered with small indentations from the pebbles around the tracks. She beat her dress with the back of her hand to shake off the dust, then turned toward the rail. Ali stood facing her. A small bird came and landed on the rail between them, its eyes darting first toward Samira, then Ali. Another bird landed nearby. The first shot back up into the air, flapping its wings and chirping. The second one moved its eyes as had the first, until a third came and landed nearby. The second one flew off. As Ali was about to speak the third alighted and a fourth landed. Samira started to say something when the fourth shot glances at both her and Ali, then flew off as a fifth took its place. The birds continued to succeed one another, staring at the two of them, then alighting. At first they were confused, but then they felt a rush of giddiness and they laughed together. They had no idea why the birds were putting on this performance. They kept laughing for a while, each holding on to one of the poles that supported the rail. The group of birds flew off to a distance and formed a circle, then they broke up and flew in all different directions, while Ali and Samira continued to laugh.

"You don't hunt or fish anymore?"

"The birds have become experts in avoiding traps, and the fish ignore the bait now."

For some reason, he was lying and talking to her as though she was not aware of what was happening in the settlement.

"But have you tried?" she asked him.

The question confused him. He answered, "I will this winter."

She stared at him for a while. "You've grown up, Ali," she said.

She began to run her eyes over him again. His confusion began to peak. He looked around him. There was no one else around. They were in a wide, open space with silent, sleeping houses on one side, and the switch house and the tranquil station with its sleeping inspector on the other. No trains, nor people. Even the birds disappeared. And the clouds evaporated as though their guard had gathered them up and locked them away in a far-away place for the day. The heavens were pure, and Samira turned to face Ali with her face glistening from the afterglow of her tears.

Ali felt something warm climbing to his throat. It was like the first time he had bitten into his pillow, but this feeling was slower and more ample. His throat began to dry, and his eyes widened. He asked himself, "Could it happen? With Samira? Here?"

"We don't see much of Laila anymore," she said.

Ali turned his head and stammered, "That's right."

She smiled. "Laila is very beautiful."

He didn't understand, could not answer.

"Ali, everyone says you're bright." She came closer to him as she spoke. "Everyone says you have no fear at night, that you throw stones at the foreigner trains—" she began playing with his shirt buttons—"that you've begun to wear grown-up clothes"—she smiled and he smiled back full of anxiousness—"I love you, but you went far away and left me. You love traveling atop the trains. You say this is your work"—she grabbed at him with a violent fury—"You want me to search for you until I die searching, and come out like a spirit from the lake waters, or come down from the heavens as though in a dream"—Ali was overcome by tension—"why do you do this to me? Don't you know I love you?"

She began to claw at his face with her fingernails and pull his hair. He tried to push her away, but he couldn't. She was too strong. Finally, he gathered all his power, and in a move that would cause him great remorse later, he slapped her once, twice, three times until she broke away and stood in front of him crying. He ordered her to go back home, and she acquiesced docilely.

As he panted for breath, he looked again to the wooden railing. Why? There were no birds there now. The sky became dark as the shepherd of the clouds opened his gates, and the clouds thickened until they had covered the sun and sky with their grayness. He caught up with Samira who was walking away shattered. He took her hand and said,

"It's going to rain. We should hurry."

And they galloped toward the twenty houses.

Ali could not understand why his heart fell. He had said to Samira as they were running, "why don't you go and look for Mursi?" but that couldn't be why he was dejected. As he neared the houses, the problem became clearer to him. He thought of how hard it must be to be separated and how much it would affect him. He had thought about separation more than once before, but had pushed the thoughts out of his mind immediately to ward off unease. But now the idea latched onto his consciousness. The pounding in his chest had been nothing more than a preternatural dread. But could he go through with it? Could he even talk to anyone about leaving? And who would agree to it? What was the source of the whole idea anyway? He would shock everyone by leaving. Perhaps some would not be shocked. Suad, however, alone, out of all of them, would be overwhelmed with shock, perhaps even more than his family. Still, he felt surrounded by a strange urgency pressing the idea upon him, although it could not yet be executed. So, then, he would leave it all for later; for now he went inside as the rain grew into a torrent.

ZEINAB

Friday came to an end. Zeidan's wife had barely left when everyone went back into their houses. No one had even gone out for the Friday prayer. That had been the case ever since Sheikh Masoud had died on a Friday morning the previous winter. The men did not gather anymore for Friday prayers. The mosque no longer hosted the heated exchanges between the Sheikh and his followers. But Abdullah still went to the mosque. He always found himself alone. Only once had he felt the presence of another and turned to find Zeidan. But Zeidan only made it halfway through the prayer before he bolted from the building.

Everyone had gone inside their homes, pushing their children in front of them. But no matter how hard they tried, they could not keep from turning and looking out into the vast emptiness that had swallowed the train that they knew would never come again. At that time, Ali was in the switch house, watching for a chance to turn the arm of the breaker. Samira was circling around behind the house so that no one would see her heading toward the railroad track to sit under the wooden rail and run her fingers through the dust-covered pebbles. But it had been a different Friday at the bridge.

The bridge bore a long, wide road that split the lake into two halves. Crowds gathered on it on Fridays, when pale-faced and pencil-thin hawkers from the North, or the tall, wide, and dark southerners almost drowned among the throng of buyers pouring forth from the nearby city on the sea, including city women concealed in long, black shawls, covering their entire bodies except for a scandalously revealing bit at the top or bottom. There were also women in short, shiny dresses moving about like butterflies, and men, young people, and children wearing every sort of costume. The bridge was full of piles of fish: eel, catfish, mullet, perch, and blue gills—all the most famous of the fresh water fish. The fish salesmen all wore baggy, black shorts and tattered vests, and every now and then their wet hands, which were covered with fish scales, would reach out to dump water on their piles. This bridge was Zeinab's final destination, as though she had been created to sell things on it. She knew how to call out and how to whisper, when to dump water over the piles of fish and when to lift one up in the air and open its gills before the customer, when to prod the eel or catfish so that it would flip around in a circle and announce its freshness. Zeinab threw herself into the teeming crowds without her husband (who called her the daughter of virgin nature) trying to stop her. If he had noticed, he would have said something. If he had been able, he would have dived into the water and come back up in spite of all the sins committed over the bridge.

Zeinab relished the hell that swallowed her. The bridge was stony silent and aware that Zeinab left every day at the end of the day and returned the next morning.

Haneya, whose name Zeinab only learned later, asked her, "Are you here for fish?"

They looked into each other's eyes and each found in the other the answer to a secret question. Haneya came closer and found Zeinab's eyes projecting fire and sorrow.

"Where are you from, sister?"

Zeinab for her part saw harshness in Hanya's eyes. She thought to herself: "You know where I'm from, you slut." She felt as though Haneya was stripping her with her eyes. Again, she thought to herself, "God knows I'm decent, so why must I suffer this?" She remembered having heard Sheikh Masoud say, "Glorified is he who knows himself!" She began repeating to herself, "Where are you, Hamed? My poor lord, you're still chasing the unknown; you're still running behind the inspector's car."

Her lips betrayed her and began to tremble. She knew Haneya picked up on it. She stretched her hand out to her. She took her into the reed hut. Zeinab sat down then cried. Each one began to understand the other instinctively. Haneya said, "What sort of base man would leave a woman like this?"

She brought two cups of tea over and asked Zeinab, "Where is he right now?"

Zeinab let her tears flow. She had no idea that weakness would overcome her in this way. She dabbed at her tears and spoke sharply, in a rancorous tone she didn't realize she was capable of: "I don't know."

At that point, Haneya's corpulent mother walked in. She took one look at Zeinab, then walked back out, and Zeinab knew the whole secret. She stood up to say goodbye to Haneya.

"Stay with us, Zeinab. Work with us. You can come every morning. You can come back at night. Buy and sell things. Make a living and feed your children."

"And feed old Um Gaber as well," Zeinab thought to herself. She was grave and direct now. The last of her money had gone.

Zeinab learned everything about buying and selling. She learned for example that no matter how much she bathed, she was unable to rid herself of the foul fish smell that was starting to cling to her. The old woman's stares tortured her every night when she returned to the house. She became accustomed to the special taste of her tears after she had hugged the children, the old woman had gone to the entry way, and the flames of the fowarika had started to warm the house somewhat.

She often asked herself why she did not resist. Why this absolute certainty that Hamed would not return? How was it that every night, when the buyers and sellers emptied out of the bridge and it became like a large black serpent, as darkness began to overtake everything, and the roving moon with wandering eyes ascended and bequeathed a light breeze that swayed the cattails, and black bats appeared and hovered in the skies, and a chill came over her body so that she convulsed in a shiver, and the universe appeared like a deep, dark center of a conch shell—just then, nature spoke to her to tell her with unadulterated certainty that Hamed would not return?

Why was it that every morning—when she would go out early before everyone else, before the sun had risen, and its rays painted the horizon rose-colored behind the bridge, and the small birds began to circle after one another aimlessly, and fog filled the skies, and Zeinab headed out toward the bridge wearing a light pair of slippers that offered no protection from the cold, when she felt that the cosmos was a huge egg that she walked inside the shell of, unable to break through its walls and into the light—nature began to speak to her to say Hamed would not return? And now all that was left for her was this old woman, resisting death, to whom fate had attached her. And children growing up beneath the mark of original sin; three souls developing before her every day, and a fourth soul expiring— but still a soul.

Zeinab despaired before a universe that swallowed her feet in the mire. But she gave no thought to trying to extract them.

Abu Haneya was the first. She saw him wink at Um Haneya, and she saw the woman smile and then get up to leave. She looked at Haneya who came in carrying a portable stove. Haneya looked down and then walked out. Fire erupted in the reed hut.

She tried after that to enumerate her stranger lovers. She was unable to, and she hated what she had done.

She asked herself why she didn't take the children and go out with them into God's wide land. But she forgot to answer her own question. Later, when she remembered the question, she would forget it again immediately.

She told herself that the universe was a liar that peddled its falsehoods at least twice a day. When it appeared in the morning like the center of an egg and again when it turned itself every night into a dark conch shell. It lied also when it told her Hamed would return, but she forgot about this, and when she tried to remember why she didn't leave, all she came up with was that the days passed quickly without giving her a chance to think. All she knew at that point was that she was caught in a standoff between the egg and the conch. As for the day, it had ended. She had no idea what had gone on in the twenty houses. But she remembered what had happened in the tumultuous fish market.

As she walked back to the hut, she felt as though her heart sank to her feet. She took off her clothes and slept with a jittery middleman from the City, who did it as though he were going through the motions. He spoke with Um Haneya for a while and laughed, until finally, she came back and stood in her place behind the pile of fish, so she could head back to the hut. When she took off her clothes and slept, she tried to envision his facial features as he climbed on top of her in a breathless frenzy. But her rapidly beating heart distracted her, without diluting her from her constant comment to herself that it was no use, that they are all alike. No one knew why she always examined the faces of the invaders in detail, or what she was looking for. She felt as though her heart were about to pop out and dart around in space, as though it had sprouted two large agonizing wings that flapped violently. She shuddered under the man. This irritated him. He scolded her, asking, "Why are you crying?" and he cursed his luck and the day. Her lips managed to form a smile. She wiped away a tear and tried to encourage him. But her heart betrayed her, and she began to tremble anew. She wished he would simply leave her. But he did not. He became vicious, looking away from her face, and acting like someone pursuing a blind vengeance.

Zeinab knew that Suad was baking when she saw the smoke coming out of her house before she entered. She remembered Sheikh Masoud telling her that she should get up and ask Hamed where he's going. She suddenly felt a rush of nostalgia for the old man who had believed his self-evident advice would stop a river of tumult. She asked for God's mercy on him. She and the children ate the food she had brought. Old Um Gaber ate at a crust the size of the ends of her fingers as she arose to light the fowarika stove outside. A light drizzle started to fall.

When she stretched her hand out to the fowarika and lifted its grate. Its pink flames burned her. She looked around at the other stoves in front of the other houses with their smoke filling the air, and she said to herself, "Hamed's fowarika burns out before the others. It lights quickly and goes out quickly." She picked up the stove and went inside. Before she made it all the way in, the heat of the stove seared her hand. She looked at the scattered rags around her; she smelled the odor of the toilet; and she suddenly remembered why her heart had begun to beat, and she shuddered and cried.

She had seen him . . . Hamed himself. Unable to run or even walk. His feet bound by strips of cloth. His legs swollen. His face sunburned. His hair and beard filled with dust. His eyelids sagged, and he could barely lift his arms. He spoke with difficulty and could hardly move his tongue. Drops of dark blood trickled from his teeth. He screamed out into space. This time the dark center of the conch. That time the huge egg. He spun around in a circle and fell. He moved his two tired eyes toward an anonymous object and he cried without tears, then his head fell down on his chest. Then she saw his tears plow a canal of blood in the ground that the dogs came and lapped up.

Um Gaber came out of the inner room toward the entryway, which suddenly lit up in the light of the fowarika stove. Zeinab watched the old woman bent forward so much that her head almost touched the ground. She was dragging along an old, thick woolen blanket weighed down by the crusted urine of the small children that had collected over the past years. Neither one of them said a word to the other. Zeinab went back inside and covered the sleeping children, but she did not sleep herself.

She had told him, "Hamed, tell me what's bothering you so you can rest," but he could not. "Hamed, why must you waste your whole life running?" she had asked. He told her, "I am not in a rush. Something is pushing me from behind. I'm condemned to misery." Then he added, "When I asked Sheikh Masoud I thought he would beat me. I asked him to give me some idea where our people had come from. From where had we migrated? Were we children of Satan who were suffering because of it? What was the meaning behind the train? I told him he was a learned Sheikh, devoted to the faith and that he should know such secrets, but he came at me as though he would beat me." "You're getting into things you have no business with," she told him. "That's what the Sheikh said," he told her. "But can't Zeidan know something about Arteh? Doesn't the Sheikh himself know about Fareed and his wife?" He added, "what hunger are we trying to feed off of? With what mildew are we trying to nourish ourselves? Here we are trying to restore the railway, and we don't even know why the trains run on it."

She said to herself, "Maybe you're at peace now, Hamed. Maybe you see other people. Maybe they meet you in that secret place that you would never talk to me about, and they talk to you and Gaber about what's going on. You've left me for no reason I can understand. You've dealt with me ruthlessly, with me—the one who followed you faithfully over the tracks and past the rail guards. You left me in the morning of that deceitful night. At the time I thought you had left me nothing but myself, but now I understand that you left me all that you had. Most nights you left me alone, but you would come back, and I would forget. You would come back worn out and exhausted, but I would forget. I felt you were my protector, my guardian. The abandoned woman is cursed and haunted by her four walls. Even the heavens give her no relief. You left me for long nights that burned with anger and remorse. But I never despaired, I never blamed you. You would get used to life and I would forget. Then he came to you to stand next to you for a bit in the hut and repeat to you the idle talk spinning around. I asked myself why he didn't talk to you in the morning. Each of you infected the other. He left his ancient mother, and you abandoned me to total barrenness. No letters. No news. Not even a pigeon carrying a message like the ones in our old songs. Neither the wind nor the sky brought word from you. Maybe if I had asked someone where does the person who wants to escape this place leave from I would have received an answer. Hamed, did you know that I figured out the way to the bridge? The one you used to climb during the nights of darkness streaked with moonlight?

"During those nights I used to love you in spite of everything. But now, I think if you came back I would put my neck down under the wheels of the train with the soldiers and foreigners. I wouldn't wait until the children develop a consciousness or the old one lets us know she has one by exposing what's going on. I'd leave this loneliness behind and search for another. Have you come to know loneliness, as well? The old one has retired. The children are sleeping too. The light of the kerosene lamp is becoming drowsy, and the fowarika's flames are asleep in its hearth. Everything around me draws farther away. Even that image of you that came to me while I was underneath that man today no longer keeps me company at night in spite of the fear that spreads through my body. The night is a tyrannical friend who does not appreciate partners. And the morning! I have no idea what pains it might bring. I no longer know what's going on here while I'm up on the bridge. The old woman refuses to speak. I've become the property of Haneya, her mother, and her father. The three that were your property for so long. Hamed, you were ruthless. The discovery of lies will carry a heavy, bitter price. You're still ruthless—choosing to come to me on the bridge in the clear light of day, but you have no thought of joining me in my nocturnal loneliness. You are just as you always were."

As Zeinab stood up to go to bed, she knew what she would do the next morning. She was ready to have the image of her husband come to her again, but only to drive it out this time.

LAILA

Ever since Sheikh Masoud died, Suad began her day at dusk. She had spent the mornings in the past winter climbing up to the roof and opening her shirt up so that the rain could fall on her bare chest, but she would not be doing that this winter. She spent her days either by herself in the house sleeping, or sitting doing absolutely nothing without even a thought crossing her mind. She either went to chat with Laila or waited for her to come to her. But she always watched young Ali as well. Then as the sun set, her day started. In the evening she cooked her meal, washed her clothes, had whispered conversations with her dead husband, with whom she tried to engage in the rituals of love. She also baked, if it was time to bake.

These days, several hours after everyone goes inside around mid-morning and the evening is just settling, Suad begins her day. She starts with baking, exactly as she had done before Sheikh Masoud had died, when she used to bake at the start of each day.

She said, "Why don't you ever come anymore?"

"My mother and father have forbidden me. I don't know why."

Suad didn't press the issue. She had suffered during the past few days from Laila's absence. When Suad had tried to go to Laila, she had noted a hostility in the eyes of Laila's father and mother. Nevertheless, she was fully aware that at that place at that time anything was possible and could actually happen, and thus, there was no point questioning changes of any kind.

"Where is Ali?" Suad asked.

"He'll be here in a little while."

She had no idea why she was asking about him. In the previous winter he had stopped coming with Laila. It had been a winter devoid of late nights and mirth. In the summer Laila had not come and spent the night with her, and she didn't know whether she would spend the night this winter or not. She asked about Ali without thinking of the strangeness of the question, and then justified it by saying that she used to ask after him whenever Laila came by herself. Besides, no one in the world felt the things she was feeling.

The two were sitting together on the floor of the entrance to the house. On the ground in front of them was a large pan containing the dough and covered with an old piece of cloth. Suad lifted the piece of cloth to expose the surface of the rising dough. The air bubbles around the edges of the small round pan.

"Start rolling the dough while I stoke the fire," she told Laila.

Laila curled herself into a ball in front of the round pan. Suad encouraged the fire while Laila began to unfold herself over the baking sheet in which the balls of dough would be baked.

"It's started to rain again," Suad said from the entryway.

"It won't quit until morning. You'd better see to the chickens."

"The ceiling of their hut is fortified with mud. The rain won't fall on us at least."

Laila plucked out an appropriately sized handful of dough with her right hand. She put it between her two palms and began to roll it. She dropped it onto a plate lined with flour. She then passed it between her two hands several times. The flour facilitated unencumbered movement, so that it quickly became a smooth round ball. Laila put it on a metal sheet and grabbed another fistful of dough with which she performed the same ritual.

It was a simple process that Laila was accustomed to performing with alacrity. She played the same role when her mother baked. Her mother put the prearranged balls of dough into the fire. The mother didn't like for Laila to sit in front of the fire much. But Laila herself enjoyed it. She loved the chance to help Suad bake. Suad alone allowed her to sit in front of the oven. There was a great deal of pleasure in this. It was pleasurable to pull the loaf off with first her fingers, then her palms, or in tossing it up several times over the baking sheet. She usually passed the baking sheet to Suad who slid the loaf into the oven, but sometimes she put the loaf into the fire herself and watched its surface inflate instantly. Occasionally, she would draw close enough to the fire for its flames to set her face aglow. Her complexion went red, then took on a light incandescence. Her body would shiver and then experience a burst of warmth. She did not experience any of these things when she baked with her mother. But whenever Suad baked, each of their faces was glowing like a red rose by the end. Suad used to pinch her on her cheek or thigh and then they would both laugh. She sat rolling the loaves, listening to the sound of wood breaking as Suad smashed it with the small ax.

Suad could do the things that men do. She pressed with her right hand on the nearest end of the piece of wood and struck the wood with the blade of the ax lodging the blade in its middle. Then she would move the blade from side to side until it had split the wood into two. Laila listened to the sound of the splintering and cracking of the board. Suad's hand often slipped off the wooden arm of the ax. There was always an uncooperative piece of red wood to face, but Suad would become stubborn. Her face would turn red and the veins of her neck would bulge. Her breasts shook with the convulsing of her body. And she laughed when her hand slid off the handle of the ax and she nearly fell.

Suad threw the right-sized pile of wood into the oven and lit it. She stepped away from the oven a bit. At first, thick smoke curled out of the oven, and she opened the door of the hut to allow it to slither out. Laila had completed her rolling. "Only four plates of loaves? Suad doesn't bake as much anymore," Laila said to herself and a trace of sorrow appeared on her face.

"What's wrong?" Suad asked, noticing her sorrow.

She had just come into the entryway to take a tray of loaves over to the hut where the oven was. She pinched her on the arm before lifting the tray. When she leaned over to pick it up, her breasts were exposed to Laila who was sitting. Laila didn't answer. When Suad stood back up carrying the tray, she asked Laila, "Why are you laughing?"

Laila had broken into a smile when the ravenous whiteness of the tips of Suad's breasts had sparkled in her eyes. She didn't answer. She picked up one of the trays and stood up behind Suad. They set down their two trays and spread out a large piece of frayed cloth after Suad closed the door of the hut and smoke began spilling out around the edges of the door. They heard the creaking of the door to Zeinab's hut as it opened and closed. Suad sat directly in front of Laila. The trays were to their left and the oven to their right.

"That's the sound of the door to Zeinab's hut," Laila said. "She must have come back already."

Suad remained silent.

"Haven't any messages from her husband come yet? Hasn't anyone come to her?"

"The letters used to come with the trains. Now the only trains that come are carrying soldiers or foreigners."

"Will she stay there though? The Authority empties any houses whenever someone in them retires, is transferred, or gets fired."

Suad smiled sarcastically. She was a bit frightened but made herself speak. "The Authority is ignoring us."

Laila began kneading a ball of dough over the cooking sheet that she set down over one of the folds in her knees and said:

"That Zeinab is such a good person. She's taken in old Um Gaber."

Suad remained silent as she rolled dough along with Laila, then she said, "I've seen Zeinab more than once walking home. She seems preoccupied about something."

Laila threw a loaf up in the air then deftly caught it with the cooking sheet she was holding and said, "What do you mean?"

"Zeinab's thinking about leaving. Her eyes have told me so more than once."

Laila threw her loaf into the oven. She was beginning to feel the heat of the flames seep into her body.

"Let me put the loaves into the oven," she begged.

"Oh no!" Suad suddenly shouted.

"What's wrong?"

"We forgot to clean the floor of the baking chamber."

Laila stood up quickly and brought in a pail of water and a piece of burlap. She wrapped the burlap around the end of a long iron prod. After plunging it into the water and pulling it out, she stuck it into the oven and dragged it across the metal grill where the bread baked and over the flames of the fire. Turning the cloth by twisting the other end of the prod, she began to clean the metal pan. Suad had pulled out the loaf that Laila had already thrown in and tossed it over on top of the chicken coop, while the sound of water dripping off the metal pan into the burning wood popped. Laila felt the glow of the flames on her face. When she finished cleaning, she put the prod and the burlap in the bucket of water and set them off to the side.

Suad began thinking about Laila's oft-expressed desire to dive into the flames with the bread. Suad herself experienced pleasure when her face drew near the opening of the oven to pull the loaf out off the grill and a river of perspiration gathered under her arms, between her thighs, and behind her ears. Baking day was always a day for her and Sheikh Masoud. Sheikh Masoud always went out before dawn to call the faithful and lead them in prayer. He came back to bed and didn't awaken again until mid-morning. Since Suad would begin baking in the early morning, the Sheikh always got up after she had finished. He always woke up burning with desire, and she always finished her baking on fire as well. He always bathed before going out to call the faithful to the noon prayer and to lead those who gathered in submission to God.

"But who can Laila go to for satisfaction on baking day? She has loved a stranger who died after only a few meetings." Suad said this to herself as she rolled another loaf then tossed it to Laila to be rolled more, then tossed into the oven.

A silence reigned over them that was only broken by the frantic attempts of the chickens to reach the half-baked loaf over the chicken coop.

Suad nearly asked about a topic she knew Laila hated, but she managed to stop herself. She said to herself, "Who could remember the train at such a time? Who could be saddened by its absence, or yearn for its return?"

Laila had spoken to her often of her hatred for the train and for the people that went out to meet it. She had once said that the train was the cause of Fareed's abandonment of her because she came back from it so dirty that it would take her three days to clean herself completely. She spoke of Fareed often after his death. She said that he had told her not to feel sad if he was found dead or murdered. But she never spoke of her tears in the depth of the night, and she didn't realize that Suad already knew everything. Laila said:

"I've come to hate Fridays."

Suad was surprised by this at first, but quickly realized what Laila meant. All the incidents had occurred on the day of rest.

"Today, Neama left," Suad said, as though she were completing her thoughts. Then they each were overcome by the feeling that they were discussing senseless things. But Laila continued, "I wonder who will still be here after all this."

She almost asked who would be leaving. Suad was tossing an unbaked loaf up in the air that only half-landed on the edge of the baking sheet, so that she had to reach down and gather it into one piece with care so that it would not fall apart.

"Fareed said everyone must leave immediately."

"You told me before that he said that, but you didn't explain why."

"I don't know, but that's what he said."

Suad turned her attention to sprinkling flour on the baking sheet she rested on her lap. She began placing balls of dough on it. She arranged each of them with her fingers so that they touched each other. She ruined the first loaf she tried to spread, and ended up tossing it on top of the hen house and setting off another flurry of competition underneath in the form of attempts to eat at the loaves from below. Then Suad uttered involuntarily: "Are you still crying, Laila?"

" . . . "

"Ali told me about it."

She said it in a low voice as though she were apologizing. Laila smiled and tears sparkled in her eyes. She brushed them away with the back of her left hand. She sensed the warmth of her hands and face, and said, "He doesn't seem to leave anything be without telling you. He's become a real devil."

Something about this comment made them both happy, although neither one knew the reason. The steady stream of rain intensified outside. The chickens in their coop began hopping to and fro like frightened birds. A crack of thunder pealed off in the distance, and they heard the sound of feet racing, then a rapid knocking at the door of the hut.

"It's him!" Suad screamed with pleasure as she jumped up to open the door. Ali darted in panting for breath. Laila was sitting with her legs crossed and the ends of her galabeya falling back around her thighs a bit. She pulled at the galabeya to cover her knees. He noticed his sister's face go red as if about to burst into flames. He looked at Suad, who was staring back at him, and whose face was also aglow.

"You're baking, are you?" he said.

They both laughed out loud, and he joined in their laughter.

"What do you want?"

"Mother wants you."

"Sit down till we finish."

"She wants you now."

He stamped his foot to the pleasure of Suad. She was staring at him and listening to his argument with his sister.

"Sit down, Ali, and let me give you a fresh loaf sprinkled with sugar and shortening."

"I don't want one." He regretted his decisive retort as soon as it had escaped from him.

"Sit down, Ali."

Laila pronounced the sentence as though saying, "Have some shame, Ali." He stood staring around him in confusion.

"Do you want a chair?" Suad asked, smiling at him.

"I'll sit in the entryway."

Ali knew that during the baking the women would bare their legs. From time to time, they forgot themselves and dried their faces with the ends of their dresses. To Ali's discomfort, their legs were exposed even more.

He stumbled toward the entryway and sat on the ground near two large trays of dough. Suad came in behind him and set in front of him a jar of shortening and a jar of sugar and a spoon and turned around in front of him letting him observe her strong, well-shaped figure. He noted the dazzling flesh on her legs, and her thick, full hair hanging over her back.

He averted his stare when she turned around, but she felt his eyes piercing her back and knew that he watched her in spite of his averted glance. And her blood boiled with pleasure. Suad went out to the hut and put the sugar and shortening down on a plate. She rolled out a loaf of bread and asked Laila to put it in the oven but not let it get overdone. Suad sat down facing Ali in a spot where he could see her from the open door of the entryway. He was unsettled a bit at the sight of the bare flesh around her thighs before him. He decided not to look in her direction and to answer while staring at the ground if either one of them should speak to him.

"The rain's heavy," Suad said.

"No, it's only flooding the whole earth," he answered. All three of them laughed while Ali still stared at the ground and Suad watched him with ecstasy. He sensed her stare.

Laila removed the piece of bread for Ali. She gave it to Suad who put it on a plate and began to cover it with sugar and shortening. She got up to give it to Ali. She made a point to look into his eyes as she leaned over and put it down in front of him. He lifted his face up, and she saw that he was on the verge of tears. She felt sorrow coming over her like a flood. "What are you thinking about, Ali?" she whispered to herself as she looked at his black eyes sparkling with a sadness she had never seen in them before. Ali was thinking about how there would soon come a time when he would rarely—perhaps even never again—see Suad's face. He remembered his question to Samira that morning about why she did not go and look for Mursi herself, and he said to himself, "Why did you ask her that?"

Suad went back to the hut carrying one of the remaining trays. She put the bread in the oven and then placed the empty trays over it. Then she went back into the entryway to prepare the last tray. This time she didn't look at him, but she knew he was eating without any appetite. She asked herself, "Why did you drown the loaf in shortening? It will be heavy on the boy's stomach." But she knew that there was another reason for his lack of appetite, even though she didn't know what it was.

The baking came to an end. Laila stood for a while in the doorway to allow her body to cool off so that she wouldn't catch cold when she went out. Suad handed her a shawl to cover her face and the top of her head. Ali refused to take anything to protect him from the rain. Suad listened to the sounds of their feet rushing away and began to cry furiously in front of the oven.

When Laila and Ali reached their house, they found that their parents and younger sister had gone to sleep. Ali slept in the entryway after he had brought out a wool blanket from the inner room. He would never sleep next to Laila again. He had become a man.

As she climbed on top of her bed, Laila thought to herself, "I was really strong tonight. Perhaps, I have really forgotten Fareed."

She almost felt like she was outside of herself when she spoke to Suad. When she cried, it was in spite of herself. She did not force herself to smile to cover up her tears; rather she genuinely felt like crying and smiling at the same time. Up until the previous day, she had been crying every night, and now she was asking herself if all that crying had been pointless.

She knew what the source of her confusion was. Since his death, she had been mulling over why he never said anything to her until the final night.

"Laila, I'm going to tell you something you shouldn't tell anybody else. I'm neither proud nor arrogant. I'm just sad, and my sorrow is unique. You won't understand all of what I'm going to tell you. I used to see you as you went out to meet the train, or came back from the railway. My heart would rip itself into a thousand pieces and let flow a river of blood; but I told myself I can't stop anyone. I knew that fact well. No one can stop all of you from going out to the train. At the same time, no one can bring the train back to all of you, and no one of you can go after it. Do you understand what I'm telling you? You're heartbroken and don't want to hear what I'm saying. You want me to stare into your eyes. I know your love is powerful; so is mine. Just as you loved me in silence, so I loved you silently. Silence is the sky we all live beneath. Even Suad, whom they accuse of transgressions with me . . . I never had her in the way they presume. I see her in a different light than you all do. I hear about her dancing and her ample spirit. Yet I see her as a sad riddle. You and she are the same. Each of you are near to the other, but I love you, even if I don't hate her. Can you understand what I'm saying, Laila? You're silent, and that's fine with me. You know that I study in the city. Do you know the city? Have you ever been there? In the city, we talk a lot, and we don't sit around waiting for things. There I know everything. When I come here I'm engulfed in sorrow because there in the City, I know what will happen here. You are surprised by the trains with soldiers and foreigners, but I know who they are, where they come from, where they'll go. I've tried many times to speak here but something rough always cuts me off. Something tells me my words will be drowned in the steady waves of the lake and the desert's stagnant sands and the wind. Even Sheikh Masoud was more dazzled by my presence than attentive to my words when I tried to talk to him. He didn't seem to follow anything I said. This night begins a long torment for me. I know what the rain and the earth's revolutions mean. Do you understand? You cry. You just cry. If only you could have your fill of crying."

He took her two hands in his. She could still feel the warmth of those hands. She wanted to talk to him, but she couldn't find him. She sensed something burning in her veins, and she asked aloud, "Did the government really kill you, as your father claims?"

No one knew what had happened between the two of them that night.

She bore the secret alone. She remained frightened for days and weeks whenever she met him after that night. Although she believed him, she still asked, what is there to keep him from lying? But he was right when he said she would not become pregnant. Had he done something she didn't notice in order to spare her the worst of the scandal? When she gave herself to him, she wasn't enticed in the least by his saying she would not become pregnant. On the contrary, she hoped he would make her pregnant and bring down a scandal. She would have devoted herself to the struggle against the others, and nothing would have filled her with fear. How she would have loved to be able to say that she was Fareed's woman, even after his death. In that case, she wouldn't have cared if marriage proposals never came. She couldn't see the world except through him. The problem was that he had not left her anything. Had the City taught him this? He didn't talk to her much about what he did in the City. All she remembered was the front of the cinema.

"The lake and the desert. Dead fish and sinister birds and a treacherous sun and a station through which alien trains pass. What patch of earth is this?" But she did not hate the place as he did. Here she had grown up, lived her life, and loved the fresh winds.

He told her he would die and she did not believe him. But he had done it, and he had left her crumpled papers that she had been trying her hardest to decipher ever since. Laila had merely memorized what Fareed had read to her, and she had memorized. Her atrophied powers of reading could not help her understand his writing. That night, she had realized that she didn't really know what she had memorized. Was Fareed just a mirage? She took out the papers, but she could not comprehend a single word. She was starting to forget what she had memorized. She shriveled up under the covers until she was about to disintegrate. Then she saw Fareed before her.

Do you know what's happened to me? I am a virgin again. I felt it in my sleep. I saw people made of rays of light surrounding my bed and bringing it back to its place. The next morning I put my fingers in and felt it. I was hoping you would live, but you died and left me. You taught me how miserable we are, and you opened my heart up to fear. No one knew the secret of my tears. Do you know what happened today? Ali told me as we were eating our lunch that Samira had gone mad. He asked about the City, and I didn't know how to answer him. I saw in his eyes a confused questioning, some ambiguous desire. Several days ago, I saw him trying to read your papers. I had removed them from my bosom, put them under my pillow, and forgot them. That was my first time to forget. But I gathered the papers up from him and figured out why he had been hovering around me before. Can you see him reading anything from them? He only knows a little bit of reading. But once he sets his mind to something, he must do it. For more than ten years he's been sleeping next to me. No one knows him the way I do. If he wants, he'll decipher spells. Suad asked me without Ali hearing as we were baking why Ali has become so morose. I almost let it out. I was the woman of a man who left me nothing, who died leaving behind only some worthless papers . . . yes, I knew she was asking about Ali. How could I no longer remember a single word from your papers? They were so full of beautiful writing, but they might as well have been a blank slate.

She sighed.

Why have you left me in this wilderness? Many things keep me away from you. My virginity has come back to me. I'm not lying. Everything draws me away from you. Everything.

Migrations

ZEIDAN

Winter came to an end. The women did not mention to the children that the waters of the lake were rising ominously toward their doorsteps at night. A deadness settled in as they all watched. Even the trains carrying foreigners or soldiers stopped coming through. So many had completely forgotten the train that it had become a mere vestige of a bygone era for them. Still, none of this meant that children could stay outside until late at night, nor play during the day, nor, in the case of the boys, fish or hunt. None of the men, however, showed any desire to return to their old ways. All of life took one form. With the sunrise, the men went out to the rail line to work on whatever needed to be repaired. In the evening they returned. Because there was no longer an inspector in the area, the men didn't work too hard. Everyone forgot who had died or disappeared. Even in the case of disappeared relatives, the relative who stayed tried to forget the one who left. But Suad didn't forget that she had seen a desire for flight in Zeinab's eyes. Ali didn't forget that he'd asked Samira why she didn't go look for Mursi herself. And Laila remembered that Ali had asked her about the City.

After Neama moved at the beginning of the winter, Zeidan disappeared completely. No one ever saw him again. The old guard met one of the local men and talked about Zeidan, describing how he had met him and heard from him directly that a jinni had possessed him. Even though the rail worker told the story with fear and trembling, full of sorrow over Zeidan's sad fate, the man spread the news throughout the twenty houses, two of which (the house of the inspector and that of Zeidan) were now abandoned. The children began to gather at these two dwellings and use them to relieve themselves, so that Um Gaber, who had gone to live with Zeinab, had to lock her old house. The women were too frightened to tell the children that the waters were creeping toward the doors of the houses. So instead, they told them that Zeidan came out of the lake at night to stalk the children so he could offer them as food for the jinn. More stories grew up around Zeidan. He was spending his nights under water. He came up during the day to wander in the nearby fig groves and around the mills until his clothes dried, and he had gathered enough figs—although the fig harvest was normally in the summer—to bear them as a gift to the jinni in the evening.

Zeidan became a figure that appeared suddenly at any time of night to snatch whomever he wished and pull them to the depths of the water. The jinni had endowed him with superhuman strength with which he was able to overcome any mortal. Plus, as a mortal, Zeidan had been beaten down, and he had a duty of blood vengeance that forced him to return to the houses at night for revenge.

As the days passed, the tales grew. Many men began to swear they'd seen Zeidan diving into the water. Many women swore they'd seen him coming out of the waters of the lake early in the morning. Men swore that as they returned over the bridge at dusk carrying the supplies they'd purchased that day, they heard a rustling in the cattails; then they heard a large flock of quail and a swarm of bats escaping up toward the sky; then they heard a slapping sound in the water, a thick sound as though a huge stone had been flung into the water from the seventh heaven. When they looked in fright, they found something long and vast stretching out over the water, something with a broad back, a huge head, and two giant feet. This immense thing slapped two consecutive blows on the surface of the water, then dove. Each blow sounded like the blow of two oars, but it was much stronger. The thing dove, raising its huge, bare feet in the air and then disappearing, sending a bevy of large bubbles gurgling up to the surface for a long time.

Everyone who told this story said that they believed this creature to be Zeidan, but when they'd seen his feet, they'd found that the toes had melded, the feet were webbed, and the limbs were those of a strange creature. When whoever was listening asked what the strange creature could have been, the storyteller would hesitate momentarily, then say that it could be none other than Zeidan. Then they added that this new shape of the feet was natural, now that he had come to live with the jinni in the middle of the water. It was inevitable that this would happen to his feet in order to make swimming easier. The jinni herself must have done this to his feet, so that he could come to her quickly. Everyone became convinced that Zeidan went back to his new house underwater every night.

More than one woman related having the same experience. When she went to the rooftop in the early morning to remove the standing water after a rain by pushing it toward the drains (all the while cursing as she worked whoever had built these roofs tilted away from the drains), she saw an awesome thing, long and curved like a huge inflated wine skin. She would become frightened that it might be a corpse, but before she could scream, she saw it rise up. As she caught her breath, the thing would begin to go down. She would say to herself it must be the gentle waves and the thick, standing waters as they awoke in the morning since everything slept at night including the lake waters. Then a large coconut, or something like a coconut, although it was black, rose up before this huge object. Before this object, two gigantic arms rose up, with broad fingers—not webbed, as on the creature the men saw. It rose up first one arm then the other. Then the large coconut rose up bearing a face that was a wild distortion of Zeidan's face, which had grown as large as the mouth of the brick oven. After this happened, the woman would explain, her heart thumping in her chest, that it would escape back to the ground. Some of the women made the story so horrific that they wet themselves and froze. One of them said she hadn't even realized she wanted to urinate, but then had suddenly felt the urine burning her thighs as it ran down the inner walls of her legs and through narrow folds of cellulite. They all reported that they were unable to move or scream or even blink, as though the whole scene was something they were destined to live through. After that, according to their reports, Zeidan started to push the cattails and the thick brush apart with his huge arms. The birds that had been sleeping in their hiding places flew. The whole scene in the end was mesmerizing because the sun, which was rising up from behind the bridge, was behind Zeidan as he ascended from the water. The water appeared as though it were desert—reds and yellows that dazzled the eyes. Zeidan appeared with his wet, yellow clothes sparkling like a gigantic piece of amber, and when he rose out of the water and the brush and came up on the beach, he came out far from the houses and headed toward the fig orchard, and it was as though the moment he took his first steps, his body shrunk to a natural size.

The conglomeration of the tales that the men and women told was totally incomprehensible. Why were his hands and feet webbed at night, but with fingers and toes in the morning? Why would he come out toward the houses and then turn around and walk all the long distance toward the fig orchards, even though if he came out of the lake by the bridge he would be closer to them?

No one could answer the first question. But Abdullah's wife suggested an answer to the second by saying that he was homesick and came out of the lake by the houses each morning in order to see his old house.

There were also those who remained skeptical. Suad still remembered what Sheikh Masoud often said to her: that men reap what they sow; that every earthly misfortune has some mortal behind it; and that God Almighty is surely not to blame for their handiwork. He said that there were no more jinn, although they were mentioned in the Quran; and that if they could be found in this day and age, they would be subjects before the sons of Adam. She went so far as to say that he had told her about a friend of his who had taken command of a jinni, and how this man had given him a magical key that had allowed him to do this, and how Sheikh Masoud himself had been able to use this key once. A beautiful jinni appeared in his hands, crying and saying that she was in love with the friend of the Sheikh who had taught him the secret of the magic key. She said that the friend knew she loved him and that he was the only mortal who could subdue her since she loved him so much that she would obey his every command. Even so, he did not wish to marry her. After Sheikh Masoud heard all this, he took pity on her. He released her and found that her tears had turned into small piles of salt on the ground. Suad also remembered that the Sheikh had described to her how he had managed a few times to subjugate a jinni.

Sometimes Suad was confused. She didn't know whether to believe what was said about Zeidan or not. Whenever her mother had told her about her long search in pursuit of her father who had disappeared after being possessed by a jinni, she had almost believed it, but when Ali came to her and said his parents were talking about the jinn to scare him, but that he wasn't frightened, she decided the stories about Zeidan were bold-faced lies.

Neither did Zeinab believe it. When she heard what was said, she just smiled. She returned every day in the evening and had never seen Zeidan diving in the lake as the men claimed. She also got up every morning at dawn and had never seen Zeidan coming out of the lake the way the women described. Sometimes she reminded herself that in the evenings she was so tired that she didn't see what was around her, and the cosmos that seemed at that moment like a dark conch shell made her shrivel inside herself and feel nothing. In the morning, she would still be overwhelmed from the shock of her visitors who visited her over the bridge. And the cosmos, which appeared like a huge egg, made her walk along as though anaesthetized, not feeling a thing. But she told herself that she would not believe what she had not seen with her own eyes.

Laila still believed what Fareed had told her: that what was being said amounted to complete lies, that Sheikh Masoud was struck down by a will-ful hand though they did not know the killer. But then again she almost be-lieved it all when she remembered Fareed talking to her about preordained fates and inescapable curses that no one could know until drawn near to them. Then she remembered how her virginity had re-turned to her. But then again she would go back to saying, if even love is a lie, how can I believe what's said of Zeidan?

Ali, for his part, devoted little thought to Zeidan. He hated his parents when they began talking to him about spirits and jinn in order to scare him. He told Suad that, if he saw Zeidan, he would walk up and talk to him, and that if he tried to dive underwater, he would dive after him and follow him all the way to the magic castle if need be.

Suad, on the other hand, no longer rushed to go out at night. She even began to light the fowarika from inside the hut whose door she opened in order to let out the smoke, as she told herself that the jinn feared fire. Laila would visit her now only if Ali accompanied her all the way to Suad's front door. Their mother would then wait at the doorstep of their house watch-ing her until she had made it all the way to Suad's doorstep. Then she would watch as her son came back by himself all the way back to her house, never leaving him to linger outside. Then when Ali went out to bring her back from Suad's, Laila would hang on to his arm with force, not letting go of him until after they had both made it back into their own house. Zeinab, meanwhile, wished more than once, as she was heading out in the morning or returning in the evening, that Zeidan would come out, snatch her, carry her off, and dive with her down to the dwellings of the jinn. That would be the most merciful future she could imagine.

The men began to buy all the supplies they needed from the bridge before sunset. They began buying what they wanted in the morning, or at least by the afternoon. They no longer discussed seeing Zeidan in the evening as he dove back into the lake, but the women still climbed up to the rooftops in the early morning. Many of them wanted to see the creature. They believed that he would grant anyone who had suffered the shock of seeing Zeidan any wish. Abdullah's wife went up to her roof the most. She believed, that Zeidan could fulfill her wish of bearing a son and of bringing back Mursi, the fiancé of Samira the beauty.

Once the winter came to an end, they all tired of all these tales. Suad forgot that she had read something in Zeinab's eyes. Ali forgot what he had said to Samira. Laila forgot what Ali had asked her about. Moreover, the men began to go back to hunting and fishing, particularly when spring was renewed, and the reins were loosened on the young boys and the children. But during one of those spring nights in which the dust and sandstorms were in abeyance, all the rooms of every house were light until late at night, and the windows were left open to take in the soft spring breeze (especially since it was a mild night after an unseasonably warm day), suddenly, stones were hurled through every window at the same time with a superhuman strength. A stone came into each room and fell in the midst of its occupants. No one realized, however, what was going on, since they were all unaware of the stones that had flown into the other houses at the same time. Every house simply imagined that some wayward child had been let out by his parents by accident and that he had hurled the rock. Soon, the whole matter was forgotten.

Not too long afterward, another stone was thrown into each home. Still, no one kept the windows shut. There was nothing noteworthy going on in the houses that night. The women were busy with their chickens or kneading the dough they would bake in the morning. The men smoked thin cigarettes, and some stretched across the ground or over the old couches. The children of each house gathered together talking in a language no one else understood, and laughing and fighting without anyone paying attention to them.

As night grew darker, many of the children went to sleep. The women had finished their evening tasks. Suad, suffering from loneliness, paced between the inner room and the entryway, thinking that she should not wait for someone to come sent by her husband. She had to go through with what she had been thinking about for some time, now that Ali had become a man, and not just an ordinary man. Zeinab had finished cleaning her clothes. She had prepared a large traveling bag and packed it with everything she would need to travel, although she had told no one of her decision to leave. She hid the bag in a corner of the entryway awaiting the appointed time to leave. Laila waited for her parents to sleep so she could flip through Fareed's papers one last time and then rip them up. As for Ali, he stretched across a blanket on the ground in the entryway with his eyes fixed on the small kerosene lamp his mother had set on the other side of the room from him out of fear that he might be burned in his sleep. Abdullah lay anxiously in his bed after having suddenly discovered that it did not matter a bit whether the sun was behind or in front of him and that he had wasted his life complaining of something that he had no hand in. His wife, still awake in spite of the late hour, sat and watched their small girls sleep almost completely exposed, covered only by bits of torn clothing.

At that moment, a flying ball of fire came through the window of each room. It darted between the narrow iron bars on the windows with its burning flames fizzling. Startled screams came up at the same time from each house. The families were struck with fear. Those who had been awake rushed to put out the fireball which began rolling along the ground into every corner as though determined that it burn whatever was in the house. Those who were asleep woke up to the tumult caused by the invasion. Some who tried to stamp it with their feet, jumped about screaming. Others tried to beat it with a small broom, kicking up a cloud of dust as the broom in their hands went up in flames. Others ran to the toilet to gather water, which they poured onto the fireball. Once most of the villagers had managed to extinguish the flame in their house, a new ball of fire, even more incandescent, flew in.

The children woke up horrified. Ali was the quickest on his feet in his house. He leapt up and closed the window after the first fireball flew in. When he heard the screams rising up from the other houses, he burst toward the door. His mother ran after him, hanging on to him and trying to stop him. Without thinking, he shoved her so she fell back on her rump, and she watched him powerlessly as he jumped out the door.

After the second ball of fire, everyone rushed to close the windows. They stamped out the second fireball, and the men rushed out toward the space behind the houses. Each one of them thought the two fireballs had come only into their house. None of them except for Ali noticed the screams coming from the other houses. The women pushed their way out behind the men once they had locked in their children. When they all found themselves running together to the empty field behind the houses to look for the hurler of the fireballs, they realized that they had been tossed into everyone's house and they stood stunned in amazement.

Ali was the first to arrive and he found the space deserted. He kept walking until he had gone all the way to the train station without realizing it. There he saw a train in the distance with its lights dawning on the horizon. He found the station inspector sleeping on a bench near his office. He heard bits of an incomprehensible language being uttered from behind the tightly shut office door. He knew what was happening inside. The train was the foreigners' train, but it had stopped off in the distance. Ali remembered that the trains full of foreigners and soldiers had not come for some time. He reflected on that strange ball of fire. He knew that he had been carried off far from the houses, and he headed back slowly and deliberately wondering how one person could have thrown balls of fire into all these houses from which screams had arisen. Maybe, it was more than one person, he told himself. But if this had been the case, how could they all have disappeared so quickly? He began to burn with anxiety. The moon hung high in the heavens, and he noticed for the first time that it was not completely white. It had small dark spots on it that he had not noticed before. When he got back to the field behind the village, he found the villagers pulling back into their homes. In the open space in which they used to gather to celebrate, they stopped and began to converse. Ali heard their voices as he approached, but without distinguishing what was said. Until suddenly, a man in their midst screamed, "It's him! It's him!"

He repeated it over and over again and waved toward the lake, mesmerized like a madman. They all looked toward where he was pointing and saw the cattails spread wide. Some huge, gigantic being was running among them and splashing its feet in the water. It stirred up a spray that sparkled white before them in the moonlight. The women all raced back to the houses, while the men froze in their tracks. Some of them thought to themselves, "How could our Zeidan be doing this to us . . . and why?" Then some of them asked the question out loud, so that Ali heard it as he came toward them.

He didn't wait, however, to hear anymore. He made his way to the house, overcome by a crushing drowsiness. At the doorstep, he felt something grabbing his collar and nearly choking him. His eyes bulged until he thought they would leap from their sockets, and his face puffed up with consternation. In his chest, water filled with hot stones boiled.

He looked behind him and saw his father still standing in the open space with the other men. He let go of the strength that seemed about to explode inside him. Methodically and with deliberate determination, his feet began to plod toward Suad's house.

ABDULLAH

Abdullah had willingly given himself up to sleep the night before. He got up the next morning forgetting what had happened at night. He threw his pack over his shoulder and embarked on the daily routine that he had been repeating for more than twenty years now. For the first time he didn't feel the heat of the harsh sun on the nape of his neck, even though it was the heart of the bitter sandstorm season that came every spring. Only once while he was walking, did he remember the fireballs and the chaos of the previous night. But he quickly repulsed encroaching feelings of fear by thinking to himself, "We have no hand in anything." Then he went back home at night to find his wife screaming and wailing in his face.

She was sitting in a pile in a corner of the entryway surrounded by other women and their five small girls. They had barely heard the sound of his approach and entrance. When he put his basket and pole down on top of the oven, they began to exit silently. Abdullah looked toward them with surprise. Then he became frightened. He sensed that the hump on his back had grown. He had entered calmly, even surreptitiously, only for his wife to break into her wailing, "Samira . . . Samira, Abdullah . . ."

She began to slap her cheeks, and the five small girls around her burst into tears. Meanwhile, Abdullah headed toward the inner room. He felt a long time had passed before he had covered those four meters and made it inside. Abdullah was over fifty. He had tried again and again to produce a son but was unsuccessful. God had saved him from the smoke of the smoldering coals. The sun had relentlessly chased him for twenty years now. His wife's face had green inscriptions spread all over it, and he had asked himself often how he had managed not to see them before they married. The hump on his back had not been there since birth either. It had begun to appear after he had turned thirty, once he had begun to stare down at the two rails all day searching over and back for defects in them. In the end, he had lost everything. He collapsed on the nearest bench as his thick shoes made his feet throb with pain.

He had always asked himself why it was that his daughter's heart had fixed on Mursi in particular. Why this figure who traveled day and night, the wanderer in the eye of the sun and the heart of the wind between the people and the open spaces? Often, he thought of the accidents that had befallen the train travelers. In one of the villages, a band of thieves had come up with an ingenious way to rob trains. They came with a long thick rope and tied one end of it to a large tree or a telephone pole near the tracks. Then they tied a large iron hook to the other end of the rope. When any train filled with freight passed by, they tossed the hook over an open car so that it caught onto one of the burlap sacks full of whatever product it was carrying. They would tie a number of ropes to trees and poles all around to toss them all toward the cars of the trains. Once the train had pulled the ropes to their full length, its own motion caused the ropes to drag off a bag of supplies so that goods fell from the train without anyone having to jump on or off or expose himself to danger. In one of the village's dark nights, when the train was passing by with a load of sesame, a band of thieves attacked the train. As they went to gather up the bags that they had pulled down, they found a guard had been accidentally grabbed by one of the hooks, pulled down, and killed. The hook had stuck right into his belly. The whole village heard the story, and they were all shocked at this strange new form of protection for the trains.

Abdullah had heard this story while he was still small, and he remembered it often as an adult, when he pondered his daughter's fixation with this strange boy who guarded the trains. He himself had had an odd experience with a guard that he still remembered from time to time. He had been returning late at night after doing some emergency work on a train wreck. His co-worker was with him, and they stumbled upon a freight train carrying sugarcane. The co-worker suggested that they pilfer a few stalks of cane for their sons. His co-worker began to pull at a couple of stalks, but he had a hard time with them because they were tied with huge straps. Abdullah decided to take a shortcut. He climbed up on top of the stalks and let loose the entire stack. It was night, with no moon or stars whatsoever and with heavy daunting winter clouds. Abdullah climbed up into the car and stood in the middle of it. He bent over to pull up one of the belts. He wrapped his arms around it but found it too heavy. When he finally yanked it up violently, he suddenly found a screaming man between his arms, grappling at his throat. Abdullah's heart stopped for a moment from the shock, but then he quickly gathered his wits as the man showered him with blows while falling across the cane stalks. Abdullah was bent over him, unable to right himself as his adversary squeezed relentlessly at his throat with both hands. The guard had been sleeping inside the stack of cane. Abdullah always called that night a night of horror, even as he laughed about it later. Then he would laugh more and tell of how the situation ended with the two of them making up, and the guard giving both him and his partner a large stalk of cane. He would say that he was so scared he thought he would lose his ability to have children; then he would laugh and say God had already blessed him with three girls at the time and he had gone on until they were six. But Abdullah stopped talking about this story once Samira fell in love with the strange train traveler. He thought about her and went silent in his sorrow. He often said to himself, "The same thing could have happened to Mursi that happened to the guard that was hooked by the train robbers." Theft increased and the bands of robbers spread all over, according to the people at the bridge and the workers that he often went out to meet who were shipped in from other areas to deal with train wrecks or other emergencies. He suspected that a sugarcane thief had frightened Mursi to death.

But none of this talk had any attraction for him now that Samira herself had vanished.

Why such a harsh punishment? On the day when Abdullah almost gave up and resigned himself to the fact that he had no hand in anything, Samira the beauty disappeared.

That damn sun which he had not been able to see now for twenty years managed to seal the conspiracy from behind his back.

A year passed from the first time they had said their train would come tomorrow and it did not come. A few months ago, when they began once again to say that it was coming, and it seemed that no one would believe them, Samira got up to take a bath and disappeared into the bathroom for a long time. Her gaze wandered when she finally sat down to eat her dinner with them, and she didn't eat as she should have. He watched her grow pale like someone preparing to depart from this world, and he quickly expelled this thought from his mind. He saw her gripped by fear. Full of pity, he asked himself what he might do to help. The train that no one except Samira was still waiting for would not come. The winter progressed with a senseless lethargy. The sandstorms of the early spring encroached with an uncharacteristic gentleness, as though it were some cosmic trick. Abdullah's wife, to whom he had not spoken the entire evening after learning the news, began to beg him to go out after her. He wanted to do just that but had no idea where to begin since his two damned feet only ran in one direction each morning and in the opposite direction each evening. Basically, Abdullah had no choice but to wait until God set a course of action before him. He began to go out to the lake every night in case Zeidan might help him. He couldn't forget how he had felt sorry for him when he saw him stark white in his room the night his wife left. He neither saw Zeidan nor heard his voice. He saw only the heavy, fetid waters of the lake. The cattails had thickened, and the moon was no longer rising.

Over the water's surface, however, he would see a small flame, a glowing ring like some sort of strange nighttime sun. The circle would transform into a color that mixed blue with red. Then he saw Samira's face appear inside the ring. She laughed at him, then chortled loudly as the peals of her laughter echoed in the darkness. He had just enough sanity left not to dive in after her.

He would see her running back toward the bridge, then turn back around to meet him. She almost jumped over him and burned him with her flame, then turned back behind him again. He would stay there holding his knees against his chest until midnight. "You've become a jinni who seeks to kill her own father," he said, and he continued to go out every night. In the end, all he saw was his daughter's beautiful face. In the morning, he remembered his daughter's illumined visage that he had seen in the middle of the ring of fire. He would tell himself that he would see her face in the eye of the sun, if only he were able to look at it. But since he could rely on neither his two feet nor his thin parched neck, he ended up spending his day crying without tears. He looked at the tracks but didn't see them. On rare occasions, a tear or two might fall. Abdullah knew that the old were the only ones to cry tearlessly. He remembered how as a boy he saw his old father crying. He would look at him and not find a tear in his eyes. He saw the wrinkled skin and depleted eyebrows surrounding them. It surprised him that his father tried to dry away tears that weren't there, and he looked at his old father as though he were watching a small child.

"Abdullah, where is Samira?"

His wife became sick. She slept helplessly and then interrogated him at night when he came in.

"They say that she's started to appear in far-off stations selling drinks in the trains," she would say after questioning him. He looked at her in silence.

"They say she appears sitting on top of the signal lights singing to the trains that pass and to the night guards riding in them," she went on.

He looked over at his other sleeping daughters who no longer played or told stories to one another.

"They say that Mursi saw her and came to her, and they rode together on a train pulled by a stallion toward the land from which the trains never return."

Abdullah felt like a worthless stack of firewood.

"Abdullah, where is Samira? Where? If only she had a brother, he would be searching for her right now!"

He thought for a moment about the son they had never been blessed with, then he quickly pushed these thoughts out of his mind and sunk into an all-encompassing sorrow.

"She was so beautiful, Abdullah."

She had been as beautiful as the full moon. More radiant than the stars. More rapturous than the morning breeze—or the faint rays of the early-born dawn.

She had been beautiful, that creature who hung her heart on a traveler through the interminable space. In fact, Samira's dazzling brilliance kept him from believing that she could end up selling sodas in a train car. But he saw her as a songbird atop the signal light. A bride ascending out of the heart of the train cars, like the bride rising out of the lake depths with light beaming from her train quenching the thirst of both passengers and traveling guards with milk and honey. But why couldn't this sparrow alight at their doorstep, flutter her wings, and dance into the house?

"Have you seen Samira?"

No one answered.

"Have you seen Samira?"

No one answered him. They told him to go look at the bridge or in the City. None of them realized that he walked in only one direction. Zeinab reported that she hadn't seen her around the bridge. The City was only a distant hope, and his wife's health was failing.

When he thought about asking the station inspector as he passed by, either in the morning or at night, if by chance he had seen her riding one of the trains, he remembered that he was always sleeping. Nevertheless, he went and woke him up, only to have him stare at him without answering and then go right back to sleep.

When Zeinab told him that she had not seen her around the bridge, he remembered Hamed and Gaber, then Sheikh Masoud, then Fareed, then Arfeh, then Zeidan. He told himself that Samira was different from all of these. She would definitely be coming back, even if she came on the last days. He continued to go out to the lake every night where he saw her over the waters.

Abdullah thought hard for an entire month about going to where the sun—that had woven its plot for those long years—came to rest. In the evening he decided to start the next morning on that anguished journey behind the tracks in front of the sun headed westward. He remembered that at midday with the sun directly over him, he had usually made it to an abandoned wooden shack where he took a midday nap. When he woke up, he would walk back with the sun behind him. But he would never be able to break off this journey, since he could not make his feet keep going in the direction they had gone in the morning. They would return on their own. He said to himself in a tone of strength and determination: "Until midday my feet go west, after that they turn and head back east. In neither case am I able to turn and see the sun. At midday itself I can't turn my eyes straight up to heaven to see the sun straight over my head since I can't take my eyes off the rails. They've been that way for more than twenty years, and they will remain so. Yet I must find some way to manage to make it to where the sun sets instead of turning back around in the evening." Finally, Abdullah hit upon a solution that filled him with joy. Once he had finished his nap, he would not return; in fact, he wouldn't even get up. He would stay there until the next morning, then arise and continue walking westward. That way he could keep walking half a day each day and continue in the same direction without backtracking and get all the rest he needed at the same time. But at the same time he stumbled on this idea, a raucous clatter rang out in front of the buildings. He came out to see what had happened and found Um Gaber surrounded by Hamed's three children in the midst of a group of men and women. She saw him and he looked back at her.

One of the men said, "No one can go to the bridge at this hour in this darkness. Take the children back, Um Gaber, morning will bring another day. Who knows? Maybe she'll come back on her own in a little while."

The crowd dispersed and Um Gaber and the children followed them toward the houses. He realized that Zeinab had failed to return from the bridge.

Abdullah realized that he had made it to a point miles beyond the area and sensed that his plan was succeeding. He could feel the proximity of those western lands where the sun spent the night only to be launched out the next morning from the opposite direction to start once again its despicable toying with him. But he was bewildered when he realized there was nothing to be found there but two tracks stretching toward eternity. There were no signal lights except at stations spread out at a huge distance between each other, and he wasn't going to be able to find Samira on the tracks that only one train ever passed over. She could not have been selling drinks in that one train, especially since all the stations were abandoned and no one was getting on or off the train. And if she had really become a small, warbling sparrow, she wouldn't have been able to fly over all those long miles between one signal light and the next. But Abdullah still knew that his internal decision had been correct. It was inevitable that he got to the land where the sun sleeps, so that he could find those who captured the sun at night and see it while it was docile instead of searing. They would surely have the patience to listen to his plight. He would be able to tell them what he should have verbalized years ago. "Take this sun and give us a new, more sensitive one." It was this new, tender sun that would return his daughter, the dove that had abandoned its nest. But this, this cursed sun was devious . . . devious . . . devious from the dawn of time. Abdullah was going to tell them that the fraternal sun would end the torture of himself and all others; and if they said no, he would ask of these fine people — who had to have been fine, since the sun came to them tenderly and departed from them in the same manner and only grew fierce once it had cleared its way into space — he would ask them to let dawn break to the west, even it were only once, so he could stare straight at it, end his torture, and bring back Samira. If they refused this as well, he would ask them to keep it locked up for eternity and let the world run its course in the deepest darkness. In the end, they had to agree to at least one of his pleas. They must know him even before they saw him. It was inevitable that this treacherous sun beating down on his back had spoken of him, of what it was doing to him, and of his own doings. He had to find among them at least one man who would comply with one of his requests. Finally, if they all refused each of his pleas, he would speak to the sun itself. It would have to respond to him by taking pity, once it had seen him up close and seen his torture. How could it not, after being his companion for over twenty years? Anyone who could forget such a longtime companion was not of this world and did not deserve to go on.

UM GABER

When one of the men told Um Gaber to come back and that Zeinab might return after awhile, she said to herself, "What can I do? I saw her eyes this morning."

She had, in fact, seen her eyes that morning, through the constricted vision that she had left which allowed her to survey the world through a black filter. Zeinab's two eyes were there before her, wide and full of enchantment and a deep resolve. She knew that Zeinab would not come back that night, but inevitably she clung to the false hope. Who else was left to watch the children now that she was old and hunchbacked, with a permanent bow that nearly made her head drop to the ground?

She was always saying to herself that Hamed and Gaber had met up together at some long job. They had been seen running at length, pushing the inspector's car. Their disappearance was what had brought her and Zeinab together.

Since her son had disappeared, she had fallen silent. The others spoke of her as being pent up with sorrow. They said she had surrendered and was just waiting for her miserable death. When day after day passed with no hope of the absent one's return, her silence increased, until she might as well have been mute. They began to say that she was possessed by a jinni and lived in another place, and they backed it up by recalling her old energy in making charms and amulets for women once the train had disappeared. But through all of this silence she still saw Gaber before her. She saw him in each step she took. She was not surprised to see him confined between four walls with the whip's lashes raining down on him from all sides; or screaming in a barren wasteland containing nothing but snakes and vipers. Sometimes she would see him crying and would tell herself that he seemed to be remembering her and her fumbling with the needle and thread. Back when she fumbled trying to thread the needle, until he took them from her, threaded the needle, and stood to leave the room, she knew he was walking out in order to weep over his mother, who had grown old suddenly.

She begged the Lord repeatedly not to deprive her of these sorrowful visions of her son, but rather to make him her thoughts' companion night and day.

Once she sensed a heightened alertness in her ears and realized that her hands went out in front of her involuntarily whenever she heard a sound, she realized she was approaching blindness, and she asked herself when had these visions of her son had any need for her two eyes?

She continued to see him night and day as though he were moving within the very whites of her eyes. She also began to follow closely everything that happened around the bridge. She knew about every ugly twist or turn that befell Zeinab. She saw her the day her heart pounded under the salesman as she shuddered, but she remained silent.

Once midnight arrived and Zeinab still had not returned, she was certain that all her suspicions had been correct. She really had begun to foresee events before they happened. She remembered seeing Abdullah come out of his house while she stood in the midst of the men and women. Abdullah looked straight at her that day and she saw in his eyes the same thing she had seen that morning in Zeinab's. She said he had surely migrated with the morning. That man who suffered through because he had no son would never be able to bear life without Samira. That man who never ceased to amuse the others with his complaints about the sun had surely left on a quest for it. She closed her eyes to sleep with the knowledge that she too was burdened by a ritual she would have to carry out.

Three days passed, during which she shuddered with exhaustion from her efforts to watch the three children. The house contained a bit of bread and some old cheese. They kept asking about their mother, and she said that she had gone on a trip and would be back in a few days. She had forgotten that Zeinab repeatedly told them the same thing about their father. Once she remembered, she was struck with fear. The children used to ask Zeinab about him every day. They never got tired of asking just as Zeinab never tired of giving them the same response. In the end, the children gave up first. But, Um Gaber could not outdo the children. She lacked Zeinab's resolve.

In the evening of the third day, she asked herself what it meant that some men had stayed and worked although the cream of the crop had migrated. Then she heard a loud commotion outside: screaming and crying. She heard the sound of footsteps passing in front of the front door and Suad's voice saying: "That's enough Laila. Ali will surely come back."

Even the golden boy, she thought to herself. With the first rays of that dawn, leaving the door of the hut open, she walked slowly, shuddering, with the children behind her.

Morning was ushered in with the clamor of the village men gathering in the open space before the dwellings. The women were standing at their front doors conversing. No one paid attention to the cats and dogs meandering in and out of Zeinab's front door. Some of the men noticed the fish flying over the surface of the lake and then twisting and crashing back into the water. Others noticed the whooping cranes hugging each other in the skies. The morning was possessed of an enchanting beauty, but the spell was broken by a man asking, "Where is Ali's father?"

Ali's father appeared in a shambles. He was standing behind a stranger. The men who had asked for Ali's father asked the stranger, "Who are you?"

"I'm new here," he said. "Just yesterday, I was dispatched by the Authority to replace Zeidan."

The men looked at each other in shock until one of them said, "What are you saying?"

"I'm replacing Zeidan."

A third man asked, "How exactly did the Authority know that Zeidan had disappeared . . . and his wife had gone off as well? And when did you come anyway?"

"My wife and I came during the night." He pointed to the doorway of the house that had been Zeidan's where his wife was standing, and then added, "I know nothing of this Zeidan or his wife."

A fourth asked, "Did you come alone?"

"I heard that they will be sending an inspector to the area, and two more men in place of"—he seemed to be trying to remember something—"in place of two men whose names I don't remember. They said that they were following the inspector's car."

"Hamed and Gaber?" one of the men suggested.

"Yes, Hamed and Gaber," he answered.

Ali's father broke in mournfully, "You've all forgotten what we're here for. Where's Ali?"

Suad, whose house was far from the opening, could hear nothing. But she carefully watched the men who seemed confused. She looked over to

Laila standing next to her. Suad had stood by her side all night as she wept and thought of her brother. Suad comforted her and concealed what Ali had said from her. She looked over to the strange woman standing at the door of Zeidan's house. There was only the open door of Zeinab's hut between them.

"Who are you?" Suad asked her.

The woman smiled and said, "I'm new here. My name's Ihsan. That's my husband there," and she pointed excitedly at the stranger.

Suad realized then that the rest of the women were looking at the new woman. Laila had left her spot and headed toward the open area where the men were standing. Suad watched from afar until she came back toward her. Then, she watched as the men went back behind the houses on their way to work while Ali's father went back inside.

"What happened?" she asked Laila once she drew near.

"My father's sick. He won't be going to work today. I'll follow Ali to the City. I'm sure he's gone there."

As she said this she pointed at Zeinab's empty house.

"What's there," Suad asked.

"The door of Zeinab's hut is open."

Suad approached the door. She wasn't sure why, but she sensed that the old woman had died. She crossed the threshold and went into the front room. There was nothing but small bits of wood and some scattered rags. She called out, but no one answered. She crept into the inner room. It was also empty. She left without knowing what had happened. When she came back out a little way, she heard a slow movement to her right. She looked over and saw a black cat and a white dog lapping at a chicken's blood. The chicken had been slaughtered and was floating in blood. The fowarika stove was overturned, and ashes and smoldering coals were scattered around it.

The bridge was long—longer, in fact, than the old woman had expected. The treacherous sun had ascended quickly. The old woman knew that today the sun would be giving up the last of its fires. She tied a black band over her eyes saying, "One can either see or not, and since I can't see, I don't need the light." She gave up her hand to the oldest of Hamed's sons. The two other children walked behind them. They were barefoot like the old woman and the older brother and wore only some tattered cloths. They stopped in front of a lean-to covered with reeds. Haneya came out to them and spoke to them before the old woman could say a word.

"What do you want, Auntie?"

She surveyed the three children and smiled. The old woman motioned toward them, and Haneya understood.

"I don't know whether to tell you she's in the City and send you back or that she isn't there and send you forward. She disappeared without telling me a thing"—then after a moment of silence— "but how did you know me, Auntie?"

With a weak voice the old woman spoke, "Do you have a cane I could borrow?"

Haneya went back into her shack and picked up her father's cane. She put some bread in a bundle. She gave the stick to the old woman and hung the bundle on the back of the oldest child. Um Gaber began to move forward, leaning on Haneya's father's stick. After she had taken several steps, Haneya called out, "Auntie . . . how did you know me?"

The old woman wanted to tell her that she was a prophetess, but she knew that her feeble voice wouldn't carry, and she ended up saying, "Because you are a harlot," forgetting that this wouldn't carry either.

When it was almost midday, she decided to take a rest. She sat next to an abandoned shack that the oldest son had pointed out to her. They sat down around her, and she spoke out loud without even thinking that they might be listening to her, "She gave me the cane and the bread!"

They had no idea what she was saying and the oldest asked her, "Where are we going, Auntie?"

"We are going," she said.

"Where to? Won't my mother come back?"

"We will find her."

The boy was confused and remained quiet. After a while, he said, "We've come a long way. There's no one around."

She didn't answer. She knew he was right, but didn't know where the bridge would finally come to an end. It seemed to stretch to infinity both before them and behind them. All she could do was go. She asked herself why she went on silently. Why couldn't she just cry out to Zeinab until someone—perhaps even Zeinab herself—heard her cries. And was that really even why she left? What she really wanted now was to find someone to take the children and raise them. But was it possible that that could happen while she was with them? She would have to die first. And yet if she left them behind, no one would take care of them. She was not wrong, therefore in bringing them along. There was no room for anyone anymore. Survival had become everyone's goal. She was well aware of that. She also knew that if she died the earth would throw up someone to take the children. In spite of it all, she had to bring them far away from that place surrounded by the lake and the desert with the alien trains passing back and forth.

By the time she got up after their brief rest, the sun was tilting toward the horizon. She felt the soft brush of the early evening breeze. She told the oldest of the children to take her down to the lake for a drink. She asked the children to drink as well and they all began lapping up water voraciously.

"The water is salty," the youngest said.

He spat . . . and the old woman began to weep for the first time since her son had disappeared. "What could you possibly have gone to do under this sun, my boy?" she said to herself.

"Who are you talking to, Auntie?" the oldest of children asked.

The night was drawing near. She turned to him to answer. "I'm begging God to let us find your mother."

"Why can't we just go back and wait for her?"

"Do you know the way back?" she asked.

He looked around him and found that the evening's darkness was coming in a flood. The sun had left its morning heights. It was now in the distance at the other end of the bridge. It loomed before him as a large red circle. He became afraid. The frogs croaked loudly as though inside his ears. He did not answer her. He moved closer to her, clinging to her as they walked. At the same time, she could see Gaber coming toward them from afar stretching out to her a large, white, protecting hand. It came to her, bigger than the cosmos, to cover and protect her, until the voice of the older child broke in: "The baby is sleeping."

She decided to sit down again. She moved nearer the edge of the bridge next to the water. When she got up the first time, she had pulled off the black band over her eyes. She said to herself that she could not see in the dark. When she sat down the second time, a black expanse was projecting darkness over the lake water around the beams of the moon in ascent. She could not see herself in either the moon or the water. She was happy that she could hear the rustling of the cattails, the seagulls landing, the frogs croaking.

When she had first come to the area with her husband many long years ago, they were the only ones there. He complained to her of his loneliness at work and she complained to him of her loneliness at home. He wondered at why the Authority would have sent him to make railroad tracks and lay them by himself with no co-workers or overseers, and she wondered at why there were twenty dwellings although there was only one family occupying one house.

But when morning broke, they found the twenty houses full of families. Neither she nor her husband thought to ask one of them where they had come from. The husband cried out with joy, "I have co-workers now," and likewise, she proclaimed, "I have neighbors to chat with."

The following morning, she told him that she was pregnant. Then Gaber came, but she went barren after his birth for some mysterious reason. The workers and the families changed many times over, but she and her husband never asked about what was happening, or where the departing people were going, or where their replacements were coming from. And the other workers silently followed their lead.

Life came to have definite limits. The men went out in the morning to repair the tracks. Due to the paucity of trains, they never had much work. In the afternoons, they went fishing. The children went bird hunting in the mornings, then fishing in the afternoons. Some days, they reversed the two, especially in the winters when birds migrated away from the area. In the evening they played their games, while the women gave birth, kneaded dough, baked, talked, and quarreled on account of the children but then made up right away. A huge war broke out while Gaber was still a small child. The trains carrying soldiers and foreigners multiplied. Her husband said that the Europeans were fighting each other in their country. She had forgotten that she even had a country. She no longer knew anything but the twenty houses, nor did she see anything beyond the lake, the desert, and the local station. Her husband came home most days with substantial quantities of tea, lentils, and fava beans; and some days with clothes, chocolate bars, or large boxes of cookies and crackers. He said that the foreign soldiers had given them to him at the station. He added that the foreigners were infidels without a religion and that some of them swapped wives and others drank whiskey. She asked him how he could take gifts from such people, and he would say that they were all-knowing devils whom he could not resist. He would tell her about the strange and wonderful things in their possession. A small piece of lead that lit cigarettes, watches that glowed in the dark, a small box with a long, thin wire attached to it sticking up in the air that talked and sang and brought them the news of the world. He told her that they talked to one another in a strange tongue and alternately fought and laughed together.

One night he told her that he had become friends with the station superintendent and that he would invite him to come and spend the evening with them. The inspector quickly became used to spending his evenings with them. Then he suddenly stopped. When she asked him where the inspector had gone, he told her that the inspector had started sleeping around the clock and refused to speak to anyone who dared to awaken him. She noticed, however, that he seemed to be hiding something from her. He had started to come back every night from a round of fishing at the lake full of fear and trembling, and he would go to bed repeating over and over, "Cover me . . . cover me . . ." Yes, she remembered now. What was it he was trying to hide from her?

But Gaber was growing older by the day. The trains of foreigners were coming few and far between. Likewise, the trains of soldiers first diminished then disappeared completely until no one even remembered them anymore.

Throughout that time, the workers and their families changed around. Then suddenly ten years ago all changes stopped. At the beginning, the salvage trains came pulling one car loaded with goods. Then the number of cars being pulled multiplied, and the locals became aware of the value of their cargo. They would come out to the train in the hope of finding things to sell in the City. But then a salvage dealer started passing through the site during the middle of every week and purchase whatever they had managed to gather from last Friday's train and take it to the City. Thus, the locals never thought of going there anymore.

The bridge was the place from which they bought their things even though it was only lined with a few shops. But these shops gradually began to multiply. The number of inhabitants living in the area increased until they learned that the government had to expand the school and the hospital over it. In spite of this, no one could bother to attend the school. They lived in the spirit of the travelers, knowing that the railway workers were always following the tracks without settling in any one place. When the inspector moved to the area, his son, Fareed, spent the whole of the school year in the City, although no one knew exactly where. Some said he was with his relatives and others that the inspector had rented him a room, fearless of what might happen even though he was still young. Fareed settled permanently in his father's house only once he became a man and entered college and was able to come and go by himself. Abu Ali was the only one who sent his daughter Laila to the small school over the bridge, and even he withdrew her after four years. Ali, on the other hand, withdrew after two years, even though the school was renovated and the teachers praised Ali's intelligence compared to the other students.

Five years ago, her husband died. The Authority ruled that she had to leave their house and move on. But the inspector was able to offer a job to Gaber, who had grown to adulthood, in the place of his father. At that point they remained in the house eternally grateful for the inspector's mercy upon them. She begged God to bless his son with success in all his endeavors, especially since the inspector had given Gaber relatively light work and set Hamed to work alongside him transporting the coach that he sat on as he moved around from one work site to another.

But Gaber had always been restless, and she had hoped in vain for him to marry and become more settled. She worried about him even more when she heard him in the middle of the night calling out Suad's name in his sleep. She considered him her husband and her father, and now she asked everyone why he would have left without telling her where he was going. And where was this person named Masaad that he had told her about? He had spoken to Gaber of new, rich lands, full of money, to which he would travel and from which he would send for Gaber. She wondered that she had failed to remember this earlier from the time her son disappeared. She told herself it would be ridiculous for Gaber to go to these rich lands. This was not something that could explain his sudden disappearance.

She prepared to sink down into the water, but she heard Gaber's voice calling to her from a very deep void. She sensed his acute need for her. She decided that she would go on resisting the last rite left for her. She would walk with the children in the morning. She would find Zeinab. She would live.

SUAD

The women did not know the secret of the sudden illness that afflicted Suad. They circled her during the daytime cursing her misfortune and wondering how it could be that she remained healthy after Sheikh Masoud's death but became ill now. One of them suggested that perhaps she knew that there were new residents coming in, and she was afraid that she was about to be evicted from her home. But Laila knew it was something else. She was the one who spent evenings watching over her. Suad called out Ali's name in her delirium so that Laila started wondering whether Suad could have really been the young boy's lover. Since he had disappeared, Suad had been constantly reassuring his sister that he would return. She knew Laila realized he had gone to the City, but he had told her before leaving that he would not spend more than a few days there. She begged Laila not to tell her parents that she knew anything. She implored and explained that it was Ali's sincerest wish that no one else know his intentions.

Suad said that the idea of going to the City had consumed him since the night that the flaming balls had flown through the windows. She asked Laila if she had not noticed as well. She answered that ever since he had tried to decipher the secrets of Fareed's papers, which she had subsequently torn up, and since he had asked her about the City, she knew that he was planning on doing something. She was afraid that he would leave. Then she added that she would let her parents know Ali was coming back just as Suad wished.

But the days passed. The winds changed and the heat pulled back. They made it through an entire summer, and a cold autumn had settled upon them. The winter seemed to be mobilizing on the horizon. Through the whole summer, neither Ali's father nor mother was able to do anything. A new inspector was dispatched, and he began his tenure by threatening them all that they would have no chance to miss even a day's work. There were many tracks that needed changing after having been eaten by rust and also many crossbeams sunk into the ground that needed to be raised and the ground under them packed so they could withstand the train traffic. Two young men had come with the new inspector. They lived in the houses of Gaber and Hamed with their own families and spent the workday pushing the cart that the inspector rode over the tracks. The inspector told Suad to look for another place to live. Once winter started, new workers would arrive and move into her house. He could do no more for her, he said. He had given her a block of time in which to look for a new house. He had done the same with Abdullah's sick wife. He told her, "We'll wait until winter. If your husband comes back, you'll stay. Otherwise, you're out." He said that he had not yet informed the Authority of his absence from work. Laila's mother was thinking about going to the City to look for her son. But her husband forbade her forcefully, and she also fell ill. He assured her the boy was coming back, but internally his crying was like pangs from sharp daggers. Laila asked her parents to let her go to the City to look for Ali, but they screamed in her face, "What are you going to do in the huge City where you don't know a damn soul?"

In the end, it was agreed: they would wait for Ali to come back. But Suad began to feel that he would not be coming back. She stopped eating and drinking and fell into a depression. Then a strange fever overtook her and transported her as though she swam through space. She could no longer utter anything comprehensible to any of the women gathered around her. But she said to Laila, "Don't you find this strange?"

"I've thought a lot about it," Laila said. "They say the inspector has a son living in the City who'll enter the university after a year and come to live with his mother and father here."

Suad smiled a pale smile. She looked toward Laila sorrowfully. Laila had floated through beautiful times. She had met Fareed in rare stolen bits of night that had seemed to form an entire epoch that the masses lived through. Finally, the incomprehensible lie awakened her from the poignant dream.

"What about the two new men the inspector brought," Suad said, "One has an old mother with him, the other a wife and three kids."

Laila shook her head: "And the man living in Zeidan's house. His wife Ihsan looks like a slut."

Suad asked sadly, "Will a sheikh be coming to our house?"

Laila was silent for a moment. "My father says he won't abandon you. He'll ask you to come and live with us."

They were alone at that moment, and they each were overtaken by a keen sense of their need for the other. Laila bent over her to give her a kiss, while Suad was still stretched across the bed. She told her that she had to rise up and oppose her illness. She also said that Ihsan had mentioned to her the train had been coming toward them for years carrying all kinds of freight including iron, brass, and aluminum, and that she asked her why this train did not come anymore, and why they didn't try to bring it back since the men made such paltry salaries and their lives were so hard and there was no hope of the men ever getting a raise. Suad was overcome by a wave of amazement, but then collapsed involuntarily.

Suad was able to resist the illness as Laila had asked her to. As the winter neared, she wanted to know who had implicated her in such a harsh plot. The old Sheikh had abandoned her, as had the young boy whom she had been awaiting for so long. In the night that Laila did not come, she knew the full extent of the crime her lord had committed toward her. She said that she had been mistaken in waiting for him to send someone to her from that other place, or to have God send someone. For a long time now she had been expecting to end up surrendering herself to Ali. He had come to her the night of the fireballs. He spoke at length about this journey, which she hated, and about those departed, who had been the pride and joy of their place and time. She told him she was afraid he would not come back. He was sitting next to her on the couch. She wanted to take him and offer him the secret of the eternal flame of passion that could not be quenched. But she saw in his eyes a fire and a determination directed at something she didn't know. Her desire appeared stillborn. She took a long look at him, and he buried his face in her chest. She comforted him as though he were her son. He raised his face to her with contrition and said he was afraid he would never see her again. She kissed him on the cheek and said she would wait for him; then she smiled and added the condition that he understand the reason that she was waiting. There next to him she felt a heat surge through her arms and her chest. She wanted to act on her feelings, but her pessimism swallowed her. She told herself she would have to see him another time. He left her. She spent the many long days that followed this meeting thinking of him and crying in secret. When she found herself alone in her room, she cried so loudly that the walls shook. The last thing he did on the night he left was commend Laila to her. He told her that if they waited for him he would return and that if he came back and did not find the two of them, he would embark on a journey with no return.

She asked her lord to forgive her, then said, "You abandoned me so why do you want to judge me now?" She saw his eye overlooking her from the top of the ceiling like the furious eye of the sun.

Sheikh Masoud had told her that God had done it all. He said to a thing "Be," and it was. Now, everything was, but she did not believe God had done it all. It was a huge lie. The Sheikh himself was a lie. Finally, after her long illness she had come to a point of unique clarity. She remembered clearly the day she looked into his eyes when he called her and her mother to eat at the shop. It wasn't love she had seen. It was a messianic wink. An invitation to flight. A spell that could not be resisted. His eyes were deceptive. She knew now with an unwavering certainty that could not be crushed, and was even stronger than the mountain where the Holy Quran was revealed. Sheikh Masoud hadn't slept with her a single night. The two of them never drowned in rivers of sweat, or milk and honey, or blood and fire.

While Sheikh Masoud was on top of her, she would always see him in an opening in the ceiling, as though he were watching her, exactly as he watched over her while Ali wept on her breast. How could she have not noticed until today? She remembered the sight well. His eye looked down upon her and his mouth gaped like a dark inverted well. She would see him wave from above to someone, who then came through the front door. He was tall, broad, and strong and emanated light. He was the one who threw her over the bed. He was the one who climbed onto her. It was he who made her scream, writhe, cry, and laugh deliriously and sink her teeth into him. She never once saw any marks left by her teeth in the body of

Sheikh Masoud. He always asked her to help him bathe. He was clean and loved bathing and washing for prayer. As she scrubbed his back with a coarse red sponge, she inspected his shoulders for the marks left by her teeth but found nothing. When she took off her own clothes and slipped into his arms, she found his chest also unblemished. But she always forgot about that. What exactly made her forget and why? What was it that stirred all these memories inside her now? Who was this man she had cohabitated with all these years? And why did Sheikh Masoud always have to bathe himself after the notorious act? Yes, it was a grave, notorious act. It was in no way her master with whom she was engaging in intercourse. She always found him next to her fully clothed. From his long, baggy underpants with their drawstring that hung down between his legs to the vest he closed around his chest. What kind of misery had she been living in? In what sort of well had the flame of passion that could not be quenched been drowned? Who was this that came forth every night to yield a heavy, burnt seed that she felt advancing its salty way from her loins all the way to her mouth? What had Sheikh Masoud done to her? Why had he brought her from the platform of the station to bring her here? Why did he leave her to this illuminated, fiery, nocturnal visitor as he watched from the opening in the ceiling? Why did he believe that she was the flame of passion that could not be extinguished? It was like when she danced and saw the whole cosmos as a light in her eyes, and she wished as the sweat burned her that the universe would turn into a huge penis. He had told her that the eternal flame of passion would never decline, and she believed and killed many.

What she had done began to weigh upon her, but it weighed upon her even more that she had not followed through with it, and thus lost the young boy she had coveted so much. Laila did not come to her that night; she left her alone to confront a vicious self-accounting. She knew how much she had lied to her.

She, and no one else, had killed Fareed. He came to her every night circling around her window more than once. He kept circling until he heard the predawn call to prayer. She saw him from behind a peephole in the window frame. Even on rainy nights when Laila stayed with her, she would get up at night without Laila sensing her movement. The wooden window frame emitted a delicate lapping sound like the chirping of the locusts, or the sound of raindrops gently patting. Despite the frost of the cold night, she opened the window for him bare-chested. As she offered her breasts to him outside the window, the sturdy young man latched onto her nipples. He fondled them for a long time while she bent over and laughed, or suppressed her laughter if Laila happened to be there. While drowning in a sea of pleasure, she never allowed him to go farther. She never let him go around and come through the door. The young man raised up to place his mouth once on each of the two nipples. He shivered like a small puppy under his mother's teat. She felt the cold press of the frames of his glasses against her chest from over his nose, and she took them in her hand laughing. The sturdy young man pulled his hair and cried in pain. He told her to let him come around to her. If he came in to her, he would conquer the essence of what was written. He told her, "This way we'll all die." She told him to come around if he could, but then he cried and said he knew he couldn't, that he would die under the window. But he did not die under the window. They found him far off many yards away over an old, rusty rail that a thick electrical wire had fallen on. But it was she who had killed him. She couldn't forget it, just as she couldn't forget that she was the flame of passion that could not die, but that had killed many.

She killed Gaber who used to come to her openly in broad daylight. In the late afternoon, while Sheikh Masoud was snoring like thunder, she opened the door and he pranced in like a tiger. He hopped around her for a while but stopped short of jumping onto her. She told him he must come during that particular time as she gestured toward the slumbering old man. "This is the time," she said. He suggested they meet at night; but she told him the night was scandalous, while the daytime could give cover to eternal perfidy for those who understood. He told her, "Truly, you're the opposite of women of this world." She told him to come closer and she pulled off her clothes. She stood there naked while Gaber's throat went dry from the fire caused by her frontal assault. His legs trembled, and his chest shook with desire, but his arms betrayed him and stayed hanging at his side. His tears fell like a child who had been forbidden to touch a delicious dish right in front of him. He felt as though he were bound by some higher power. He mumbled several things that she couldn't understand. She opened for him the door to the hut, completely naked, but he ran out broken, full of remorse, and ready to cut his tongue beneath the pressure of his teeth. She would never forget his gaze as it pierced her body as he moved across the house to open the front door. She remained the flame of passion that could not be extinguished. Thus, she was described by her master and she believed it and killed many people. The only one she had not killed was her master himself. She now knew that he had been killed by the one who came to her every night awash in light. But why had he killed him so barbarously? And why did he no longer come to her? Why had he left her so many times to go through the rituals of passion with a corpse completely bereft of life?

In front of her, the lie grew. Both her days and her years were turned upside down. That night she wanted to know. When she saw the cats and dogs feeding on the meat of Zeinab's chickens, she felt she was near the end. She wanted to scream in the face of something she didn't know. That night she wanted to scream. The days of rain were encroaching. The faces changed and the houses filled back up, or nearly filled. But the changes didn't make the winter easier or less harsh. It progressed to end quickly a base season filled with sorrow and madness. Meanwhile, she was the flame of passion that was not extinguished. She knew that God, whom she had said could not delay more than two years, had decided to delay for a long time. There was a debt hanging over her that she had to pay, and only Ali in his raw intelligence could save her from it. He was growing before her eyes everyday and ascending toward the summit of manhood. She was convinced that he would come to her quickly on top of the Alborak, surpassing the other young boys, his peers. She had seen this vision many times as she climbed up to the roof and exposed her chest to the rain. She still remembered that small chariot in which Ali would swim between the clouds and throw down on her bouquets of flowers from above. It was like the inspector's cart except that it wasn't pulled by men. It was pulled by the completely invisible Alborak. There was no Gaber and Hamed either in front of or behind it. Poor, miserable Hamed ran after the inspector's cart by day and after his raging lust by night. When he told her, "Something is pushing me toward you," she didn't discourage him. She told him to come to her at the evening call to prayer. Sheikh Masoud would be holding his nightly vigil in the mosque, clinging to his beliefs while Hamed was clinging to her breast. She laughed and the world began to spin around him until he almost fell. He came to her like a hedgehog circling around the huts in burning, frightened hops. When he found the door of her hut opened, he entered in a leap that frightened the chickens. When Hamed crept into the entryway, he found it lit up with a light he had not seen the like of. He was frightened. He thought about escaping as fast as he could. She was inside laughing invitingly. As the sound of her laughing wafted toward him, he almost split into two halves, at the same time craving escape and raging with lust. He didn't know which foot to step with; each one pulled the other forward for a step, then backward again. She let out another laugh and he leaned forward until he almost fell because his feet remained planted in the same place. He boldly gathered himself and, determined to take decisive action, he leapt forward. In the course of this enormous leap he felt as though he was hanging in the air for so long that he almost screamed for help before his feet finally came back down to earth. Finally, he managed to make it to the inner room that was only a few meters off. He saw her sitting on a couch beneath the open window, and the room was lit up with a light like the face of the prophet visiting in a dream. Or like the face of a corpse. These were his feelings, though he had never seen a prophet in his dreams or a living corpse. She was naked with legs crossed. There was a dry crust of bread in her hand. Why a dry crust of bread? This is what he thought about later. The wretched creature had no idea that she watched him from the inner room with a magical power, or that she read all of his inner thoughts and his pain. Her eyes were wide like two stars. Her breasts were two protruding globes. Her arms reached out like the arms of the inspector's cart. He knew he would never make it to her. He was always behind the two arms of the cart and he would never be riding it. Even if he could get in front of the two arms, he would never ride in it. He went out running like a madman.

She knew that night that he wouldn't stop running until he had arrived at the bridge. He would go there looking for Zeinab but end up finding someone else, for Zeinab was in the house waiting for him, and she would always be in the house waiting for him. "Ah, Sheikh Masoud! How you've fooled me! But where are you so that I can avenge myself? Where are they all? Even the boy has slipped through my fingers."

Suad, wearing all the clothes she possessed, appeared comical. She slept buried under all her covers. She would never appear naked before Sheikh Masoud. She would remain rolled up until the return of that young man who had asked her to wait for him. That young man with the fine chiseled features: the delicate nose, the broad, sparkling, amber-colored eyes that relayed a thousand secrets. The dark, black shiny hair, the tiny mouth. She was filled with remorse that she had lost so much time awaiting a messenger from her husband who never appeared, although she herself should have known from the beginning that he was her final refuge. This was how she had always felt as she saw him maturing day by day. Why then had she grasped at fraying strings? But never mind that for now. The boy would return . . . certainly, he would return.

For the next several days, Suad formed this comical sight with all her clothes piled on top of her. The women looked at her then exchanged glances with one another saddened by what she had fallen to. Laila was shocked by her friend and did not know what to say. In one surprising day from the final days of the fall, a day in which the sun shone in brilliant colors, a day in which sparrows gathered in the west and then alighted all around the houses, all the birds gathered in the heavens over the lake were white, and there was not a single black one among them, on this day everyone was shocked by the intrusion of huge vehicles carrying heavy equipment that came to a halt a good distance from the houses. The men were at work. The women and children watched men they hadn't seen before, with long, red, and pale faces. They said they were aliens. They came out of the vehicles and began to unload the equipment. Then they saw them unloading a huge stack of wood, and they began to work at no one knew what.

In the evening the inspector told Suad that she would have to move in the morning so that someone else could come and live in her house. She went to Laila's house where she found Ali's parents waiting. They told her, "We knew about this and we were waiting. If you would like, we can move your things here now." She kissed the father's hand and walked out with Laila. The two of them began moving her few small possessions.

"What are the foreigners doing?" Suad asked. "My father says they're filling the lake with dirt."

Suad felt her heart drop; she felt it jump back up again. She did not know whether to laugh or cry. But she was certain based on her feelings that a corner of the world was collapsing. Then she remembered something she had thought about before. She saw the face of the stranger who would be coming to occupy her house the next day, and a tear flowed down her cheek like a quiet rush of a river. The house had a place in her heart that was being shattered. In fact, it was her whole heart. How had she come to see such times of misery? When her father had decided to become a vagrant, could he have known the sorrowful fate his hand was drawing for his only daughter? Suad struggled a great deal not to fall when she was moving her things. But now as she collected the last remaining items — these decorative Qurans and framed posters displaying holy verses that Sheikh Masoud had hung on the wall — she felt that without question she would collapse. When she walked into the entryway, she fell. She had wanted at least to make it to the doorway. Laila rushed to her and bent over to support her. But Suad was pressing her lips against the doorpost, clinging to the Qurans and the framed verses, and kissing the doorstep and the floor of the entryway.

She slept in the new house where they had taken her in. Actually, she spent the whole night awake on her bed, which now found itself in the entrance to Laila's family. In the morning after the men had gone out to work, she climbed up to the roof and sat by herself. She was afraid someone would see her observing the new entourage. At mid-morning a small, mule-drawn cart appeared bearing some furniture and an old man in his fifties. It was exactly the way she had observed Sheikh Masoud for the first time. His wife concealed her face with a black scarf. When the cart stopped, the old man got down and then helped his wife. He began unloading their things with the help of the driver. The wife stood for a moment, then lifted her scarf and looked around. She saw all the women standing in front of their front doors, but she did not see Suad watching her from up on the roof. Suad was staring at a young woman who looked like a girl in her twenties. She possessed a beauty that was mesmerizing. She stood in the nearby opening as though she owned the world and its contents. Suad smiled as she thought of what this woman might do and of what might be said of her. She shuddered violently and said to herself, "This isn't the way things really are"—and, she kept repeating—"the houses have all been filled now and people are determined to forget." The world spread out before her, and she realized that she understood everything now. Then she saw a vision, as though the wind were unfolding her and the houses toppled above her, and she told herself forcefully, "But Ali will come back."

PART FOUR

The Desert

GABER AND HAMED

No one knows the secret of the desert. God made it an eternal riddle. Epochs and nations have traversed it; time and humanity have endured it since the creation. The sun travels over it pale from excessive repetition, neither burning it nor firing its sands until they burst into flames. Its brilliant stars in the dome of the still night are pure imagination. The mournful moon flashes for only a moment, then is quickly forgotten by two lovers. The winds clamor beneath the sun and moon, but they move neither the serpents nor the desert beasts nor even its insects. Millions of sand dunes unfold beneath the force of the winds. But no one can say that the desert will ever run out of them. This prodigious desert bows to the small child running behind two sheep who have wandered away from the tattered tent where humans have sprouted like weeds. What intelligence has conceived the enigma of this barren land? What force has thrown Gaber and Hamed into it?

The two were thrown out onto the land surrounded by vast space. Both the yellow earth beneath them and the blue sky above them seemed to stretch to eternity. It seemed as if God had suddenly tossed them onto that spot. It didn't really matter whether they had come from heaven or hell: they were now outcasts.

They knew that well now that it had been a year since their departure.

Their Bedouin guide knew it as well. As sure as he drifted all along the way, he knew. He was leading a guided tour of deflated hopes. Gaber told himself, "After a year's worth of work and solitude, we'll have to cross the border on our feet, walking at night and sleeping during the day."

But where was this border? They couldn't overtake it. One looked up at the heavens and saw the eye of the sun that bore down on them every-day, as though he were seeing it for the first time. A fiery disk, it emitted crimson rays with yellow daggers attached. The disk moved along with the daggers stretching toward the two men spread out over the desert. He and Hamed were partners in the race across the train tracks. He always forgot the guide. He was no companion of theirs. He had a short fuse like that detonator that the workers put over the tracks on foggy days. As the train approached the station, the conductor, whose view of the flashing lights and the signal was blocked by the wall of fog, would know when the train wheels overran the detonator and he heard the bang of its explosion that he was nearing a station. He would begin to slow down. This guide was on a fuse, like the detonator. Once the train passed over it there was nothing left of it except bits and pieces that could not be gathered up again. Perhaps in the morning, the children would come and play with it. In any case, it was useless once it had performed its task. And what would be left of the guide once he led them to safe ground . . . to that hope which seemed increasingly foolish, or perhaps even a mirage? Gaber swooned. Would they really get there? He had never known on that night, now a part of the distant past, that he was deciding upon a journey of anguish.

His elderly mother had told him, "The winter is fierce. It's a good omen."

She was coming from the chicken coop carrying in her hand a kerosene lamp that swayed in the wind. She had just checked the chickens and made sure that the rain wasn't leaking from the roof of the pen.

He didn't answer her. He was sitting in the inner room that was separated from the chicken coop by a living area that they called the entryway. It was covered and included a washroom, the top of which they used for a storage area where they would leave their bread. Around the walls they set plates of old cheese and some empty sacks, and all their necessities of life. Thus, the inner room was reserved for sleep, entertaining guests, and late night sessions. Whenever Gaber passed through the entry way and saw all the paraphernalia scattered about, he felt it surrounding him and closing in on his lungs. His mother could not see him well that night, although a large kerosene lamp lighted up the room.

She said to him, "My heart had been whispering to me about its return constantly. They say it will come the day after tomorrow. This time though, it really will come."

He did not answer. He was sitting on the one couch that he also used for a bed ever since he had left the real bed to his mother, who was very attached to it. He had folded his legs up against his chest and rolled himself up in a thick woolen blanket so that nothing was visible except his face.

His mother constantly surprised Gaber. She was obsessed with the train, although she was an old woman who neither went out to it nor benefited from it in anyway. Yet he saw in her one of the residents most pained by its absence. She spent the entire summer praying for its return. She bet everything on it, just as she tied all misfortune to its continued absence. If the women sought her council after some dispute, they would find her cursing the train as the root cause. If some chickens were stolen, or an illness swept through the henhouse, or they were attacked by foxes, she would comment, "The train will come and end all our problems." When Rawaieh, a newcomer who had never before seen the train, came to her, Gaber heard them talking in the entryway.

"Wait until the train comes back."

"But he can't have an erection, Um Gaber."

"The train affects everything."

"What's it to me? I came after it stopped."

Seven days later, he saw Rawaieh standing in front of the chicken coop as he was returning home late in the evening.

"Don't believe my mother," he told her.

She smiled and said, "It never came back."

He knew who the alley cat meant. He looked around furtively, like a weasel, then pushed her inside. Before she could say anything he had knocked her to the floor of the chicken coop. He told himself, "Poor old mother, you don't know how to treat people." But Rawaieh was nothing more than the apparition that one sees sitting in one's room alone suddenly. She was that sort of sly apparition that intrudes on a person's privacy, giving him a brief sense that there's someone with him, until the moment ends and all that remains is a broken train of thought or a hanging set of worries. Yet the brief moment reminds the person that no matter how much he tries to distance himself from people, the apparition is still able to touch him.

That night, his mother sat in front of him on the ground and began to pray. He could not understand what she was trying to say. It seemed to be the same thing she would say while making her charms. Gaber had not known that his mother made charms before. But after the trains stopped, he saw her one day walking at sunset toward the two tracks that the train ran over. He followed. He called after her. She signaled to him to leave her and go back. Gaber had no idea what he was looking at as he watched his mother moving through the world like a vagrant by herself. Once she got to the tracks she sat down on them. She began dusting them with her hand and then wiped off with her hand dust or whatever scattered white remnants were left by the train. After she had gone back to their house, she sat in the entryway and began using the cloth to make charms. Then he saw all the other women of the village, as though they had a previous appointment, flocking to their house in silence. His mother began handing each a charm and stammering incomprehensibly for a while before telling the woman, "Read upon it the Sura of Salvation from the Quran."

As she prayed, there appeared before him a black spot from weakness. He would never forget the first day he had realized that his mother had grown old. Her hands shook as she tried to put the thread through the eye of the needle. Her fingers kept failing to get the end of the thread through the eye. Finally, he took them both from her and put the thread through the hole. *The rooster and chickens watched him from their cages while he was on top of Rawaieh, swimming as though he was on the waves of the sea.* Two tears sprung to his eye shed for his mother. He handed her the needle and thread and went into the entryway to cry. He knew he wouldn't be able to leave his mother, but he began shaking with Suad's name echoing all around him as he slept.

In the morning the old woman said to him, "Watch yourself, Gaber. Her husband is one of God's holy men."

A few days later, she spoke to him again: "What's troubling you, my son? Why do you let yourself bear such a burden? Get married, my son. Virility doesn't last forever."

That day, he felt as though he could shake a mountain. His frame was long and full. His arms were huge and his head hard as a rock. His full, black eyes were sorrowful and projected his intelligence. But he was surprised at how Suad's name could shake him even after he had left her unfulfilled and full of frustration and after he realized that he would not find satisfaction with her, could not turn to her like a Mecca to face during prayer. He thought at length about the tales Masaad told of the lands flowing with oil and riches. Rawaieh remained a dalliance that he repeated mechanically from time to time. He himself remained gravely depressed ever since his mother's problems with the needle and thread.

As his mother prayed, he was thinking of the letter that came to him from Masaad. She had almost finished her prayer. She asked God to bless him, as was her habit. The blessings she asked for at the end of her prayer were usually the only thing he understood.

She turned to him and said: "If only you would pray, Gaber!"

For the first time, he lost himself. His tears began to flow freely. He answered her choked with sorrow: "I'll leave you, mother. . . . I'll come back a rich man."

Then he heard the voice of Hamed who had covered his face with a white kufiyeh to shade his eyes from the sun's full strength. Hamed told the guide, "A month has passed, Fatouha. Haven't we passed any villages that could give us supplies?"

The guide nodded to reassure him. They would be starting to move more rapidly. They would draw nearer their paradise of riches. But Hamed was tired. . . . He thought they would walk again, once the sun passed over the horizon and back to its anonymous place of rest. God created it that way. He created them as well to rise out of the hole they had made for themselves to sleep in during the day, in order to reinitiate their journey at night. Hamed knew God then. His chest pounded from the lie. He was the one who had dug his own hole. He had made for himself the deep hole that he now fell into. This was how the guide had taught them. He explained that they had to bury themselves in holes so as not to be run over by scorpions, snakes, and vipers. He warned each of them not to snore and to hold his breath if approached by a desert lion or hyena or any other animal. He warned that the end of the hole for the feet would have to be deeper in order to make sure the feet did not stick out and draw the attention of the wild animals. These things were said to them by Fatouha the guide, who now added, "There's not much more to go. I won't leave you until you've both found a job in the largest of the oil fields."

Seven days passed during which they ran out of food. There was only a small bit of water left. The small pebbles were the only thing left to ward off thirst and help them conserve their small amount of water until they could make it to a well. They each put them in their mouth and sucked on them for all they were worth. They were like a hot iron at first, but they eventually got used to them. Then, the pebbles cracked their tongues and made them whiter and drier. Finally, the saliva flowed. But how long could they continue that way? It had been ten days since they had seen a well. The water that remained amounted to two drinks. Hamed looked up at the stars in the sky and distracted himself by counting them. "There are many stars tonight," the guide said. "What about it?" Hamed said to himself, "Why can't the stars see us as we see them?" He knew that his feet wouldn't be able to carry him after that day. Ah, for the inspector's car that moved constantly without swelling his feet. The shoes that wore to tatters without swelling his feet. How many times had he collapsed exhausted under the berry tree next to the inspector's office near the train station and pulled off his shoes to air out his feet, and Gaber did the same while they each looked at the other laughing? But his feet didn't swell, nor did Gaber's.

He was lean but strong back then. He raced with Gaber, who appeared even stronger than him, and he won. Gaber laughed and said, "You're all bones, like a weasel." And he answered, "What about you? What have you gained from having flesh as well as bone?" They laughed. He told Gaber he was sleeping with three different women. He asked him to come with him to the bridge, but Gaber declined by saying he was saving up his strength for the day he would conquer the world, while he stood over one of the rail lines holding onto the other pole of the inspector's cart. After the inspector had sat in his cart, opened his parasol, and raised it over his head, he would signal to them with his finger and say, "Let's go, boys," and they would pull his cart swiftly toward his destination. Even when he wanted to go to the main engineer's office in the City, he would go riding his cart along the rail tracks. They pushed him there running. Once Hamed said to Gaber, "Why doesn't the inspector replace us for a while?" Gaber answered, "We're too young," but Hamed spat and said, "Why must the young always be miserable?" Gaber said, "We've got to leave here. I'm arranging it with Masaad. He's always talking about people who leave and come back with money and cars, and the life of luxury in the City. He says one can't count all the money . . . that they spoon it up with a ladle. They exchange this foreign money whenever they come home for a big stack of Egyptian money. Thousands and thousands. . . . They're only a few people in those countries, and they love Egyptians."

Hamed was always torn. In the end, he decided though that there was no turning back. Still, when winter fell upon them, and he heard the train would be coming in a few days, he hesitated. He waited for Gaber. In the evening he went out to bring in the fowarika stove from in front of the door to the hut. He looked at it like it was something he was in love with. Its thick zinc siding was pure white; he knew that he would be leaving. Why else would he be exploding with feeling toward a stove that burned wood and coal, as though he were saying farewell to an old friend. The whiteness of the fowarika stove balanced off the blackness of the night, the lake, the bridge, and the black creeks flowing around it. He cast his glance out over the dark surface of the lake. He focused his eyes on a pale choking light in the distance over the bridge. Haneya was sleeping there without him.

He had grown tired of Haneya and her mother, and of her father's drugs and the inspector's cart. Let Haneya sleep her miserable sleep alone that night. Let her father smoke his hashish until he's wasted and her mother has to get high too and masturbate. It had started to rain. These were his scattered internal thoughts, as he lifted the fowarika stove up with both arms. In this way, the winter pounded the fall's heart and occupied its days, and summer was almost a memory. In the heavens above him, night's darkness waited in ambush like a past that has become oppressive. From a deep source it spread blackness through the night and glowered at him. And he, Hamed, clung to the fowarika stove with determination. Its flames singed it to the point that he wished he had stuck it into the heart of the flames a long time ago and settled the matter. It would have been cold and dead and final, but Death never chooses villains. It is always the true believers who are pure that it afflicts. In his case, all was against him. He used to go to Haneya's hut walking in backward, with his eyes still watching across the lake. His ears heard the pounding of the waves on its bank, which mixed with the gurgle of the hookah and the coughing of Haneya's father. He sees his own hand stretch toward the mother's lap to pinch her as the man laughs.

The lake at these moments appeared like the basalt of the hills near his home village, or like the houses they slept in. Hamed knew that tomorrow they would celebrate the train's return the following day. From that night, they would start congratulating each other on the train's return. But he knew that only Gaber would spend the night the same way he did.

A commotion arose suddenly out of a wind that seemed like ghosts. He felt surrounded by things trying to keep him from that cursed bridge. He would never be back to see that thing he had seen before him in the depths of the night.

He had snuck out after Zeinab had lifted her leg up off his midsection. He tried pinching her leg, and if she had awakened he would have gone back to sleep, but she never did. She would always go to sleep completely destroyed, as though she had cleaned and watched over the whole world, rather than a small house with three children. He covered her and then moved away as he climbed out of bed. He felt like a lead weight over the shaky boards of the bed, even though he was really as thin as the edge of a razor. He told himself that he was Hamed, who had still not surpassed age thirty with three children scattered at the foot of his bed. He stepped around them and opened the door to the outer room slowly. He shrunk into himself and almost rolled into a ball as he approached the bridge. He saw the faint light like blood pumping out of a heart. He began to run, although he knew that he spent the whole day running. He always said that no one could run like him. Even Gaber who ran with him along the other rail track did not run as swiftly. Then there was Zeidan, who worked little and farted much and was laughed at by everyone. There was also Abdullah who resorted to bribes and was in the habit of paying colleagues to pass him the easiest work. He walked along the tracks methodically. Where were all the chinks that Abdullah seemed to find every day? He spent so much time complaining about the sun's pursuit of him that he played with people's minds. What prevented a person from just turning around and looking at the sun? And why did he want to see it anyway? Also, no one mentioned the fact that he had originally paid a bribe to get the job. People had come and gone and none of the original group was left except for Um Gaber whose husband was dead now, and she knew nothing of the men's matters. There was also the superintendent, but he was always asleep; and when he did wake up, he never said anything comprehensible. But Hamed himself knew that Abdullah's soft job only came to a person through a bribe. This left everyone else to lift the metal tracks and rail guards, dig up the dirt and fill it back in, and to come out at night to repair damage after large accidents in which trains collided or jumped track. Sheikh Masoud also did no real work. When he first came to the area, he was near retirement age. Once he did reach it, he stayed in his house, even though the Authority never left anyone in their dwelling who didn't work. He had also paid a bribe, to the big directors in the City. "Then he spent half his life in the mosque praying and left his wife, the slut, at home to keep me suspended between heaven and earth." Meanwhile, Sheikh Masoud did nothing but recite Quran, call the faithful to prayer, and declare Hamed an atheist for hating that place and his work and the train—the long absence of which had caused women to abort, they all claimed. Children had stopped growing, and fishermen all came up empty. Chickens died. Bread did not rise. But Hamed himself only knew one thing: that every night his lust increased . . . for Haneya, for her mother, and for his wife . . . and most of all, for some unknown thing that none of them could divert him from, something that drew him away from them all.

Hamed stood there holding the fowarika stove in the middle of the entryway. He could see through its open door the wide spacious darkness outside, and the far-off bridge and the light drops of rain. He spoke to Hanya as though she were in front of him. He told her he did not love her in the least. He didn't love her mother. He loved his wife because she was tied to him by the tragic cycle of life. He would leave it all though. He would not wait around for the train that would only bring police who screwed the women, intimidated the boys, and flirted with the girls. He asked her whether she knew that Arfeh was now a friend of Zeidan, much less that he was the only friend Zeidan had left. Then he told her that this was something of no use to her and that he wouldn't visit her again. Trying to run through the mud would be dangerous that night anyway, and neither she nor her mother was willing to visit him. The bridge stretched all the way to the City that she and her mother loved so much. She loved the alien and frightening faces that came to her everyday en masse, and the city dwellers that walked in circles like chickens, and looked all around furtively like a cat, and took random steps like a rabbit. He closed the door of the entryway and looked around him at the garbage piled in the corners. If not for the fowarika stove, he would be able to see nothing.

He set it down and picked up a metal poker. Without knowing why, he began poking around through the holes in the chicken coop, until he had stirred up all the chickens. The rooster's cackles mixed with his own laughter. Back in the inner room, Zeinab stirred. She came running out afraid that she would find a weasel in the coop, but when she got to the door of the entryway, he met her with the fowarika stove in his hand throwing light onto his face. Zeinab almost fainted from shock. The air rushed out of her lungs, and her blood flooded into her face and left it red like the flames of the stove. In that moment, he felt Zeinab's total love and concern toward him. She walked in behind him. After he put down the fowarika, he looked at his three sons, covered by their tattered blankets.

"Tonight they can sleep on top of the bed," he said.

She stared at him in embarrassed confusion.

"We'll sleep on the mat."

She still stared.

"The fowarika will keep us warm."

She remained suspended in confusion. She could not understand what he had in mind, but he looked at the white stove with an unconcealed sorrow.

Ever since that night the passing of midnight found them walking. He felt that his feet would bear him no longer. He still clung to the hope Gaber had planted, and the words of the guide continued to reassure. At the same time, hunger was going to obliterate him, and the water would run out after two more drinks, and he wouldn't be able to suck stones forever. What really disturbed him was this guide, as thin as he was, who seemed not to suffer from hunger or thirst as though he were carved from the heart of the desert. Finally, Hamed collapsed, and the guide calmly remarked,

"Why don't you both rest for awhile then? Maybe in the morning your strength will return."

Then he started to sing. He sat at a distance and sang in a Bedouin dialect of which neither of them understood a word. He looked at them stretched over the surface of the desert and said, "We've got to dig first."

"We'll dig in the morning," Hamed answered.

"Who's going to awaken you to dig?" the guide asked. "You might not awaken until the following evening. Besides, the snakes can bite at night as well as they can by day."

The two began digging. Hamed worked his fingers into the sand and Gaber followed his lead. They began to pile up mounds of sand to their side. They saw that their nails had grown long and their fingers had turned to stark bone. Gaber, who had always possessed a muscular frame, now looked sorrowfully at the protruding bones in his hands. The guide had worked quickly and dug himself into a hole where he stretched out with his arms folded behind his head and continued to sing, as though he had thrown all the world's troubles behind him. They were annoyed to no end by the sight of him.

"Rest assured," he told them, "you are not the first ones to try to cross the border."

They did not answer. They were still digging laboriously.

"But you two are the first to wear me out along the way."

They answered in unison, "This way is long."

"It isn't so long for those who really want to cross it," he answered.

They had no answer, and so he went on.

"The last person I took across was an Upper Egyptian with a wife and child."

Finally, they finished digging. The night was cold, and they each took a blanket to cover themselves out of their backpack. They had not been able each to dig their own hole. They dug one wide, shallow hole that they shared. Meanwhile, the guide kept talking.

◆ ◆ ◆

He said that there had been no problems with the Upper Egyptian and his family. He had had twenty pounds left to his name, which the guide had taken as a down payment for his services. The Upper Egyptian had given them to him in complete confidence that he was doing the right thing and that the guide would be worth it. He said that he was handing over those twenty pounds that he had saved over the course of his life as a way of cutting all ties to his past. At first, he had gone through the cities and large ports, but had eventually decided to leave the country altogether and emigrate to the lands that people claimed were filled with oil and gas and that his countrymen were returning from bearing expensive gifts and money. He had decided to bring along his wife and son because he did not want to come back bearing money and gifts; in fact, he did not want to come back at all. He knew that the trip would be arduous, that they could all die before they had crossed border, but he was certain that God would not abandon them. If they were hungry, he would bring down from the heavens a table full of food, and if they became thirsty, He would let flow before them a wellspring of holy water . . . and even if God did not do these things for them, he himself would. He would capture birds with his bare hands, and eat the desert snakes, serpents, and hyenas. His son was no less of a son than Abraham's son Ishmael. His delicate feet would cut through the ground beneath them. His wife was no weaker than Hagar, and she would struggle courageously against hunger and thirst. He would stay at their side and never abandon them, just as the Prophet Abraham had been stalwart and faithful. But a sand serpent bit the son, and he died instantly. It was a horned serpent that they called the *tareesha*, known to be the most dangerous breed. The guide admitted to being shocked at the father's response. He had shown no signs of sorrow. In fact, he proclaimed, "In all things, praise Him Who chose to take his life in a strange land," because that meant they had made it across the trail.

After this, he said that he had handed over the Upper Egyptian and his wife to one of the Arab contractors in that land of oil—another Upper Egyptian with a long handlebar mustache, raised like two flags. The contractor told him, "Welcome, stranger," and the Upper Egyptian insisted he was no stranger. He said he was strong and healthy and nothing was strange about that. Both the contractor and the guide were annoyed by this comment, which they found impertinent. The guide explained to the contractor that the Upper Egyptian had given him only twenty pounds, but that he wanted another twenty, which the contractor should take from his salary, thereafter. The contractor paid him, while the wife of the Upper Egyptian asked the guide, "Why couldn't the serpent have bitten you?" He laughed. He said the wife went into a daze after her child died. Before that when her husband commanded her to catch up, she would run; but after the child died, whenever he called her, he had to repeat the call several times. He commanded her and then repeated the command more than once. In the end, he began dragging her by the arm so she would keep up with him. But she would still fall back and then burst into tears of agony.

By then, neither Hamed nor Gaber heard what the guide said. They fell asleep and snored powerfully, while he let his discourse flow freely. Surprisingly, he didn't seem to hear them snoring at first. Then he had the idea that he would awaken them. He tried to, but they would not wake up. He thought about stuffing their mouths with sand and then lying back down, but he thought better of the idea. He went back to his hole and decided to sleep. Yes. He felt no need for rest. He still felt strong and was neither hungry nor thirsty. He knew that the remaining strength in Gaber and Hamed was the last gasp of their souls and that they would not make it to the following noon without surrendering them.

The night before Hamed's disappearance still endured in his mind, especially the vision. That night, Zeinab had put the children up on the bed as he had ordered and then climbed down next to him on the mat with the fowarika between them. They warmed their palms over the fire for a while, then rubbed them together, then warmed them some more. Then they both put their hands against their face.

"Is it true that whoever chases the foreigners' trains never returns?" she asked him.

He didn't answer. She drew one of her hands back to her chest, moved back, and opened her legs a bit. They started up the exhausting, sweet ritual.

Hamed could tell she had wanted to be alone with him, and he wanted her as well on a night whose details could not be erased from his mind. The luster of her wide eyes was subdued. The bones of her face protruded beneath her skin. Her neck was long, like the neck of a young hen. Her belly sagged. Zeinab was a dark-haired mountain woman. She was a wild product of nature, sharing with him a physical support rail during life's journey for provisions; she was like the arm of the inspector's coach. And when a woman becomes like the coach arm, she stings like a whip. She gasped for breath, but he couldn't tell whether it was out of passion or some trauma in her lungs.

He asked her that night, "Are you happy?"

She answered with the solemnity and the sorrow of a winter night, "Of course, the train will be coming tomorrow."

He told himself, "but we're still wrapping our sons in tatters. That's how we've been, and that's how we'll be. Fate must really exist after all."

They suddenly heard violent pounding at the door. Zeinab went into shock, while Hamed leapt to his feet. It was not yet midnight. The winter night always began at midnight, and this year, winter had come early, as had Zeinab's fear. She grabbed his arm imploringly, and he immediately shook it off. She went silent acquiescently. Zeinab somehow remembered this later. He went out and opened the door of the hut. Gaber took one step and stopped.

"Come in, Gaber."

"There's no need."

They had barely seen one another and were listening to the clucks of the chickens. Gaber, panting and wet from the rain, said, "I've prepared myself. We'll go out a bit before the workers. Don't forget the letter I brought you, the one that Masaad sent. He will guide us during the trip, and of course, don't say anything to anyone."

Hamed wanted to speak, but he was befuddled by Gaber's disorientingly rapid and frightened speech.

"I've decided. Today will work better than tomorrow. There's no turning back . . . don't let anything distract you from our mission."

Gaber retreated and quickly disappeared. Hamed went back and stood in the middle of the entryway thinking. Why had Zeinab seemed to plead when she grabbed his arm? Did she sense something as he went out each night? If so, she did not show it. But why had he pushed off her hands so violently? Could it be that he hated her? He went into the bedroom, and she smiled a strained and frightened smile at him.

"Make us a dark, bitter pot of tea."

After the flames of the fowarika had calmed and its ashes had been smothered, the room became like the hearth of a stove. Zeinab became warm, like the smooth corrugated tin side of the stove. She stood up and staggered as though she had drunk one of the glasses of arak that Haneya's father was always swigging.

"The lining of the fowarika is intoxicating me," she said.

He stood up before her. He pulled up her galabeya. Just as he lifted the end of it over her head, he saw tears collected in her eyes. He took her by the waist and pulled her toward him forcefully until her body snapped like firewood. A flame of mad passion passed between them and tore through the remaining drunkenness. Zeinab writhed over the mat in genuine pain, and yet she did not let go of him for an instant. She bit and dug her nails into him. Her feet struck the smoldering stove, knocking it over, and scattering its ashes. The opening near the roof above the window emitted a ray of light revealing to each of them lines of sweat and blood running down their partner. One moment he saw Um Haneya's face in hers, then he saw Haneya's, then he saw all three at once. The old man, Haneya's father, quaffed the rest of the arak and collapsed on the ground in exhaustion while his rotten teeth scattered over his chest. *The back end of Suad's cloak swept over the rooftop as it had the first time he saw her, and he caught a glimpse of her supple shining calves, and even her black lace panties, which he was sure that day that only he had seen. He even believed Sheikh Masoud had not seen what he had. He saw himself in a state of agony over her. By the time he finally reached her he was hanging in space, not knowing whether to*

try to ascend or to come back down. He cursed Sheikh Masoud and his ser-
mons, the inspector and his car, the summer and the train, the lake and the
foreigners. Another strong ray of light entered the room. Then he saw a bolt
of lightning come from over the bridge, where it wreaked fire and havoc.
He saw Haneya and her mother running along with flames shooting off
them until they made it to the lake and plunged in, causing its waters to
boil and steam to rise up into the air. A shooting flame even shot up and
overtook Abu Haneya. He began to run like a madman over the bridge,
until he dove into the lake over the other side of the bridge and slapped
against the water like a person dropped in boiling oil. Flames shot off him,
setting the cattails on fire. The fish that had seemed dead the whole year
since the train had stopped coming surged in harrowing leaps up to the
heavens and then crashed down pieces of charred blackness. At the same
time, the birds that had been resting among the cattails flew up in flames,
screeching and crashing together in a frightful struggle in the heart of the
endless sky; lit by the lightning that crashed into the water like a meteor.
Then the sun observed him, and he saw himself standing alone under it in
the midst of a wide desert. Gaber was tied to a stake on the highest moun-
taintop, screaming, with eagles picking at his heart and ranks of scorpions
crawling toward him from every direction and being overtaken by long
snakes. He felt his feet gradually sinking into the ground until only his
head was still exposed, and a large snake crawled toward him with its
forked tongue leading the way. The sun's rays had gained strength and
awakened Gaber, who was unable to move. All this time during Hamed's
vision of the final night before their departure, the entire previous year
and its trials passed before Gaber's eyes. When he awakened in a fright,
he found something heavy on top of his stomach. He could not get up. He
felt that he was experiencing that end which he had long to push out of
his mind. He did not consider calling to the guide or trying to shout. The
only person in the world that he knew was his partner in toil and travel,
Hamed. He grabbed his hand and listened to him snort like a bull. Hamed
opened his eyes and took a deep breath that seemed to put him at ease

and exorcise his horrible dream. But when Gaber pointed at his stomach Hamed looked up and saw a gigantic, long snake slithering over them.

At the beginning of their trip, the guide had told them that he had been able to smuggle one thousand Egyptians across the trail so far. He had been counting how many he had smuggled, and he said he would be starting on his second thousand with them. There was no reason for them to be afraid, since by now, he knew all the strong and the weak points of the border area and had even become good friends with the border police on each side.

The smuggling kingpin had originally told them, "I am assigning this special guide to you in recognition of your great service to me. Now do you remember any of what's happened regarding our agreement?" "No," they said in unison. "Was there any agreement to begin with?" he then asked. "No," they said. "Hasn't the year gone by quickly?" "Yes," they both answered.

Before this year that he asked them about had started, he had told them, "Let me see this letter of yours." Then he laughed and asked them, "Who is this Masaad friend of yours?" He began to drown in wild laughter. "Why is there no stamp on it?" he asked, and he took an ecstatic drink from a bottle of whiskey in front of him. "He sent it to us with the private mail carrier on one of the trains." He looked at them with disgust and said, "Do you think trains really come from the place to which you are trying to escape? What idiots!"

They stood speechless in front of him. This man that they had come to meet in this large city near the border seemed to know everything. He was telling them something they had never thought of. The letter, in fact, bore no address where they might write to Masaad, nor the name of the work site where he was stationed, nor even the city where he lived in that other country. How could they have not realized this? What good was it for them to have his full name, and who in this great, wide world might know of him? "We must go back where we came," they said.

Hamed stretched his hand out to take back the letter, but the man folded it and put it in his hand and said, "You need not go back. The two of you have made a decision that you must go through with. This is how to be real men."

They were visibly upset, and so he told them, "I myself can send you across the border into that other place, but on one condition."

They both asked what the condition was.

"Do you both know the story of Moses and Shu'ayb?"

They answered yes, for they had heard it many times from Sheikh Masoud.

"Work for me for one year," he said. "Your compensation for the year's work will be a trip to one of the greatest of oil wells."

"But that's not fair," they said.

"I believe you know that Moses worked for over a year," he answered violently. "His compensation was the right to marry Shu'ayb's daughter. But I'm asking for a year of work from you in exchange for something that will allow you to marry any woman in the world if you like. Plus there are two of you; Moses was by himself. Besides, why don't you at least ask me what the work is to see if you might like it?"

"What is it?" they asked.

"You'll eat and drink whatever you wish," he said. "If you want women as well, you'll have them. If you want wine, you'll have it. The important thing is that you not talk to each other and engage in conversation with others; you must forget everything you see here."

They were both confused by his proposal. They were both determined to complete their odyssey, and so they asked him, "Is it that you want us to work for you for a year?"

"Not a day less," he answered.

"We agree," they said.

They saw that they were burning their bridges, but the whole world behind them seemed a huge lie, and they had decided to confront the one that lay before them.

Gaber laughed and said, "All our running around with the inspector's cart has given us a love of running between countries."

He felt as though he were tricking himself.

The man moved them to a lone villa in the middle of the desert, far from the city in which he had met them.

After they entered behind him, he told them, "Be sure that if you break your agreement with me, God himself will not have mercy on you. There's not a force on earth that can save you from me. You should also both know that I have neither religion, nor scruples."

In fact, he appeared to them to have neither. He was short, fat, and sported long sideburns in front of his ears and long flowing hair that he kept idiotically disheveled. He had a double chin, a flabby face, small narrow eyes, and thick bushy eyebrows.

They could not watch the city in which they were to meet the smuggler very well. They had met him accidentally on the same day that they arrived. They had just wanted to ask him where they could find Masaad, an ordinary question such as any stranger would ask.

They remained in the strange villa he had moved them to for an entire year without going out. They ate and drank everything they had ever desired in their lives. The villa had two floors, one of which was underground and was used as a sort of secret meeting place in which shady deals could be made. Each weekend, fancy cars full of beautiful women would suddenly appear, and men whose appearance suggested that they were important. They wore elegant clothes and gave off a mesmerizing perfumed scent. They passed huge stacks of money back and forth on a small table in front of their large potbellies without calculations or cares. Then a big party began in which wine flowed and the smell of hashish wafted through the building. The men each took a woman up to the second floor, and their employer, who—they now knew—led the smuggling ring, sat in a corner of the bottom story surrounded by his lackeys, counting piles of money and putting it in black pouches.

For the most part, they abstained from these parties. They learned their role well. They prepared things and set up the place and served the food that the ringleader had brought readymade from the city. All they had to do was serve it with the wine. He taught them how to prepare the lump of hash, how to carry the waterpipe with its long stalk so that it wouldn't break, and how to set it at the feet of the honored guests.

After everyone had gone, a dark emaciated old woman came to them. She came out of a closed room that she had gone into before the first visitor had arrived, and that she only came out of after the last one had left. This old woman had been assigned to them as their object of pleasure. She had a big, flat nose, a wooden eye, gray hair, and only a few scattered teeth left in her head. The sight of her so turned them off of the female gender that they never went near her, in spite of her disgustingly bald advances. She always left in the end without a word of good-bye. They watched as a small jeep swept her away from in front of the villa. This went on for a whole month during which four parties were held, and they rebuffed the old temptress four times.

The fifth time she came out of the room after a party, she was followed by four dark men each as solid as a brick wall. Neither of them had seen either the woman or the men enter the room this time. They were sitting by themselves after the party, remembering the good old days. It was impossible for them to go on that way, but there was no going back on the agreement either. Suddenly, they were surprised to find the woman in front of them with the men behind her. Each man had a long thin chain in his hand. They were so thin that no one would ever believe that they might tear the flesh of a human. But the chains tore their flesh. Four enormous hands holding four thin chains crashed down upon them. Gaber and Hamed were left with no refuge as the circle of men grew tight around them. They hung them from the ceiling. Neither of them had even noticed the hooks hanging down. They were hung up together and their feet were bound with rope. The light flooding into the large hall from the corners prevented them from looking up. Once they were hung there, the hook seemed like something especially for them.

They hung there naked for five days. The old woman brought them food everyday and fed them as they hung pathetically. After they had voraciously devoured their food, doing all they could to keep it from falling from their mouths, she brought out a long pole with which she stuck them in the butt until their screams bounced around the corners of the room. Then she left them, only to come back the next day and find them in a state of extreme hunger and repeat the same thing over again.

Neither of them could explain exactly why they were consumed with desire for the old woman after that. Was it fear or a genuine desire for her? All they knew was that they both began to wait all week for the party to come and go, so they could go visit the old woman. They paid no more attention to the deals being concluded around them. Even the beautiful women around no longer did anything for them. When the year ended, the kingpin asked them, "Do you remember any of what's happened this year?"

"No," they said.

"Wasn't everything on the level?" he asked them.

"It was all on the level."

Then he announced, "Here's the guide that will take you across the border."

He gave them some extra food and water, then hesitated for a moment, then gave them some money.

Gaber had seen the whole thing again shortly before the sun's rays awakened him. But once he awakened and saw the snake crawling over them he could not tell whether it had been reality or a nightmare. The entire trip had revisited him as a set of ugly images while he slept. Yet he was sure that the snake was real, and he awakened Hamed, who was in the same bizarre state of confusion about whether the snake was a reality or an epilogue to his frightful dream. The immense weight of the snake over their bellies confirmed that the creature was real, and their faces went pale in horror. They remembered what the guide had told them and they held their breath. They were now sorry that they had only dug one shallow hole.

If they had made two deep holes instead, the snake might have gone around them without noticing anything. Of course, the gigantic snake had no sense of what they might be thinking. It just crossed over them. It crossed so slowly that they thought it was a train passing and not a snake. Its head past over Hamed while its tail had still not reached Gaber. It was a glistening yellow color, and it had shiny black stripes running its length. The sun's rays were drawn to it as though it were attracting them, and they created a nauseating glassy appearance—especially when the sight was combined with its loud hissing, or when they saw its head turning to the left and the right turning up the whistle of the wind and sand in front of it. They saw its tremendous tongue spilling out of its mouth with its forked end, each side of which was longer than a ruler. The ends of the tongue lapped up objects they could not see from their prone position.

In these rare moments, Hamed remembered Zeinab. The good daughter of virgin nature. His three children wrapped in rags. How tragic for her husband to die so far from her. He knew how ugly his harshness had proven as she went through her daily routine. How much bitterness had poor pathetic Zeinab tasted.

One of the forks of the snake's tongue appeared to Gaber like the thread that his mother had fumbled trying to put it through the eye of the needle. He remembered her narrow eyes surrounded by bags and wrinkles, with their narrow whites behind dark pupils that were turning a pale yellow. Gaber did not know why he always seemed to lose his memory of his mother when she was still young. Why did he only remember her as an old woman? He knew his mother had been young like other women, but he could only manage to see the picture of the beaten old woman.

They finally remembered the guide after the snake had almost passed over them completely. They heard a braying sound in the distance. They looked toward the noise. The guide had grabbed a gazelle from behind and was leaning his upper half across its back and grabbing its horns with all his strength. It was a small, brown doe, and it was dancing back and forth in terror. The powerful guide forced the animal's knees apart then went up on his toes and forced it to the sand, gripping so tightly that it couldn't think of escaping.

As soon as the snake had passed over Hamed and Gaber, they stood up. They didn't worry for a moment that the snake might sense their movements and turn back to them. They raced to help the guide with the doe. These were days of delirious hunger. The doe instantly erased the memory of the horror of the snake. But just as they reached the guide, he let go of the doe, which shot off like the wind and left him panting.

There was nothing in their entire thought life up to that point that prepared them for what they saw before them. They had often heard that some of the desert Bedouins had sex with young camels or mules or goats, but this wasn't the sort of thing to be preserved in one's memory. The guide stood in front of them with his exposed penis dangling and covered with blood and mucus. He had pulled his caftan up over his waist. His tongue dangled from his mouth like the snake's tongue, while his eyes shifted around in every direction deviously, and an eerie yellow smile stretched across his face. The sun's rays fell down on his face to reveal a cunning, old enemy that had finally exposed himself to them after all this hardship.

Neither of them knew exactly what happened in these following moments. They lit a fire from some dry brush after digging a pit for it. They started to grill bits of meat over the fire starting with the heart, then the liver. That was a good enough beginning after so many days of hunger. They drank the rest of their water carelessly.

They emptied what was in Gaber's pack into Hamed's and put one of the legs in the empty one. They could not carry the rest of it. They left the rest of the guide's body to the vultures, hyenas, and snakes, and they began walking again by themselves without bothering to wait for nightfall.

Neither of them realized that the circle would inevitably close, that the cycle would run its course, and that the sequence would be consummated with an eternal closing. For now, they could merely search for the fountain of life, even if that in itself was an absurdity.

Had they thought carefully before leaving?

They both knew that they had been enflamed by fire. How could someone in flames think properly? And if they had thought more would that have corrected anything?

All of this was a shot fired from the realm of the impossible. All the mind games they engrossed themselves in only led them to the core of a ball of flame. They realized that the flames always won even when they are extinguished and their embers are smothered. The fowarika stove, that utensil of no value, as it began to fade, let its flames evaporate. All its energy was extinguished, and it died after it smoldered for most of the night. The universe finds itself having to gather its own energy in response. The clouds scattered in every direction across the heavens and random winds and rain beckoned, and they all collected in an unjust celestial plot, and they fell upon a place in fearful, blind tenacity to conquer all smoldering ashes and subdue their heat once the flames had been extinguished. Thus were the fires a filthy instrument without significance and with no known name. Its subjugation required the full force of the cosmos and the full duration of the night. How then, could they presume to emerge victors over it?

Now, they tried to think, but this was only after they had grown weary and impotent. After the marrow had been sucked from their bones and their hair had turned white. The skin around their face and thighs had wrinkled, their movements slowed, their gaze wandered, and their limbs became drugged.

Neither one of them expected to find themselves refugees in barrenness like this when they found themselves in the basement of the villa again in the middle of the desert. On the ceiling the two grotesque iron hooks hung down before their eyes from two distant corners. In another corner, the huge pole with which the old woman had prodded them was leaning. A luxurious oriental carpet that they had first tread over a full year ago was spread across the ground. Red, green, yellow, and blue lights mixed together in the center of the meeting room to create a light like the color of the lake in the morning when the sun lights it up as it ascends, or like the color of the desert at dusk when the sun is choked by the horizon as it sets.

They had been staring at one another without wavering for over an hour now. This had not been their first day. In fact, countless weeks had passed. When the smuggling kingpin met them this time, he said, "You will know about how many days you will spend here before you return to your homeland." In fact, he said this same thing to them everyday, but he said it lifelessly as though he were a corpse talking. Sometimes he stared into their eyes for a long time. Once they blinked, he spoke. They had noticed that the old woman had gone, and there were no more tumultuous parties.

"What will we do here?"

"I don't know," he said. "But I won't leave you until a reasonable time has past."

At first they thought he would punish them for killing the guide. They were certain that he knew everything because when he had met them, he said, "We welcome the rabid dogs."

They didn't understand what he was saying, and when they looked at him imploringly, he said, "Welcome, dogs."

They became frightened. Their clothes had become mostly torn rags, and their bodies had atrophied. Their bones protruded, and their long beards reached down to their chests with the two ends of their mustache hanging frighteningly down either side of their mouths. Their ears were clogged full of sand. Their hair was matted and filled with dirt so that one felt it could never be cleaned. Their feet were swollen to the point that they both felt as though they were dragging the crossbeams from under the railroad tracks. They were covered with boils and filled with cracks. So shredded were the tatters they wore that they had failed to keep sand out of the cracks in their feet.

Neither one of them really believed that he would come back to meet this smuggler again. The only refuge they dared hope for after killing the guide and getting lost was death. They spent a month wandering aimlessly with the guide's leg, which they sun-dried in strips so that it would not spoil. At first, they couldn't eat any of it. True, they had no trouble eating the heart and liver, but this had been in the initial moment of irrationality. Afterward, they realized they had done something inhuman. They both began to fear coming down with some strange disease about which they had heard but knew nothing. When they were young, they had often heard strange stories about people who ate human flesh and about the illnesses that afflicted them. One had begun to speak in dog barks and sing in meows. His fingernails sprouted uncontrollably. Hair grew inside his mouth. His tongue hung out, and his earlobes began to flap. His backbone grew so long that he seemed to have a tail.

These stories had frightened them when they were young. Each of them began to remember cutting off the first piece of the guide's leg. They each thought about something else while they ate.

Gaber thought about his father for the first time. It was his father who had first told him and his mother about cannibals.

His father was a product of a time they called the Age of the Authority. He told them that when he had neared the age of military conscription, his own father had tried to arrange for him to escape by any possible means. He also heard his mother—Gaber's grandmother—tell her husband, "If only you had made him memorize the Quran!" But he turned on her and said, "And what is he supposed to do with memorization of the Quran? It might get him out of the military service, but he won't be able to do anything else other than recite for a living, and if he did that he would only eat when someone died or when a Sufi order met."

Gaber's grandfather thought about every possibility. He considered chopping off his index finger, but he decided not to try it since it wouldn't necessarily keep him from being drafted. On the contrary, they may just take him and force him to do only dirty work. He did not want his son to experience the worst of both worlds by entering the army without enjoying the honor of being a soldier. He considered sticking a pencil in his eye, but Gaber's grandmother became hysterical at this suggestion and screamed at him, "You blocked him from memorizing the Quran and now you want to blind him. How?" and she slapped her cheeks repeatedly and the two spent the rest of the night in tears.

But Gaber's father did not weep the way his parents did. All he could think about was this "Toker" place he would be sent to, and what it would be like? Was it really, as his father said, a hot country with driving rains? Was it really full of slaves and forced labor? Did its citizens really have tails? Did they really eat human flesh? He was afraid.

He told himself if only they would take him and send him to the Levant as they had done with his father back when the British were at war with the Turks. His father was in his forties then. Still, they forced him from his village. His compatriots there considered themselves lucky that they had not been sent to Europe like some others. Gaber's grandfather smuggled British weapons to the Turks: the infidels' weapons to the Muslims. Gaber's father said that he'd wished they would send him to the Levant, where he would do just exactly what his father had done: smuggle the infidels' weapons to the Muslims. At the same time he laughed and said, "This was in spite of the fact that at the time I could not distinguish a Muslim from an infidel. I had never set foot outside our village surrounded by hills. Neither an Englishman nor a Turk had ever visited us, nor even any kings or countrymen. I don't even know how anyone figured that my father had a son who was required to do military service."

Gaber remembered that his father never finished the story. He never found out from him whether he went to Toker or not, or if he saw human flesh being eaten or not. Still, he knew that there were humans who ate human flesh, and he had now become one of them. What was this strange cycle spun around by the days? How could his long odyssey end up that way. This was the cost paid by the person who listened to the beat of his heart.

Gaber remembered Masaad's letters, and how they were all full of conspiracy. Masaad himself was a conspiracy. He was a person that Gaber did not know well. He used to fish on the banks of the lake before the train stopped coming, and Gaber had met him there. Gaber knew neither where he was from nor what he was doing there. They just saw each other every afternoon. Once night fell he saw Masaad board a small boat and, after loading his net and fish and equipment, begin rowing toward the center of the lake. He did not know where Masaad went after that. He watched him cut across the lake. In his eye, Masaad's size gradually shrunk down to nothing. First he became a line, then a small spot that almost instantly disappeared, as though the lake had suddenly swallowed it. Their relationship did not go beyond some superficial conversation about fish, bait, and the fishing seasons. They went on like this until Masaad surprised him one day and said that he wouldn't be seeing him there again. He said he was off to those new lands that were exploding with oil over the past several years. People were pouring into these lands fleeing hunger and poverty, and the oil turned into countless gold coins in their very hands. Masaad told Gaber that when he arrived there he would send for him. He promised to find him a place there and to extract him from their sterile, dead, dark well of a life in the twenty houses that stifled their minds and left them without choices.

His eyes still hung on Hamed who claimed he had never seen Masaad in his life. He trusted Gaber; he wasn't the type to run after a mirage. They had come back a second time to the smuggling kingpin and that was the only thing that had saved them from death. Maybe one would have ended up eating the other. As it was, Hamed just thought about his friend Gaber. They finished the jerky they made from the guide's leg, and Hamed lost his remaining strength in efforts to keep his stomach from jumping into his mouth. Once hunger began biting at them again, and they stumbled upon no more wells, after the last dirty well that had saved them days after they had drunk their last remaining drops of water that they finished after completing their meal of heart and liver. The filthy water they collected ran out in turn, and they ended up with no saliva at all to be released by the smooth pebbles they sucked on. They ended up tossing them out into the sunlight. Through it all, he kept thinking of Gaber. He spoke and heard his own voice as though it were a dog barking. His breathing sounded like panting. He noted a hoarseness in his voice as though something were rattling. His tongue began to drop out between each word and the next, his eyes bulged, and his ears pricked up. Gaber moved away to relieve himself and hopped around on all fours looking for something dry with which to wipe his bottom. Although Gaber's hopping looked frightening to him, he thought he had to do the same thing. He had to look at Gaber the same way. He thought it was inevitable that one of them would have to eat the other. At that moment, a caravan of desert Bedouins appeared on the horizon and saved them. If only these Bedouins had not appeared. If only one had eaten the other and then fallen dead beneath the sun.

They carried the two of them on the back of a camel to a way station that neither of them could have guessed existed. They offered them water and food. Although they did not enjoy the food, they both ate. They forbid them to bathe because of the scarcity of water, and, of course, they forbid their women to look at them. Then they transported them to where they had met the kingpin for the first time. They were overcome with joy when they realized they were in the city, but then they found that he had also received the guide. He had come along behind them on the back of a camel with a rope around its neck that he clung to, and he had passed the two of them on their camel. They found this guide standing in front of the villa that they had already spent an entire year in. He told them, "You'll rest here tonight and in the morning, we'll send you back to your homes." There was no way that they could put up any resistance. After he left them the first thing they thought was that the guide who brought them back arrived quickly. It couldn't have been that his camel was so much faster. The whole process had taken less than a day. What had the first guide done with them then? But they quickly forgot about this and became preoccupied with what tomorrow held. The villa was deserted, and the guide had padlocked it from outside. At midnight, the kingpin appeared before them.

Neither one of them gave a thought to moving around. They looked like a pair of potato sacks slung into the far corners of the room. Since the first day of their return they had been trying unsuccessfully to answer the question of why the kingpin was holding on to them. He had complained to them in the preceding days of the tentativeness of his situation and how time had passed him by. Things had changed a great deal after they left, or so he said. A pulverizing war had broken out between the two great states. He was shocked that they weren't aware of it. How could they have not noticed the war vehicles passing as they wandered in the desert? That should have saved them. Military vehicles should have picked them up, but it did not happen. His smuggling channels had been cut off by the war. Constant confrontations between the two armies ran up and down the length of the border that they had not made it to. Every station along the rail line, including the one at Gaber and Hamed's old home, was now occupied by soldiers who constantly went through the dwellings with a fine-toothed comb. Consequently, their country, to which he had regularly smuggled various goods, was closed off and kept under tight watch. The city in which he had originally met the two of them was now ruins. The Peugeots, Toyotas, and Datsuns that transported passengers between one village and another stopped running. There were no passengers to be found, and they came to be sold for the price of dirt. The flow of smuggled goods cut off completely, and military surveillance blanketed the entire area. Cloth, the most innocent thing that one could smuggle, might carry a flammable substance. A spare part of some type could be used in a time bomb. Drugs could make poison gas. Not only was smuggling affected, but desert guides also had no work. Some disappeared; others became beggars. The guide whom they had eaten—neither could deny the charge at this point—was the least valuable of those working under his supervision. The kingpin suffered not so much from his loss, as from the loss of dozens of others who had left the city.

In addition, other operations that piggybacked on the smuggling trade, such as the trade in women, had come to a standstill. The big-time smugglers and the VIPs that they dealt with in the upper political and administrative echelons stopped coming to the villa. They contented themselves with the women in the cities they lived in, and they looked for other means of bringing in extra profits.

All of this talk instilled in them some hope of salvation. As long as the man was in such dire straits, he would surely let them go. But it did not happen. He was evasive when they asked him what he would do with them. They thought about trying to escape but found the doors were all bolted from outside with four solid, towering men outside them rendering impossible any hope of escape. Not to mention the possibility that they might manage to escape, only to become lost again. They had never even known exactly where the villa was, because the first time they had come there with the kingpin from the city where they had met, they were riding in the back seat of a closed jeep, which took them on a long journey during which they saw almost nothing.

Finally, in a moment of bravery, they said to him, "If things are as bad as you say, why are you keeping us here?"

But he did not answer. He simply shot them a terrifying look that stuck crystal-clear in their memory thereafter. They looked at each other, and then he disappeared. Their huge guards began throwing down things to eat from the upper windows each morning.

Despair clouded their faces, and they lived constantly on the verge of tears with no other option but to take refuge in the mist of their own nostalgia.

Suad. Suad. Suad. What was this light that trapped me in a web of perversity? Everything was swimming through a rush of pure light, which unloosed passion, sent on an aircraft through the heart of space. But it frightened me, and when I ran, I knew not where my feet carried me. I was like a flying coffin, or like a swimmer huddled on top of a handkerchief riding over the sea waves. A hand of Haneya reached out and grabbed me, then her mother's hand grabbed me as well, and a lump of her father's hash fell between them both. How did matters arrive at this bizarre outcome? I dive in the sea of shadows and run after mirages. That's what they always said of me when I was little. "He's a young boy unlike all others. He wants to grab the moon with his bare hands. He chases its light against the walls and doesn't even give up when he finds his hands empty." If only I had believed you, my father, when you came home exhausted after a miserable day slaving beneath a mountain of steel. If only I had believed you when you told me that the world is a lame harlot, yet can catch a gazelle. Father, my whole world was four women. The light over all light was Suad. When she closed the way before me, I fell into the way of Haneya, her mother, and her father, the darkness under all darkness. Then there is Zeinab, who cut off our many paths together, who bore my children, children whom I left like birds with no feathers. I wonder who Zeinab, the daughter of virgin nature, could have chosen? I wish she had chosen Suad. My heart keeps telling me though that she's chosen Haneya and her dark, dry well of a mother. This is the same Zeinab, who, when she laughed, displayed the blossoms of a field of a thousand smiling flowers. Father, you used to say that the scent of a thousand flowers was purity, and that its wide fields were like a balm that soothed the nerves. And yet, my father, I did not smell this scent of purity, nor did I experience the soothing of my nerves. I kept running behind the treacherous light of the moon, and I never stopped. Yes, Zeinab, I see you in a shack over the bridge under the craven men of the city. Wait for me, Zeinab. Throw out this beast; Hamed will come back to you. Surely, he'll return one day, even if he himself doesn't know it yet.

Suad. Suad. Suad. What sort of harlot are you? What sort of unfeeling brute? Mother, if only you had not told me that her husband was a master sent down from God. What sort of friend of God snores through his own cuckolding, Mother? I could not wrest this title you bestowed upon him from my head. You always scared me when I was little. And if you hadn't said those frightening things, I would have leapt forward. Every time I would see her naked, her body appeared to me like marble lighting up an unmarked road. I am overcome when I see the rivers of honey dripping from her white flesh, to the point that I fear drowning. I had to kill you, Sheikh Masoud. Hamed and I had agreed to it. But we left you and told ourselves we would escape. I cannot forget that night after I told Hamed that we would leave in the morning how I kept stumbling on my way to the mosque. I was going to execute the murder myself without even telling Hamed, but when I tripped, I looked up and found myself in front of the door of the entryway to the wooden house of the inspector, and I heard a sound coming from inside that I can't forget. It was a sound of passion that seemed like it had been repressed for years and now suddenly exploded. It was the panting of a vintage lust. I knew what Laila and Fareed sounded like. Neither of them drew my attention in the least. I was preoccupied with you and your husband, Suad, and I didn't even notice your blonde female companion. The needle and thread and my mother's fumbling with them, and those suspicious letters from Masaad that were all a big conspiracy, blinded me. The rain poured down suddenly, and I did not kill your husband. I came back to my senses and told myself that leaving would be enough. Yet, I was anxious to bury my hatred in someone. I thought about going into Rawaieh's house, but I knew that her husband was probably inside. Where could one, who feared warmth on a stormy night, find refuge? I left Sheikh Masoud alive. Perhaps, he is still with you. He still tries to distract all of you with his lies about the evil that encircles you. I lost my way to my own house that night Suad. If only you had invited me to come to you sometime when your husband was not there snoring away. Ugh. What have you done to me, and what has your husband, God's servant, done to us all? When I stumbled upon our own front door and went inside, I found my mother sleeping. When I tried to pull the covers up over her, she looked up at me. Where are you now, mother? Why can't I remember you as anything other than an old woman? I see you walking down a path of anguish to meet death willingly. I see you surrounded by night. You are a piece of darkness over the bridge being lowered down into the water. Your Gaber, who has spent his life up until this moment running after a mirage, will return soon. I swear to you—by the blood shed on the day I recognized your old age for the first time when you fumbled with the needle and thread—that I will return. Gaber has no choice but to come back. Whether he's behind the inspector's car or behind a gathering of clouds, he will return. This Hamed, my fellow traveler through victory and grief, will accompany me in the journey back. Wait for me, mother. All I ever wanted was a grave in which to bury my despair.

The two of them heard the sound of a creaking door opening. They knew that day all their memories would come to an end. Surely, the circle had completed its circumference and was now closing off with an eternal bolt.

As the kingpin entered, they both remained seated. There were two men with him. He waved at them, and they began to pull up the rugs that covered the floor of the hall. They pulled it out from under the feet of Hamed and Gaber and began to fold it. Then they carried them out making several trips. They turned out the lights leaving only a wan, blue lamp, and they walked out ahead of the kingpin.

When he got to the door, he turned to Hamed and Gaber who were left there in the same spot where he had found them.

"Do you want to know when I'll release you?" he asked them.

When they showed no interest in answering he told them: "Whosoever enters this building a second time does not leave it."

He left. They offered no protest. They didn't even look at him. Neither batted an eyelash. They were both well aware of their fate, and they welcomed it.

PART FIVE

The City

ALI

Ali wasn't surprised when he returned and saw what he saw. He felt it from the first day he entered the City. On that day, he asked himself if he had traveled all that way only to return straight home. He decided to surrender himself to the hidden force that he felt had beset him, that seemed to have settled in his head. He was almost fourteen. He had seen many people his age completely contented with hunting and fishing. But this force that had overtaken him since the night of the fireballs had engrossed him in a quest he could never have imagined before that night. He genuinely felt a burden but at the same time understood that before him lay a task to be performed and a path to be traversed.

He had no idea that the world could be lit up the way he saw it lit up as he made his way to the City for the first time. As he drew away from the houses and the settlement gradually faded from view, the first thing he saw was the sea, whose vastness dwarfed their small lake. Its waters twisted into huge waves that made the ripples of the lake seem like nothing. The sea spread before his eyes to eternity. It was mid-morning, and the small but lofty sun rising in the immense blue sky seemed almost turquoise, like the color of the sea.

At first, he saw a group of fishing boats, some with sails, others running over the water causing a huge commotion, stirring up froth behind it. He decided it had to have been driven by some sort of steam engine like the ones that drive the train. Above one of these lightning-fast boats there was a pile of netting that trailed in the water. The boat turned around and formed a wide circle until he felt the fisherman driving the boat must have been casting out his wide net in order to catch all the fish in the world.

He was exhausted from walking in the sun. He had neither food nor drink with him. When he came upon a group of fishermen sitting in the shade of a wooden kiosk covered by some soggy netting with tan balls of cork and gray bits of lead dangling from its ends, he approached them and asked if he could drink from their water jug. His stomach twisted when he saw the fish they were grilling, but he asked for no food. He asked how far a walk it was to the City. They said he was already on its outskirts and asked exactly where he wanted to go. He repeated, "the City," and they all fell silent.

He walked for about another hour during which the sun settled in the middle of the sky. Beads of sweat budded over his forehead and his chest, but the sea breeze quickly blew in and dried them. He was by himself walking along the beach. The group of fishermen and the boats and the netting faded from view, leaving only a faint smell of tackle and iodine infiltrating his nose, jolting his lungs, and stirring up feelings of nausea.

In the distance, he saw strange obscure shapes moving. As he moved toward them he became certain that he had come to the place he was seeking. When he entered the City, he would know what to do. As he drew closer and the vague shapes came into focus, he saw half-naked people wearing swimsuits of different colors.

He had heard much about the beaches, and about the men and women who mingled and swam together with no compunction. Now he saw it with his own eyes. He was not so much embarrassed for them; he could only think of the trains filled with foreigners whom he had seen kissing each other so many times. Now when he saw almost naked women on the beach, he supposed that they were foreigners. Until he came closer and heard them speaking a language he understood.

· · ·

"Maybe they're coming here. Take me back home."

Annoyed, he answered, "You're still afraid? Aren't all the long years you've already spent locking yourself inside your four walls enough for you?"

As she struggled against his efforts to drag her toward the water, she answered, "No one has ever stood in their way, and no one ever will. No one has seen the things that I have."

There was almost pleading in his answer: "They won't come. Trust me. Everything's all over now."

He picked her up and carried her, and she stopped resisting and burst into tears. He rushed her toward the water. Ali had understood nothing.

He let himself wander over the sand among the crowds of people. He thought they would surely stare at him. There were hordes of beach umbrellas strewn before him with bathers scattered under their shade, but no one looked at him. He saw brightly colored swimsuits, both one-piece and two-piece, wrapped around white, tan, and pink bodies. The bright, scorching sun seemed cold to him. It stirred no desire or passion of any kind. All he thought of was that he had neared the City.

The smell of food was bombarding him from all directions, but he waged a valiant struggle against his hunger. He did not regret not bringing food or money with him. He had no idea why he had not tried. As he looked at the bodies of the men and women around him, he thought that even in the moments right after he had bathed his body did not glisten that way. He was not dark-skinned, and the others like Suad and his sister Laila were also as fair as the flame of a candle, but the women on this beach gave off a different sort of light. They were dazzling; their bodies glistened with an alluring light. He approached a group of young people who were fully clothed. They sat in a circle as the men used to do around Sheikh Masoud on Ramadan nights after they had performed the long prayers. He noticed that they stayed far from the crowd. There was a young man with very sharp features sitting in the middle of them with an olive complexion and fiery brown eyes. He carried a muscular frame as though he had been created to drag the trains behind him.

"My final word. Without a war all that will be left will be a slow and painful death from fear."

"But we decided not to turn back."

"We want to go on. Three years have past already."

Once again, he had understood nothing. But now a year later he understood it all. He forgot over the course of the year, the face of the besieged woman and the man who dragged her toward the water. He had not forgotten a thing about the strapping young man. After he had heard this voice that day he felt he could not go on walking, and he headed for the shade of one of the cabins and went to sleep.

When he woke up, it was evening. There was no one on the beach. A Coast Guard officer wearing a khaki jacket with shiny buttons that flashed in the darkness woke him up. Without knowing what he was doing he said, "I'm hungry."

The officer sat next to him and surveyed his utter fatigue and brokenness.

"Where are you from, son?" he asked.

"I don't know," Ali answered as though he were in a dream.

"How can you not know? If any of my fellow officers see you, they'll arrest you. We're at war."

Ali was confused and annoyed. He motioned toward the west that stretched before him dark and interminable. "I'm from there."

"From where exactly?"

"I don't know. Believe me. Toward the end of the railway. Near the lake. Trains always pass by us filled with soldiers and foreigners."

Now it was the Coast Guard officer who was confused. After a brief silence he asked, "And what are you doing here?"

Ali did not answer.

"Don't you have any family? Are you trying to escape from something?"

He answered in a daze, "I'm an orphan, and I want to work in the City."

The officer scrutinized him further. He stared into his wide, sparkling eyes. He saw before him a muscular boy with a broad forehead, and he begged God's forgiveness. At the same time, Ali was wondering how he had managed to call himself an orphan. The word's sense and the taste of it felt strange to him.

This officer had a small commercial cart run by his wife in a poor neighborhood in the City. It sold candy to children; sugar, tea, and cigarettes to adults; and envelopes and stationery to foreigners and young lovers.

That night, he decided to take Ali back home with him. It was about eleven at night when they made it back to his modest one-story house and his corpulent wife prepared a place for Ali to sleep on the roof.

Ali noticed that there were two empty kiosks on the roof each with smelly refuse stuck to its floor that sent up an unmistakable odor, so that Ali knew they had been used as chicken coops.

Each had a small electric light bulb dangling from its ceiling by a stripped black wire covered with flyspecks. The bulb was also black. The wife looked at Ali and then pointed toward the small pen. She pointed to a waterspout and a filthy toilet on one side of the roof. In the morning, the officer told him that he would spend a few days helping the wife watch the cart until he could arrange some job to suit him.

Ali had no idea where matters would lead him. At one point while he was in the cart watching the enormous wife try to move, he blurted out, "Auntie, do you know where I could find the Railway Engineers' offices?"

She looked at him in confusion. For a moment, he thought he may have said something wrong, but he was certain that he had heard his father talk over and over again of the general authority that they worked under that was located in the City and that was called the Railway Engineers' Headquarters. As sure as he had heard his father, he was sure that these offices supervised matters related to the trains and the railway workers.

"What do you want with that place?" She gave him a long look, and her face seemed to suggest that she knew all, but how could that be?

"Nothing," he told her. "I just want to know where it is."

"That's all?" she asked in a tone dripping with suspicion.

He did not answer. She left him to sell something to a customer who conspicuously examined Ali's face in a way that unnerved him. Was there something strikingly different about Ali's visage compared with those of the City people? Did something give away that he was from an isolated backwater surrounded by the desert on one side and the lake on the other with an old abandoned train station whose supervisor had been sleeping for the past several dozens of years where no passengers boarded and where no passengers got off? The customer walked out quickly, then stopped after taking a few steps and turned to shoot another piercing glance at him before moving on again.

He had hardly had a chance to consider this final stare before the woman said, "At the end of this street you'll find another long street where the tram line runs. Get on the tram and get back off after three stations. That's where you'll find your offices. In an old, two-story, red building made of yellow brick. You can't miss it."

For some reason, Ali felt a surge of joy pump through his veins even though he had no clue what he would do in the building. His body throbbed as though there had been a quantum leap in his growth since he made it to the City, even though he hadn't even been there two days. He told himself that there was a hidden force behind his growth and joy. He would give himself over to it, so that it might infuse him with a power beyond his age and his strength.

"Shall I go now?" he asked.

"Tomorrow," she answered firmly.

In the evening, after he had eaten his dinner up on the roof by himself like a dog with mange to whom the corpulent wife had silently tossed a plate of bean paste and a couple of bread crusts and then walked away, he remembered how his father used to spend the summer nights before the train stopped coming up on the roof by himself. He would eat his dinner then lie back against the railing and light a cigarette as he stared up at the heavens. It was as though he were counting the stars. Ali found himself craving a cigarette although he had never smoked before in his life. He forgot about smoking, however, when he saw a young man coming up to the roof. He came up the steps and looked around himself furtively, then he signaled to the steps for someone to follow him up. Ali's heart pounded as he realized that this was the same muscular young man that he had seen on the beach the day before. He slid quietly backward into one of the kiosks as he watched a girl come toward the young man with an unmistakable expression of fear on her face. Once he had hid himself inside the kiosk he saw another young man, and a second girl, and then a third boy. Then, to his shock, the first boy signaled to him as though he knew he was there all along. Ali jumped up. It was the first time in his life that he was afraid of another human being.

Once the young man had come over in front of him, he lowered his eyes as though, if he did not look at anyone, no one would be able to see him. Somehow he sensed the two girls exchanging glances and smiling. For the first time since he had arrived in the City, he was overcome with a nostalgia for Laila and Suad. He felt he had to leave the City that instant, for they would surely leave the twenty houses if he did not come back to them soon. And yet had he really come just to go right back? What was making him see himself this way, as though he were a dog with mange? He called on the hidden force to reassert itself over his thoughts, and he made himself see the way before him as open.

"Could you go get us some cigarettes from the shop? Here's the key." The young man did not wait for Ali to answer. He just handed him a key. Ali figured out then that he was the son of the Coast Guard officer and the corpulent woman, and he rushed down the steps, elated with relief.

He ran down a narrow, filthy street full of children running in circles throwing pebbles at one another and trying to throw dirt in each other's faces. He looked to either side of the street, hoping to find lampposts that

children grouped around to fix broken traps or bait fishhooks. He wanted
to see children playing card games with old cigarette packs and a game
called "money" involving throwing rocks in the air and catching them
with the small pebbles from the railroad. There should have been a group
making themselves a soccer ball from cloth, or a group running out like
rays of light from a lamppost in a game of hide-and-seek, or some even
gathered in a circle and telling each other ghost stories. But he could see
absolutely none of this. All he could see were children running and smear-
ing each other's faces with dirt. All the windows and doors in the area were
tightly closed. The stark-looking houses gave the impression that none of
the children lived in them, that they descended from heaven each night to
toss dirt at each other, and then ascended once again.

He rushed over and finished his errand, completely unafraid that
there might be someone around the shop that might see him. As he ran
back up the steps, he felt he was moving with the stealth of a fox. Then he
thought about walking as though he were hunting a hedgehog. But the
stairs were too narrow for him to circle like a hyena. He went up at a slow
contented pace. As he arrived at the top of the stairs, a beautiful moon
shone down and lit up the rooftop like a lake of pure light. The two small
kiosks seemed like two distant train stations, and the moonglow was so brilliant that he felt it came from inside his breast.

When the moon had shone over the lake it made the waters glisten before his eyes. He told himself, "The fish can see each other down there.
This moon must light up their dark underwater home." He imagined the
fish swimming, so elated by the beams of light that they danced, while
their partners swam off to a distance and engaged in their own amusement.
The moon ruined games involving hiding. Anyone who tried to hide
ended up with a shadow that exposed them. But he knew how to get
around this problem so that no one found him easily. He sat on the ground
in a heap smothering his shadow under him. When he sensed the pounding of the boy who was looking for him nearby, he sprang up in his face
and ran off leaving his playmate in shock. They all asked him how he

could not have a shadow, but he only laughed in response. Once the train stopped coming and ended their games, their families put them to bed early as though they were farm animals, and he never gave another thought to telling anyone about his secret. He told himself, "Who knows? Perhaps the train will come back, and everything will return to its regular pace." When he asked his mother about those with no shadow, without hesitating she said, "Pure light casts no shadow." It made him feel brilliant, and he decided at that instant to teach his children as they grew up to not have a shadow. Thus, they too would be pure light.

As he stood there at the top of the stairs, he suddenly felt that the world really was a huge place, just as his mother had said. The human being was a scrawny creature of little value. God had cast him to earth as a punishment after he gave in to Satan's temptations. As a result, he went through afflicted and pathetic. Satan chased him; God set him right; and he hung suspended between wondering why one did not kill the other and put an end to the tragedy. But his mother had always said that only those whom God had chosen recognized the righteous way from day one. That was why there were children who were evil from infancy, and others who were obedient, who stayed between the lines, who never disobeyed their parents. The children of the devil made up the first group. Once they grew up, horns sprouted from their head and fire poured out of their eyes. The other group comprised children of God like Sheikh Masoud, or even better than him, like the Sufis of the south. He almost laughed as he remembered the day Sheikh Masoud kicked him out, and how his mother had called a plague on the man and his wife. She had even told him never to go back to the mosque after that as though she wanted him to be one of the followers of Satan. Then he almost cried as he remembered Suad. He felt himself such a puny figure in this vast earth that he never should have come to that place alone. He asked himself if he should return. Then he felt the hidden force driving into his mind like a train pouring out a black cloud of smoke.

"It looks like the war's ready to break out."

"Soldiers have filled all the streets of the City."

"Then we must volunteer. They'll leave us if we don't. Let's volunteer ourselves. The women can work as nurses, and we'll work in the civil defense."

"Do you think they'll need a civil defense force?"

"Everything's possible."

"If Fareed had not died, we might have converted him to the cause."

He spent a restless night. Was the secret of everything here in this despicable little hut? He was certain that they had referred to Fareed, the inspector's son. Were all secrets really hidden somewhere in the heart of this city of which he had only seen one narrow and filthy street so far? And what was this war they spoke of? And what was this fear that they talked of on the beach? When the boy told the anxious young woman that everything was over now, what had he meant by this? What was this war that was supposed to break out two days after he had walked into the City, and with whom would it be fought? How could his people have been so oblivious to it all. These injured soldiers that had talked to him, what did they mean? Why hadn't they explained anything to him?

These young people seemed to know everything about them. Why else would they have mentioned Fareed? Back in the village, their whole lives had revolved around a train that had stopped coming. They had just watched the trains and the mysterious soldiers. They saw foreigners of whom they knew nothing other than that they were foreigners. They fished for rotten fish and hunted pigeons that were already dead. Finally, the men and the women migrated. Now, when he asked this fat woman about the railroad engineers' offices, she became circumspect for some reason. What about the customer at the shop who had stared at him? Where did the darkness stop and the light begin? The hidden force in his head burst forward into a guided flame that almost exploded in his head.

They stopped talking after he gave them their cigarettes. He could no longer hear them. He crawled back behind the kiosk inside of which they were sitting. His ears went lax, and he could hear nothing. They were quiet for a long time until it was almost midnight. He couldn't understand how they could stay silent for so long. They had to have been talking in an ultrasonic language, like the language of the lake waters. Its smooth waves bent and broke toward the bank. The grand waves made a sound, but the smaller ones were silent. They would come in a delicate arch and gently cover the beach, then dissipate. The supremely welcoming banks took them in. Those were always the most precious waves and the most sparkling ones. The sight of the earth's pores drinking up the delicate waters always intoxicated him. Then again, whenever a moist and silent breeze was stirred up, he also felt his body grow as thin as a thread that no one could see, hung in the calm of space swerving peacefully in exquisite pleasure. He almost felt as though he were entering inside himself, standing enthralled in exuberance and rapture. He blinked his eyes. The fish were surely conversing underwater, even if no one heard them. His father had been right when he said that every creature has its own language. What, after all, was the fish's rejection of bait on the hook, other than the wiliness of the fish or its attention to the warnings of others? When fish were thrown into a basket after being pulled from the lake, the large ones always jumped out and flopped around on the ground. Whenever he went to grab one of these, a second would jump out, then a third, then a fourth. His mother told him to cover the basket, but he often uncovered it simply to watch the fish jump out one after another. He watched the scene in delight. It was as though the jumping of the large fish led all the smaller ones to jump around as well. It was all by rank. The large ones led the small ones. He was sure of it. When the large one stopped the smaller ones followed suit. The smaller ones submitted to the large ones. They only surrendered after their leaders. But he wondered why the large one gave up so soon and left the small ones to give in. His father also claimed that birds had their own language, as did all insects, even the ants. This reminded him that whenever he heard a rooster crow at dawn, he would immediately hear the rest of the roosters crow after it. They never all crowed together, even though the dawn always broke in one glorious moment. The grandest rooster always had to crow first, and thus, signal the others to crow after him. He was certain it was true. He had often heard a cock crowing at midnight or even earlier without the others following suit, and he felt this proved his point. When he asked his mother why this cock was crowing so early, she said it was the "false cock." He knew his mother spoke the truth. Why else would the others not follow its lead? This meant that roosters had their own language, and that they could differentiate between the truth and a lie. His father had often told him stories of Solomon the Wise, and how he had been able to understand the language of the birds and the mammals and the insects, and how he conversed with them all. That night he wished that he was Solomon, as he rested behind the kiosk, surrounded by ultrasonic language. But he knew that these people were neither birds, nor mammals, nor insects. So how could they possibly be conversing?

He tossed and turned over his scratchy cot until morning. He went off toward the railway engineers' offices, full of anxiety. He saw people running through hallways, huge signs and lights, windows and doors left open or closed. There were children chasing each other again, but this time, they didn't smear each other's faces with dirt. He was swallowed by the wide street full of noise. He boarded the tram and prepared himself to get off after three stops as the corpulent woman had told him to do. He thought about the train station and its sleeping inspector and Uncle Abdel Nur, the night shift man, and his son. He heard people talking about troops breaking through enemy lines, and brutal battles waged with tanks and warplanes. He saw a small radio in the hand of one of the tram passengers. He wondered at how it could be that none of the twenty houses had a radio. Only the inspector had one, and his didn't seem to make any noise. Only occasionally would it let a melody flow out behind the wooden shack. When he went to the bridge with his mother, however, he heard many songs coming out of several radios at once, so that he could distinguish nothing. The radio called out numbers that made the listeners praise God and shout for joy.

"We said they were cowards."

"The Book curses them."

"But it also says that everything has its seasons."

By the time the third stop had arrived, he had figured out nothing. He knew that the distance between the place where he had lived and the City was no small distance. In fact, it was overwhelming.

When he exited the tram, he began to look around him. He saw the huge red building like a wide mountain that had been ablaze for ages. There were many short houses surrounding it. He was surprised that these closed off houses seemed not to sense the war or the commotion around them. For some reason that he didn't understand, he thought about his lie to the officer that he was an orphan. Then he saw a huge billboard with a train on it, and he found himself wondering exactly what he wanted in the place.

He was sure no one had ever come to this place before to ask about the train. When they said that the inspector had done so, they were lying. The inspector never spoke of it at all. He himself would have to get to the bottom of things.

Ali saw a thin guard sitting on a shiny bench in front of the broad doorway and went to him.

"Is this the Railway Engineers' Building?" he asked.

"Yes." The guard's stare reminded him of the customer at the shop the day before. He thought perhaps his clothes were the reason. He wore a very baggy shirt with a large tear over the shoulder, in stark contrast to all the tight fitting clothes that the young men and women of the City wore. He wore extremely baggy pants that tightened around his ankles, but the City dwellers pants were all the opposite. His feet were clad in an old pair of sandals made out of tires, footwear these people had surely not seen the likes of.

"Where is the boss' office?" Ali asked anxiously.

"Which 'boss'? Do you mean the general manager?"

Ali asked the question excitedly, and the guard seemed surprised as he answered. Ali nodded his head yes and then decided to say no more out of fear of saying something wrong. The guard waved toward the top of the stairs carelessly, as though he were shooing a fly. Ali left the guard and carefully paced toward the wide-open door. He felt humidity in the air. He decided the weather outside had been hell without his even noticing. Then he stood for a moment, confused in the wide dark hallway. The hallway branched off to both the right and the left before him. Each way consisted of wide wooden steps fortified with steel. They were exactly like the steps at the switch house, and men raced up and down them in a dizzying hurry. Some of them carried papers in their hands or tucked under their arms. To his surprise one of them even walked with a whistle in his mouth.

He began looking around for a welcoming face to engage, but he found them all austere. Their clothes were all a dark green like the uniform of his father and his co-workers. He told himself perhaps all railway workers everywhere wore these dark green outfits. He finally decided just to walk into the first door on his right, from which laughter and loud voices were coming.

"Who are you, son?" someone asked.

He had walked into the office and found himself looking at a broad, black wooden desk that glistened like the guard's bench outside the building. Behind it was a man smoking a cigar—which he recognized from having once seen a foreigner smoking one. The man was handsome, although he looked older. When he moved the cigar to the side of his mouth to ask Ali who he was, there were four clerks surrounding him, scrutinizing Ali with piercing glances that pricked at his skin and bone like an icy needle. But Ali managed to collect himself enough to tell the man everything, as he sat and listened in shock. He thought he had found what he was looking for when the man kept relighting his cigar and listening and asking Ali to keep talking until he had finished.

Then he shocked Ali by asking him, "So you want me to set aside the state of war to focus on some freight train that hasn't run for a couple of years?"

He couldn't answer. Everything in his head evaporated, and the clerks sitting around burst into uproarious laughter. His blood began to boil, and he felt so puny that he wanted to burst into tears. The man seemed to sense Ali's humiliation and began speaking to him reassuringly.

"Look son, I won't ask why this train is so important to you, but maybe if you come back to us after the war ends, we could help you." And then after a brief pause: "Son, aren't there any older people where you're from? I mean a man, instead of you."

That night, he waited for the young man and his friends to come up to the roof, but they never appeared. He thought to himself that the fat woman had not said a word to him after he returned. He was now more certain than he had ever been that what he found when he returned would not surprise him. His visit to the Railway Engineers' Building had not gone as he had planned. But after he came out of the first office, he decided not to leave before he had solved something. He strutted into another office and found the clerk at the desk in front of him waving him over to another office without even bothering to learn who he was or what he wanted. In the third office he found three men wearing prominent shiny glasses. They unfolded wide papers over a long, spacious table. They each had a long pole that they used to point at the papers as they whispered to one another. They wore shiny white shirts and pressed slacks. The long poles frightened him, and he walked back out of the room without saying anything. In the next office he entered, he found a man drinking tea and smoking a cigarette. He told him his entire story while the man listened quietly. In the end, the man just offered him a cup of tea. He declined and walked out of the office. He then remembered that the guard at the door had pointed up the stairs, and he decided to go up to the second floor where he found himself in front of the General Manager's office. The whole floor was polished and clean. Its floor was covered with an exquisite rug that his feet sunk into. Elegant young women rushing back and forth between offices surrounded him on both sides. They carried official-looking papers and smiled at each other as they met. They wore stunning outfits featuring short skirts that left much of their legs exposed. Along both sides of the long hallway that stretched from one stairwell to another, old men sat on little stumps of chairs in front of closed office doors in and out of which came the fancy women. The old men sat in front of the doors without moving like the silent idols that he had heard people used to worship before the coming of the prophet Mohamed. At first, he couldn't tell which office belonged to the general manager, but eventually he managed to figure it out. Most of the women were coming out of their own offices and going into a centrally located one. They would saunter over to it, disappear inside for a few moments, and then come back out. He told himself that the general manager's office had to be behind that door; the women went back to it for everything. But as he approached the door, several of the old men stood up and headed toward him. They grabbed him by his arms and shoulders and dragged him to the top of the stairwell and pointed down the stairs, and he went back down.

He repeated to himself his father's proverb that God could inspire him to stay along the straight and narrow. Was it possible? Could this really be Samira?

He repeated his father's saying, "God help me and make me strong." If it was she, he would not go back. The world would have raised the veil over its own baseness. He would not forget what he had come for, or the constant hidden force in his head. His body matured by a quantum leap everyday. But was this really Samira?

She twisted half-naked on the stage in front of him. He was surrounded by bright light. Women, young girls, and children sat in the rows in front of him. He sat in the back in the midst of several long tables surrounded by men. It was a cold, dry night, and there was Samira, twisting and turning in her sheer dancing outfit. Her drummer pounded away passionately, and the accordion player was floating in another world. Meanwhile, all the men who were watching expressed their approval through gruff sounds and catcalls. The air was filled with the smell of hashish, and its smoke gathered in a cloud over their heads.

Ali stood and began to move toward the stage. This certainly was none other than Samira the Beauty. He continued to stare at her waiting for her to notice him. Finally, he decided to speak to her, but then as soon as she finished, having taken no notice of him, she turned and disappeared behind the curtain heading for the band's dressing room. He made his way to the door of the dressing room and waited some time for her to come out. When she came out, the drummer and accordion player flanked her on either side. She swung from her hand a small black purse with a gold chain for a handle. Ali noticed a thick coat of makeup smeared over her face. He tried to shout, "Samira," but the sound was choked off before it came out, and she didn't even look toward him. The drummer threw him an angry glance, however. He watched her move toward a nearby taxi that seemed to await her. Her two accompanists rode behind her. In the front seat next to the driver, Ali caught a glance of a very ugly old woman before the car disappeared into a narrow street.

He stood in place for a moment, asking himself if the earth really spun in a circle as Sheikh Masoud had once said. Or did the sun spin around the earth, as his mother had always said? The war ended after only a few days, and he knew the whole story. Safaa told him that the young people had forced the government to declare war. She said that the Coast Guard man's son had died a martyr after joining the popular resistance forces and that they had all recognized that they had lost in him an ardent patriot. He had been the one who organized demonstrations among his classmates at the university. Safaa explained it all to him. When he was about to ask her about Fareed, she raised the issue once she had figured out where Ali had come from. She claimed she had known him before she ever laid eyes on him. Fareed had painted them a clear picture of their life. She knew that Ali had a fair sister, that the most beautiful woman in the world lived with them—a woman called Suad—and that her husband was found murdered the morning after a stormy night. Then she told him not to ask her any questions, and that he should leave the City and go back home as soon as possible. Before that, on the third day of the war, she had told the son of the coastguard officer that she had found work for Ali in the repair garage owned by her brother. Ali had no idea that the son was looking for work for him. That was the same day that he had learned her name. Before then, he had just watched her come up to the roof. She was pretty with delicate features. Her hair was black and her eyes were amber. Her face was slightly curved, her nose fine, and her lips like two plump grapes. When she moved, she looked like a giddy little girl. Once he started working, she came back to him and said, "I have arranged this job, but the best thing for you to do is to go back home." She told him she was afraid.

Safaa visited her brother at the mechanics' shop several times after that. It was always Ali who brought her tea there. She let him sit with her in the office behind the big garage. He heard her urging her brother who was much older to teach him the mechanic's trade. She kept saying that Ali wouldn't be there in the garage much longer. He tried several times to ask her what Fareed had done to deserve his fate, but he never was able to go through with it. He was about to utter the words once when he noticed a tear glistening in one of her eyes. She said Fareed was not always so faithful.

He spent six months trying to get some answer from the Railway Engineers, but he kept having the same experience he had had the first day. Even after the war ended, the first man he had talked to said that after they finished reorganizing the entire train schedules they would look into his matter.

Ali maintained a faint hope, but he knew that it was indeed a faint hope. He asked himself what the trains had to do with a war that happened so far away. He began to understand something of auto repair and decided to commit to learning more. The cinema became his sanctuary when he felt choked off. He lost himself in its visions almost every night, then he would go back and sleep in the garage with the sense that the hidden force was reinvigorating his brain cells. He spent six months this way until the night some co-workers took him to the wedding where he had seen Samira dance. That night, he lost his mind. He yearned to see Safaa, thinking perhaps she could explain it to him. Could he possibly ask Samira why she had not come and searched for Mursi so that they could talk it all out? He remembered Samira's father Abdullah walking along with his extended neck and his hunchback, carrying a crowbar over his shoulder with a basket made from rubber tires hanging from the end and wearing that same dark green suit that he had stumbled over in so many places. He left right after Samira disappeared and had not come back by the time Ali left. Surely, he still hadn't. Could this really be that very Samira the Beauty, dancing before him in a strange city?

He decided to attend every other wedding he heard about in order to see Samira again and try to talk with her. If she only saw him, he was sure she would know him. He would never forget the last time they had met when she confused him for Mursi, her fiancé, who traveled atop the trains. Ali had asked about him at the Railway Engineers' Building but had not been able to arrive at anything. The man in charge of the complete list of workers told him, "You're asking about a specter. A young man named Mursi who works as a guard on top of the train cars? The security on the trains is done by contract labor. Your friend has to be doing something else by now. Plus, you don't even know his whole name. There are hundreds of Mursi out there." Then he was silent for a while before he added, "My boy, you're full of strange questions and bizarre stories, aren't you?" Then yet again he said to him, "You've started to come back more than you should. Everyone knows you and that's made you look suspicious, and God help you once you become suspicious in these times."

Strange occurrences proliferated throughout the City. People were alternately disgruntled and nationalistic. Some asked why they had waged war, only to have their enemy come and walk among them. Others said they had seen them walking around various parts of the City drinking cold bottles of Pepsi and licking ice cream cones, even though it was winter. He knew that these creatures that had come to threaten the state had appeared in the City. He knew that the enemy achieved his goals by spilling blood. Thus, he realized that Safaa was right in saying he should return as quickly as possible, but how? and why?

But he also thought, if there had, in fact, been such a devastating war that had taken so many martyrs, how had everything turned upside down again so quickly? There was a boy who used to pass by the spot where he liked to fish near the twenty houses. He would attack him, and they'd fight. They'd maintained a fierce competition, but the world never stopped because some blood was drawn. He realized he was completely removed from his environment and that Safaa was right about his returning, but how?

He knew that Safaa had left the City with her father, who had gone to work in another one. But her advice to him to return and save his family that she had spoken the last time they met stayed with him. Her words still rang in his ears as though they were hanging from them. But once again he wondered, how?

When he had lived in his family's midst he could not save them, and he even felt some loathing toward them. He had come there to the City and not known its people either. The hidden force began to vex him. It refused to release him, and the surging expansion of his flesh and bones irritated him as well.

He felt now like a man of twenty-five with various powers boiling in his veins. He began to hate the cinema because its erotic images provoked urges he could not control, especially when he went home to sleep alone in the dark garage. He did not want to have his nose blocked once again with that thick smell that used to waft up from his underpants over two years ago. At the cinema as well there were many dancers who reminded him of Samira who had disappeared again and whom he had no idea how to find.

Then one morning, he heard the workers in the garage talking about a dancer named Nana who was all over town. This was during a conversation about the elaborate tents set up among the ruins that presented circus acts, acrobats, and magicians, among which this Nana was always presenting her act.

He decided to go see this dancer. Internally, he was sure she was Samira. He had completely failed to learn anything about the train at the

Railway Engineers' Building, but he had to find Samira the Beauty and take her back. After that, he could wash his hands of the entire matter. He could leave this City. He didn't give a damn about the warring parties. They could settle things by spilling blood or water for all he cared.

He began going out every night to the largest tents he could find. He found a disgusting picture of a contorted dancer over the door of the tent. Her face actually would have resembled Samira's, if it had not looked so vampish. He would always remember her face as the innocent face of a child. Underneath, a banner proclaimed the scintillating dancing of "Nana, the human coil." He passed through a throng of peddlers of everything imaginable, including toys he had not seen before and games that featured fire or cards, or throwing things like weights and spears. He tried to push the throngs of people out of his way enough to make himself a path. He saw strange, deformed faces on people of all different colors. He saw women dressed provocatively, unveiled and wearing paint that made their faces look glassy. When he went inside, he saw one man on a stage announcing the various acts. First, there was a magician, then acrobats, and finally an exotic dancer. Finally, Samira appeared and began dancing in so disgusting a manner that he wanted to cry. When she walked off the stage he ran toward the door to try to talk with her, but now she left her venue surrounded not only by the drummer and accordion player, but also by two huge bodyguards who looked as though they could crush one hundred men. He left the tent and moved to another where he repeated the same experience.

He went on like this for several nights, each time staying out until dawn. Nothing bothered him as much as the billboards with their banners that he had begun to memorize. They announced the exotic dancer, the acrobatic dancer, the dancer for every night: Nana the human coil—plus Fire, Wind, Electric Energy. After he had spent two months in this futile chase, he realized he had completely forgotten about his family and his old home, so he decided once and for all to talk to Samira even if it cost him his life, and in the end, he did it. He saw her coming out of one of the tents and raced over to her like a bullet. He grabbed her arm and then could not tell what happened after that, or how it happened.

Even now, after an entire year had passed, and he had taken the decision to go home the next morning and the garage stretched out in front of him like a huge beast on a summer night that seemed to have gathered the heat and humidity of all the previous years and the cars parked in front of it seemed like dilapidated burial chambers . . . even now, he did not know if the long, hanging, deep, piercing laugh that stabbed into him like a dull knife, was really Samira's laugh or not.

Was it really Samira who had uttered the laugh, or was there some lewd demon inside of her who had done it? Even now, the only picture in his mind of what had happened was like a picture of a gangster movie. It was as when a swiftly moving battle breaks out in a film and bodies fly about as though choreographed, and then seconds later the battle is over, leaving behind its dead and wounded. In the end, the hero emerges safe and sound and protected from the fray. Then he walks forward triumphantly with his clothes barely wrinkled, and he kisses the beautiful heroine.

But that night, Ali's clothes were disheveled, and he never kissed the alluring heroine. He had barely touched her arm before the two huge guards fell upon him. He flew through the air faster than a bat. Ali convulsed, kicking one while punching the other at the same time and knocking them both unconscious. He stood and looked at them with fire streaming from his eyes, almost unable to believe that he had been the one that had done this. Anyone who had seen him at the point at which the two attacked him would have surely seen him a dead man. His body that had grown by a quantum leap still did not amount to half of either of these two men's bodies. He had no idea where this swiftness had come from, or how he had managed to subdue them. The accordion player and the drummer stood by astonished and gripped by fear. They each raised their instruments in front of their faces as though to protect themselves. But Ali knew exactly what he wanted. He raced back to Samira and grabbed her arm once again. She let out a scream as she felt his finger about to crush her arm. He knew the teeming crowds in front of the tent were staring at him. He was prepared for attacks to rain down from all sides. But when none came, he found himself speaking to her in open pain,

"You're Samira. Don't you remember me? I'm Ali. Laila's brother."

Samira just stared haughtily. He let go of her arm and she took a deep breath. She seemed to remember him. A translucent tear shined in her eye. Then she suddenly burst into a long profane laugh, deep and piercing like a dull knife thrust inside him. Then she left him standing there with no idea what to do.

An hour later, he found himself pounding on the door of one of his co-workers in the garage. When he came out, Ali barked at him sharply to put his clothes on immediately.

"What's going on?"

"I'll tell you on the way."

He felt base and insignificant. He was angry and driven. Along the way, he asked his co-worker, "Can we go right now to see this woman that you've said so much about?"

His co-worker burst into surprised laughter. He had always tried to convince Ali to come with him to see her, but Ali had always refused.

His co-worker took him to a narrow street after they had covered a long distance in a taxi. The cabbie had left them off along the beach toward the eastern end of the City. The houses on either side of the narrow street were closed up. It was after two o'clock at night. The narrow street led them to an even narrower alleyway. It was filthy with peelings of sugarcane scattered about and the smell of waste filling the air. They stopped in front of a house and went in through an unnecessarily wide door. He followed his co-worker up a creaking wooden staircase with broken metal supports. His friend raised his finger to his lips to warn Ali to be silent. They climbed two flights. On the pitch-black third floor, Ali stopped, short of breath with a feeling that sweat covered his whole body. He felt the hair on his head stand up like the quills of a hedgehog, as his friend gave the door three light knocks.

After a few moments, a small light which hung outside the door came on. The door to the peephole opened, and the face of an old woman wrapped in a white shawl looked out at them. Ali's friend made a signal, and the door came open. He entered and Ali followed.

It almost seemed as though something in the universe pushed him to confront its entirety all at once. The hidden force that still occupied his head and had pushed him to the City, that he had never given a thought to before, had decided to lay bare before him all that was hidden.

In these moments all that he wanted was to conceal his anger in agitated flight. He had forgotten that he had learned nothing at the only place where he might have found relief—at the Railway Engineers' Building. Samira, who seemed to fill the whole City, had laughed at him when he tried to execute his plan of taking her back to break the vicious circle of hell. Safaa, who had lit up his consciousness, had left now. She left incomplete her speech that he so wished could continue endlessly. Suad was about to be completely erased from his memory. He felt as he sat there in the long parlor looking over the rows of chairs with multicolored, flowered cloth print covers, and the small tables in the corners with bags of cotton and small glass items that he could not identify. There was a determination in the universe to crush him.

The old woman who was covered in white had gone into the room in front of them and come back after a few moments offering them cigarettes and saying, "The other customer will be out in a little while. You two are very late."

He smoked for the first time in his life. He wanted to chew up the whole cigarette and swallow it, and it didn't escape his notice that the universe was determined to crush him. When the customer came out, he was a huge, black man whose cragged face reminded him of Zeidan, whose whereabouts he had never learned. After a few moments during which he was overcome with an all-encompassing sorrow until he completely forgot the presence of his friend next to him, Zeinab, Hamed's wife, walked out and stood before them.

This was none other than Zeinab. He was sure it was her; the numbness that crawled up his leg and the pounding of his heart gave it away. This was the Zeinab who he had only ever seen modestly clad in a whole mountain of different clothes with three children with snot dripping down to their chest clinging to the end of her cloak. Now she wore only a white night shirt that exposed most of her bronze body. His friend stood up to greet her. He smiled and said that he had come for Ali's sake and that he would leave him to her. Then he added wryly that Ali was very green, and he burst out laughing as Zeinab smiled and Ali's chest and head began to burn. He felt like someone had opened his head and dumped all the coals of the fowarika into it.

His friend walked out while she stood there in shock at the sight of him. He placed his head between his hands and cast a glance to the earth between his knees.

He could feel the old woman standing at a distance in front of the door of one of the rooms staring at them in amazement. He believed that Zeinab had not recognized him at all. This body of his that had grown by a quantum leap must have fooled her. At the same time, his face, which he had not looked at in the mirror in months, surely had changed just as much as his body.

Zeinab sat down on the ground and smiled at him, slightly confused. She was beautiful, like a small white lantern on a dark night.

"How are you, Zeinab?" he asked her.

She became unsettled and asked him, "What are you saying?"

He raised his head and fixed his stare upon her for a long moment, then said, "Aren't you Zeinab?"

Her lips began to tremble slightly, and she tried to repress them but could not. She motioned to the old woman to come in and before she could speak, he said to her, "Look carefully at my face."

She looked.

Then, she spoke to him at length. Throughout her speech he kept repeating to himself, "What sort of evil is pursuing us all?" She told him he had grown a great deal, and it was as though many years had passed without anyone realizing it. He told her that he had grown old and felt his life was over. In the end, she wept.

Then she took him to a closed room. When she opened the door, he saw old Um Gaber in a pile in one corner and the three children in another corner. She told him that the mother was becoming senile and barely moved. She wet herself and prayed for death, which never came. She said Gaber had fooled her. He had called as she was about to sink, and she had decided to wait for him, only to have him not come.

Ali had no idea that Um Gaber had also left the twenty houses. When he asked Zeinab how she had come, she said the same person that had brought her had gone back and brought Um Gaber and the children. He had found them on the bridge sleeping near an abandoned hut. When Ali tried to ask her about the person that had brought them, she just said that the important thing was for them to see a great deal of him because he was a pleasant scent wafting from the beautiful past.

He walked out exasperated. He asked God why He had brought him out to chase after the unknown like this. His father had always called on God at the end of his prayer, saying, "May Your grace rise above Your loathing and anger toward us." He thought that if only he had persisted in praying at the mosque behind Sheikh Masoud, he would still remember many of the supplications that might have saved him now. There was nothing left for sons of Adam these days but supplication—ascending to the heavens or just flying through the wind. Then he said, "Lord, if you can't bestow salvation, please don't exact vengeance either." He scurried away.

Dawn had broken, and a thick fog had settled over the City, giving Ali the sense that he had ascended to heaven. He remembered going out early to fish and finding the fog enveloping the world, and he would compete with his friends to see who could exhale more fog.

As the sheets of mist began to evaporate, as the high buildings came

into view and then filled up his vision, he finally arrived at the beach, and
he felt the buildings were ready to crash down on top of him. The ground
along the way was wet, and the smell of the sea filled his nose. The early
morning chill almost folded him up inside himself. But the roar of the
waves beckoned darkly, until he stripped and ran into the sea. He dove into
the waves then stood stiffly just in from the edge of the water struggling to
fight off his trembling with his legs underwater and the waves crashing
against his torso.

The City stretched in a long curve around him as though it were hugging a mother it had just met for the first time. Small boats scattered in
front of him and behind him, moving in all directions chaotically. Fishing
nets covered the boats or were stretched over the beach on top of high
wooden poles. He remembered the day he had arrived, and the first signs
of the City that had met him at the westernmost end. As he looked at the
long, winding empty seawall stretching along the beach and the tall buildings coming toward him with their closed windows, he asked himself what
made this City sleep and what made it come to life. He sensed a thousand
and one sins filling the corners and oozing from behind the walls and
crashing with exuberance against the open spaces that God created in purity and cleanliness, but no longer paid attention to.

He walked out of the waves and put on his clothes and asked himself
when the embrace of the unknown mother had ever been tender. He went
back to the garage walking in spite of the long distance.

The City began to awaken around him. He found himself looking into
people's faces again. For the first time he saw the foreigners about whom
he had heard so much, and who had divided the loyal ties of the people.
He remembered being surprised when the last train full of foreigners that
he had seen had stopped some distance from the station. Now he thought
this train must have been preparing for something. It was just as it is when
a person or an animal hangs back to get ready to attack something larger
than itself or something it expects to be strong. There was an unusual invisible smoke filling his eyes, and he imagined it was from the burnt bones

of innocent people. That day, after he made it back to the garage exhausted, Safaa came to pay her brother a quick visit around noon. Her
brother didn't ask him to bring her tea. But she herself asked to see him,
and he went to her expecting bad news.

"Are you still here?" she asked him.

". . ."

"Don't be so proud. Your strong body can't always save you. You're
young, and this city has some hard days ahead of it."

He hesitated for a moment, then said, "I wanted to talk to you about
something."

She answered with an eerie finality. "There is no meaning to any of this."

He had wanted to talk to her about Samira and Zeinab, but she had
blocked the way with her puzzling enigmatic response. He felt a burning
sensation in his chest and a savage longing for the older, simpler times. But
he still had a few more days to spend talking with Zeinab.

His life at the garage settled into a fixed pattern—work during the day,
sleep at night. He never tried to go back to the carnival, which he later
learned had closed down. The foreigners, who were arriving in the City
now in droves, were to use former fairgrounds for huge hotels which some
said would turn into giant cathouses where the most beautiful women
from among their former enemies would work. Some spoke of the project
sarcastically, others with a lustful desire. They said there was a growing
nostalgia for this type of woman who used to fill the City many years ago.
Ali eschewed weddings. Somehow, he was certain that Samira wouldn't
appear in the City again.

After a few days, he visited Zeinab for the second time. He told her
about having seen Samira and she said that often imagination seems like
reality. She said if it had really been Samira, she would have spoken to him
as she herself had done. When she noticed him poking around looking for
Um Gaber and the children, she said they don't come out of the room during the day. Then she broke down and cried saying that the children had
stopped growing, and Um Gaber was shriveling down to nothing.

But he saw on Zeinab's face a paleness. In her eyes there was a sort of flight to an obscure thing made clear in the following visit. At the door, he met the old woman who had opened the door for him the first time he came, and he found another woman with her. When he asked about Zeinab, she said she knew no one by that name. He brought up Um Gaber and the children, but the woman simply accused him of making up wild stories. He shot past her to see the rooms for himself but only found three ugly naked women and three old dark-skinned men. On his way out, he paused in the parlor on the verge of exploding with anger. He did nothing to the other woman who came toward him with an offer of vilest prostitution.

He spent the evening asking himself where reality stopped and imagination began. Zeinab's words slipped through his grasp. Where was Zeinab herself? He began to count the days he had spent in the City and found them to be eleven months during which he had accomplished nothing. He thought to himself that the time had come to make a break.

The next morning the garage owner didn't show up. He overheard the other mechanics talking about his having left for the city that his father had gone to. He was overtaken by a mysterious sense that something was about to happen. The next day he heard the other mechanics saying that the garage owner had received a phone call from his father in which he was informed that Safaa had been arrested with a large group of students who were demonstrating against enemy infiltration of the homeland.

The work routine didn't take its usual course that day, either. Types of cars were presented to them that had not been seen before in the area. Cars with long, wide, sturdy chassis, driven by mere girls and boys—or men with grotesque visages and huge bellies. They spoke with difficulty, and when they laughed, they laughed heartily. Ali saw the mechanics battling over the privilege of greeting these cars as they rolled in, then cursing the cars and their owners after they left. They said of one of the car owners, who always rode in the backseat of his car, which was driven by a black man, that he began his life as a dockworker until he struck it rich on a drug deal and ended up becoming the biggest wood trader in the country. The odd thing was that most of these cars had nothing wrong with them.

Ali crouched in a corner and kept his distance. He thought about Fareed, and he shook with fear for Safaa. This beautiful young girl with her slight frame like a butterfly moved as though she were a raven circling around a stone covering the bait in a trap hopping and jumping and dancing around before going to eat the food in the dirt-covered trap that snaps shut over her. He felt like something was snapping shut over his heart.

His mother told him the bird didn't end up in the trap because it was stupid, but because it was overcome by hunger. Anyone overcome by hunger loses his ability to reason. He asked her how, then, one might challenge hunger, and she said he must think of how he could eat. The only thing he really understood, however, was that in the end the beautiful bird fell. He saw Safaa looking at him from behind a high wall, calling to him from across the wide-open space of the light of day, telling him they had already waited too long.

The next day, he found all the workers in the garage crowded around a mechanic reading to them from the newspaper as astonishment covered their faces. As he listened, they directed curses at a man whose picture appeared in the paper. Ali moved into the crowd until he could see what they were all looking at. There he saw a strange picture of two corpses next to each other.

The picture was so grotesque it almost knocked him unconscious. He looked over at another picture next to it toward which everyone seemed to be directing their curses. It was the picture of a man whose face suggested violence, ruthlessness, and extreme cunning. He learned the whole story from the text below.

The article under the pictures explained that the smuggling kingpin who had smuggled across the western border had lost all his money. Subsequently, his partners and employees—whose names were not mentioned in the article—abandoned him and he turned to spying. He was eventually arrested in a broad intelligence gathering operation. They found that he had built a villa in a far away spot in the desert that he used as a smuggling headquarters. He had even imprisoned two unidentified persons in it for a long period of time with no food or drink until they died and their corpses rotted.

Ali scrutinized the picture of the two corpses. He vaguely recognized the two bloated faces surrounded by wild hair and tinged with a yellow shade of death.

He saw Laila, a flower wilting before his eyes; Suad, a moon besieged by dark clouds. He saw his father bend over in prayer and never stand back up; his mother take his younger sister by the hand and head out on an endless journey across the bridge. He almost asked himself how he had forgotten them all, how he had spent this past year, until his eyes were filled with a huge black Cadillac that stopped directly in front of him. The sun blazed in the heavens, and a full year had completed its cycle.

The owner of the garage stepped out of the car and walked to his office without looking at anyone. He was followed by two men of a strange bearing. The employees all stood around in a trance paralyzed and tongue-tied by what they saw. Ali, meanwhile, was making a resolution.

Finally, he awakened to the day he felt would never come. The garage spread desolate before him as on this summer night that gathered up all the heat and humidity of the ages. Those cars that would disappear in the morning appeared before him like crumbling tombs. He still did not know if the long laugh that plunged inside him like a dull knife was Samira's laugh or not. What he had come to know well, however, was that if he kept searching in the corners of the City, he would eventually find Neama, Zeidan's wife; and he would find the inspector and his wife as well. Perhaps, he would even find Zeidan and Abdullah. He also had come to know well that the hidden force no longer resounded in his head. In fact, he began to feel that his head was a void, and that he could hear the wind swimming through its empty spaces. How this last night was just like an entire year! He had no way of knowing what it felt like for a person to be put inside an oven; still, he felt now that he was in an oven whose floor was covered with the ashes of the bones of the many who had come before him.

He thought all night about the garage and how it had reverted to another owner. This new owner was going to destroy the few buildings around it to lay the foundation for a huge hotel that everyone said would be unlike any other hotel on God's earth. Its walls would consist entirely of cut glass. From outside, whoever would look at the walls would see himself, and whoever looked from inside would see everyone outside. It would go up one hundred stories and would have a landing pad on its roof. The inner walls would also be of glass, and transparent so that all the hotel guests could see one another, in the nude or any other circumstance. The important thing was that no one outside be able to see them. Once inside they were all one family. The area was so small though that the new owner planned to buy some of the other buildings and streets around the hotel and demolish them. He planned to construct a cinema that only the hotel guests could visit, and he would cut a canal from the sea to a wide pool in front of the hotel. It would be cut wide enough that the sea waves would make it all the way to the hotel pool and even ships would be able to pass through. In fact, the guests of the hotel would all either arrive by ship or arrive by aircraft. No one would be allowed to come by car, since that would mean that he was a local. Special cars were being prepared as well to take the hotel guests on guided tours, if any of them expressed a desire to leave this magical hotel. It was said that the motivations of the new owner were not merely an excess of disposable income. This was merely a secondary reason. The primary reason was that he had suffered from partial paralysis since birth. Because he had always been unable to travel and see the outside world, he had decided to bring the world there so he could see it up close, and that is what had produced in him this concept straight from the fires of hell.

Ali did not believe it at first. But then he asked himself, why shouldn't he believe it? He saw the owner of the garage gathering up his papers and a few small things of his in his bag, and he carried them to his Cadillac. He gave his manager some money with which to pay the workers, then he shot out into the street in his car as the workers cursed him because he had not told them good-bye. Meanwhile, Ali was wondering how he might manage to ask him about Safaa.

As the car disappeared, Ali felt as though his head had emptied completely. Only in the evening did the feeling in his body gradually return to normal. He looked up toward the stars clustered in the heavens, to the moon, and he asked himself what they were looking down upon. When he got up from his fitful attempt at sleep, he went to put on his pants and shirt but could not find them. After searching for them for some time, he realized he had never taken them off. He left all the small things he had accumulated over the course of the past year and left before the inhabitants of the City, that he had arrived in an entire year ago, awoke. He wondered what would happen now. That is what he was asking himself, and all he could think of was that it would not be good. That made him want to laugh.

It was still very early. He sat down in a small coffeehouse at the corner of a narrow street. It was empty, and its attendant was still sound asleep. Ali sat down hoping that he would not awaken him. When he did finally get up, the City itself was also starting to come alive. He watched people coming out of their houses; he did not know why this pleased him. They appeared to walk in crooked lines as though they had slept for one hundred years. He noted for the first time the strange hump on each of their backs. Most of them walked staring at the ground. He did not see any of them walking in pairs. He told himself if he kept watching them that way he would go mad, yet he could not get enough. The men who stopped at the coffeehouse stood for a while then walked around in circles several times, then chose a chair far from where the others were sitting. No one spoke to anyone else. The whole City seemed to him to wake up to a sort of intense competition.

The sun rose with vengeful flames, as though high noon was ascending in the early morning. He told himself everything had exceeded its proper balance. The City was like the Coast Guard man's corpulent wife: it knew everything, and it moved with difficulty. He got up.

He made his way under the blazing sun. He knew he would not meet another soul along the length of the beach, in contrast to what he saw when he first came to the City. He asked himself why he didn't seem to remember his family very well. His forgetting helped him to be less shocked when he went back and saw what he saw.

PART SIX

The End Time

THE SUPERINTENDENT

"What will you do now?" The old superintendent, with his two small colorless eyes, his white hair, and his red face full of wrinkles, smiled and pointed to the couch.

Ali looked at where he pointed as the old man said, "It won't be long now. Tomorrow at the latest a young man will come to take over my duties."

Then he pointed to the area in front of the lake, to the decrepit build ings. Ali looked at a large basket covered with white cloth as confusion spread over his face.

"Don't worry," the superintendent told him. "There's a salvage dealer who comes from the City in his donkey cart. He can take the two of you back with him."

Ali had been with the superintendent the previous night, during which he had heard from him things he would never forget. He had watched the sun leave its place at the height of the heavens, casting its final gaze—just as he did—on the twenty houses that were turning into rubble. From a distance he could see the parched, immobile cattails. He had always loved the sound of their rustling when the cool blast of the night or the morning breeze passed over them.

He stood on the platform of the station and looked at the houses that had become piles of stones to be raised by a huge bulldozer. A barechested young man, whose body glistened from a distance, was driving the bull-dozer and dumping the rubble into the lake. He imagined hundreds of fish being pounded to death under the onslaught of rocks and sand. All those fish must have multiplied after the fishing stopped and could be har-vested some day if the devastation ever came to a halt. He could tell from the crowd of bulldozers and building equipment and glistening halfnaked bodies that he should not go near the place — especially since he had seen three people stretching barbed wire to mark off the area. But would he be able to prevent the violent convulsions exploding inside of him that almost sent him flying into space in the direction of the site.

He quickly crossed over the two main tracks that the trains ran over as they headed toward and came back from the desert, the tracks under which he used to hunt hedgehogs. When he made it to the two tracks of the cursed train, he found them deteriorated, twisting in different direc-tions, and coming off the wooden crossbeams underneath the tracks. They were falling over and lying prone in the sand. A few scattered sparrows plucked at yellow worms that sparkled under the sun's rays. He had never seen such gaunt sparrows. They had hair and not feathers.

He thought of where the people had gone. Where might he find his family now? A tidal wave inside him was asking this question. He walked faster, feeling the stares of halfnaked foreigners looking at him from a faroff distance. He saw them pointing at him and then going off to work. They were talking, but he couldn't hear them. The air was filled with dust kicked up by huge machines. To his right in the distance, he saw wooden buildings with young men and women running in and out. Beyond these buildings to the west, he saw groups of tanks and armored cars with soldiers perched atop them like idols. By the time he had made it to the piles of white stones that had once been their houses, he felt as though the sun had cut inside his skull and lit a fire. For the first time, he could actually feel the world spinning and spinning. He felt the salt in the lake and the vast sea beyond it was from the tears of the people, and he fell over and sat on the ground, rigid as though he had turned to stone.

• • •

He lay fallen over the earth for a long time. By the time he woke up, he realized the day was gone as dusk's darkness began to engulf him. He felt neither hunger nor thirst. He only remembered that he had started his day in the contentious bustling City, and now ended it among the wispy vapors of a lost past.

He realized that the gunshots he heard had awakened him. He turned and saw brightly colored rockets flying through the air. He heard the sounds of contentious laughter and ribald screams coming to him from the wooden buildings in the distance. The interiors of the buildings were well lighted, and he could see people dancing in a frenzy inside. Once the earth was bathed in an expansive light, he looked up to the heavens and saw the moon rushing toward its apex.

The lake appeared as he had known it, pure and beautiful, with the lush moon glow glistening on its surface. But the banks of the water had become disgusting due to the piles of dirt and rock that had been dumped there. He thought to himself that they would surely fill up the whole lake. He didn't know why, but he began to gaze into the distance toward the bridge.

He began to look for the light of old lamps that they used to see every night to reassure themselves that God had created other humans to inhabit the world besides themselves, even though they often went to the bridge during the day to see these people for themselves. But now he didn't see the lights or even distinguish where the bridge was. He thought about where he could go on that poignant night. He arose and let his feet carry himself forward methodically.

The earth that he pounded on seemed to urge him not to leave it. But where were the people, the children, the buildings, the henhouses, and the clucking of the chickens?

Everything arose before him as it had once been. There were the stubby little onestory buildings. The curved gutters on the roofs stared down on him. Children chased each other and hid. They began to gather up their fishing equipment and prepare their traps. He met one of them carrying a wire basket full of the birds he had caught, and his face was caked with dirt. He ran away from them, not wanting to show what he had. His mother had warned him about envy. His father had trained him not to give away everything. Still, he found himself describing all he had caught—how much, how big, what it looked like. He also told them all about his father, who snored and farted all night. They roared with laughter and slapped him on the back. They whispered to one another about Suad and her men, and about Rawaieh, who would sit off at a distance, not realizing her bare thighs were exposed. One of them said that Arfeh was a sinister soldier and a son of a bitch because he patted women on their behinds. They laughed about Zeidan who, after his wife Neama physically pushed him out of the house and threatened that she would abandon him, cried and fell sprawled across the earth. Another said that Uncle Hamed was the strongest man in the place because he was slender and was able to run all day pulling the inspector's car behind him. But one of Abdullah's daughters said that her father was the strongest man because even though he was old, he walked all day in the desert by himself without fear. Then they all decided to go together to throw little pebbles at Sheikh Masoud as he sat by himself in the mosque. After that, they were going to throw dirt at the sleeping superintendent. Ali got up to go hunt hedgehogs. He prayed to God for the clouds to cover the moon so he would not have a shadow as he walked, and for his father to buy him a pair of sandals at the bridge so that the rocks wouldn't cut his feet and the heavy grease would not creep up between his toes. Then one of the boys said that Fareed would become president of the railway soon, that he would stop the salvage trains from running and send in their stead trains full of fine food and clothing. One of their mothers came to call her son, and they hid him between them, but she pulled him out from among them and knocked him around a bit and cursed him, as they laughed and ran in all different directions.

He almost fell back to the ground, but instead he bent over, gathered up a handful of earth, and kissed it. Yes. The young boy whose body had matured by a quantum leap and now had begun to shrink once again, leaned over and kissed the earth. A hidden force had chased after him and then settled in his head for an entire year. He had dreamed of throwing a rock that would fly through space and not fall. Now he had begun to realize that the past that had fled from his consciousness had also fled from existence. The young adult had learned what old men already knew. And yet he drew near this patch of earth. If he had been assured that God had a clear design that covered the length and breadth of the universe, he would have gone to him to ask the question revolving around his brain right now. Why had he created people and Satan and then spent so many years watching them? What sort of justice was this? Where was right and wrong in all this? Why had his mother lied to him? He would also ask Him why everything around him collapsed, even as his imagination returned. For the buildings that had surrounded him moments ago flew around in space, bathed in light, and then crashed into the lake. The children that were gathered in an innocent circle moments ago flew up with the buildings and crashed down with them into the water. He heard the sound of the terrifying crash and saw the awesome sight of the lake water flying up toward heaven and then crashing back down again.

But he gathered up his strength and began to walk. His foot stumbled over something sharp that he leaned over to pick up. He had become used to kicking away things in the road that might trip people as he walked. His mother had taught him this lesson, which she always summed up in the phrase, "The road belongs to God." He grabbed the sharp object and pulled at it and found it heavy. He realized that he was holding on to a fowarika stove. Like a simple man leaning over to lift his son up off the ground, he began to dig the fowarika out of the dirt so that he could pull it up. He finished digging and knew he was right. It was made of polished white zinc. It was Hamed's stove. The inspector had owned one like it, but he had abandoned the place and taken everything with him. His heart throbbed as he asked himself whether Zeinab had any knowledge, in her carefully concealed new home, of what had happened to her husband. Did Um Gaber know what had become of her son? The fowarika stove fell out of his hand, and he walked on. He thought about drawing near the aloof wooden buildings, so he changed his mind and headed toward the station lights.

The superintendent told him, "This is the whole story from the beginning. Nothing's left besides what Suad spoke to me about."

The man seemed to Ali to have slept forever as though he had closed his eyes to the entire world. The clock had struck midnight. As the superintendent spoke, sleep closed in on Ali after the long, hard day. Suad was in her new home in a corner of the offices of the superintendent, who from time to time tossed her a dry crust of bread. Ali thought to himself that she must have gone to sleep by then. He still had not seen her face. He still had not learned how this new creation managed to sleep.

He asked himself if anyone there knew the story of the superintendent. All the people who had been there before had never been aware of anything except their own presence in that place. They had not even had any connection to the City other than the salvage dealer, who came once a week to buy from them what they had pulled off the train; and even he had stopped coming when the train did. Could he have known? Did they really need to know any of the things the superintendent explained to them about what had happened before they arrived? Perhaps . . . no, certainly, at least dozens of years before any of them were born.

What the superintendent relayed about the first train that had come a hundred years ago was a history no one could remember—not even Sheikh Masoud, who had been their teacher at the time.

The superintendent said that those trains had consisted of three cars that were each open on both sides. They were driven by a small steam engine that puffed out thick smoke like the clouds of the sky. The cars were white and carried large groups of Englishmen wearing caps with long flaps on their sides, as well as a number of Turks with sculpted moustaches that turned up on either side and red fezzes tilted backward. They had all debarked on that spot, which was an empty space at the time but had come to be the train station. They had pointed to the spot where the big wooden guardrail was now collapsed over the ground, to that spot which was empty at the time, but now the train tracks ran over it, and the rail lay beside it. Finally they pointed to the vast desert itself and began laying track over which the trains ran into its very heart, and all the way to its end.

The superintendent said that after they had pointed around at these places, they returned to their threecar train. Later, another train came, and they started to build everything. This second train brought with it hundreds of workers from the north and the south of the country who were overseen by a vicious Englishman and a few Turks carrying whips that they spent some of the time brandishing and the rest cracking across the backs of the workers.

The sand was fine, but right below it lay a firm layer of rock that had to be cut through in order for the rails to be put down. The men from the North and the South laid the tracks for the salvage train first, then they spent a long time completing the rest of the railway out into the depths of the desert.

Once they had finished building the station, the first superintendent arrived driving the first train. He was also the grandfather of the present superintendent. This first manager had seen everything. He had seen the workers from the North and the South disappearing off in the horizon behind the track they were laying down in the sand. But only a few days later, he would see them coming back two at a time each day. They were transported on the coach that later became the inspector's coach, and it was pushed by two strong men.

The coach used to stop at the station. The two strong men who had pushed it back would drag the corpses of the two dead men off and throw them into the river. That first superintendent began to realize that one of the men he saw pushing the coach would return after a few days as a rigid corpse borne by the vehicle, to be thrown into the river by two other men. When that first superintendent asked those who pushed the cart why the corpses weren't returned to their homes to be buried, he would be told,

"Here we have neither home nor country." The superintendent had watched when the English and the Turks carelessly motioned toward the lake as they spoke in their language.

After that, the threecar trains came back, driven by a new conductor. When the first superintendent asked him what he had come for, the conductor said he came to take back whoever was left. He went on with the train deep into the heart of the desert. A few days later, he came back with the Turks and the Englishman. The superintendent didn't even ask about his countrymen, who had come from the South and the North. He knew the ones that weren't tossed in the lake were buried under the sands of the desert, which covered everything. That was the reason that first superintendent had always told his son, the father of the current superintendent, that he did not want to live to see the day when the dead spirits rose again from the lake, because on that day no one would be shown mercy.

Ali thought about Zeidan and the lake, Abdullah and the desert. Then the superintendent shocked him with his powers of telepathy by saying that he would get to Zeidan and Abdullah in a little while. The superintendent said that all of this had been the beginning and not the end. A great war had erupted in the world. His father became the new superintendent and watched as train after train passed bearing barefoot men with torn clothing from the north and south of the land. They gathered in the distance in a huge camp where they went through training to learn how to kill. He saw them come back after their course wearing military uniforms, carrying rifles that were longer than they were. But their countenances remained just as yellow; their eyes still skirted about; the bones of their faces still protruded out from under their flesh; and their long legs, exposed at the bottom of their short trousers, remained thin with bulging veins that crisscrossed here and there, like two train tracks meeting at a switch point.

The second superintendent stayed there for a long time, watching the trains come with young men from the north and south of the land, who met in the camp at a distance and came back as soldiers and passing new recruits on their way out. But once a group of soldiers left, he never saw them again.

One day the threecar train came back, carrying a group of British officers. There were no Turks this time. The second superintendent understood from what they said to each other, since he knew some of their language, that the men who they were training to be soldiers would be flown off to wage war in the distant land of the foreigners beyond the great blue lake. They would die there and their corpses would be dumped in the lakes and rivers or left under the sun in the valleys or the frost on the hilltops to be eaten away by the vultures.

The second superintendent plunged into grief because the large number of countrymen he saw passing through made him feel no one would be left. But the war ended quickly, and the trains filled with soldiers in training stopped coming.

Then one blazing hot day about a year after the war had ended, the second superintendent jumped up off the couch in his office, the same couch that the third superintendent always slept on now, and began pounding his forehead with anger. He ran out of the station crazed and frightened, and he kept going until he reached the heart of the desert. He had suddenly remembered after all these months that a few days before the war ended, a huge train filled with his countrymen from the north and the south of the land came though on its way to the camp, then came back empty. No other train came to bring them back, and he never saw them pass back through.

The third superintendent said that his father, the second superintendent, kept running night and day for an entire two weeks, neither eating nor drinking nor stopping to rest, until his nose clogged up with a rotten smell filling the air. He was sure that he had remembered rightly, and in fact, he did find a huge pile of bones and skulls, exactly as he had suspected. He also found footprints even though a year had passed, and he understood that during the year the spirits had been moving across the sands.

The feet seemed to have gone off in all directions: some southward toward the lake, some to the east toward the station, some toward the west and the abyss of desert, and the rest to the north. Where the footsteps ended, he found bones. At least that's what he found when he went north or east. But he couldn't walk behind footsteps heading toward the south or the west. These either went toward the lake or penetrated deep into the desert without ending. He became exhausted and went back to the station and never explained to anyone how he had been able to bear it all. He decided to close his eyes to the affairs of the world, and he was overcome with fear every time he remembered his father telling him not to wait for the day in which the lake and the desert would convulse and throw up the dead spirits. He grew old and senile overnight. Another great war was about to ignite in the world by the time he died, just after he had told his son, the third superintendent, to sleep since there was nothing left in the world that deserved to be seen. This was after he had relayed to him all that had happened to him.

But the third superintendent decided that he would do something else — or at least that's how he told it. He practiced being asleep and awake at the same time. He managed to become a sleeper with senses wideawake. He said that he had seen Ali throwing dirt at him many a time, but he never felt like awakening. He had seen trains that he would not forget, that bore not only men from the north and the south of the land, but also Indians, Africans, Australians, and New Zealanders. The trains tossed them out and went back empty. Gaber's father and Um Gaber had been the first to come to live there. The father spent most of the day with the superintendent. He asked him why they brought him to this place with twenty dwellings, where he had neither a supervisor nor people to supervise. There was no way one man could maintain the rail lines. And no trains traveled over those two tracks that deadended at the railway bumper. The salvage train had still not appeared. The superintendent was still training himself to be awake and asleep at the same time, and he had plenty of spare time to talk to Gaber's father. But he was still asking where these soldiers were headed.

On the night of the immense siege, Germans and Italians came out of the west, preceded by their air force. The darkness filled with a thousand rays of light coming out of the lake and the desert. He knew that the spirits of the dead, of which his grandfather spoke and whose footsteps his father had followed, were rising. He could never have believed that the soldiers coming across the sea from the east were coming all the way from the other side of the sea, and the rays of light grew denser every night, because (he thought) the corpses were being thrown in the lake from a distance, or were being left out on the sands of the open desert.

He told Ali that Gaber's father decided that as long as he had no supervisor and no one to supervise he would fish. The superintendent started to warn him not to do this, but he didn't go through with it. One day, he was shocked to find Gaber's father coming and telling him about a golden sea bass coming out of the water and speaking to him. At that time the superintendent spent most evenings up late talking at the house of Gaber's father. But once Gaber's father told the superintendent that he came back from fishing shaking after every conversation and that he went to sleep begging for a blanket to protect him from the cold that racked his body, the superintendent decided not to talk to him again. He had advanced quite a bit in his state of sleeping and waking simultaneously. He told Ali that a night didn't pass without his hearing sounds coming out of the night from the lake and the desert. Laughter, screams, and extended wailings.

Instead of listening to the tales of the superintendent as bits of nostalgia, Ali sat there and asked himself where the true and the false in all of it was. He yearned to listen to the tales told by Suad. The superintendent told him that one day he had awakened for the first time to find that the twenty dwellings had filled up. He had seen the workers changing shifts, exhausted, cast across the earth behind the station after work, as though the world had forgotten them.

When Sheikh Masoud first arrived, he had not yet retired and devoted himself to service in the mosque. He used to pass the time with him after they prayed the final prayer of the day together. (He never had any trouble waking up for prayer). He often tried to warn Sheikh Masoud about coming trials and tribulations, but the Sheikh kept throwing the conversation back to old talk about the jinn and what he did with them. He told the superintendent that for the longest time, he believed that his purpose in this world was to torture the jinn. They were the enemies of all the prophets. The only one they submitted to was Solomon. Sheikh Masoud had devoted a great deal of his time to learning their signs and secrets, and through his knowledge had become their tormentor. If a female jinni, for example, fell in love with a young mortal man, he summoned her and ordered her to love whatever other thing he wished. He almost always picked some old man. And when he learned that a jinni had fallen in love with a young lady, he summoned him and caused him to fall madly in love with an old grayhaired woman. He often ended up marrying jinn of the same sex to one another, and he talked of destroying their capacity to love. Surely, it was the jinn themselves who had killed him, for such oppression is unbearable even for them. It did not help spare Sheikh Masoud that he stopped enchanting them after marrying Suad.

He moved up to the basket and looked inside to see whether Suad was listening to him or not, and he found her there smiling at him. He thought for a moment about stopping but decided to keep talking.

He told Ali that only the good could hear the sounds that he heard coming out of the lake and the desert, along with noble young men descended from the martyr Hussein, whom the prophet had called the young master of paradise, but he knew that trying to respond to it meant death, and that was something that the naive Zeidan, whose dark body in spite of the scars from the boils that covered it was carved out of an emerging light, had not understood. That was why Zeidan never came out of the lake, and why the corpse that they had found could never have been his corpse.

"Did Zeidan die?" Ali asked in shock.

"They found a corpse that resembled him, but his kind does not die."

"Whose corpse is it then?"

"It must have been one of the city dwellers, murdered by the people from the bridge and tossed into the lake. Or it could have been an old corpse of someone that had been thrown into the lake."

Ali became even more upset. "Could that have really happened?"

The superintendent answered him knowingly, "Even more than that can happen to good people."

Ali asked himself how much longer it would be until the dawn broke, but the superintendent interrupted his thoughts to shock him once again: "Not only that, but the body that they found in the desert wasn't Abdullah's either."

"Did he die too?" Ali asked sorrowfully.

"They found the corpse of a man with a hunchback."

Ali whispered back an almost inaudible whisper, "Why then, do you say it wasn't him?"

"Because I know what it was he wanted. He wanted to stop the sun or change its direction, and he could do it too."

"I couldn't be more exhausted," Ali said. "I want to sleep through whatever's left of the night."

"Do you want to ask about anything else?" the superintendent asked.

But there was capitulation in Ali's voice as he answered, "I don't know. You can go on anyway, if you wish."

"The sun didn't appear for several days," the superintendent said. "When it came back a month ago, no one was left but those people," and he motioned toward the foreigners, "and the new inspector and the replacements for Hamed, Gaber, Zeidan, and Sheikh Masoud."

Then the superintendent went into what Suad had said. After the sun had dawned anew, those living creatures that had survived the long eclipse celebrated. Gunshots were heard being fired into the air from the wooden dwellings of the foreigners, and tumultuous late nights erupted. The superintendent had seen it himself. But the question still circulated among those remaining in the twenty dwellings about the mystery of what had happened. How had all the old inhabitants disappeared and left only the new comers? They did not realize that Suad and Laila were still there.

Suad said that she had spent the entire long period of darkness clinging to Laila, and as the darkness continued, she became more frightened, and she held on to Laila more tightly as the two began to weep. The torrent of tears that poured out of the two of them and acted like a glue that covered their two faces and their breasts and turned into a sort of paste that stuck them together even more.

The superintendent said that once the sun finally came back out, a train carrying some policemen came to take whoever was left of the workers and their families to a remote site in the desert. But the policemen hadn't even noticed Laila and Suad. They had become a pair of pale, dry flakes from excessive hunger and thirst. They had ingested nothing throughout the long period of darkness other than the salt from their tears that had built up on their bodies. That's how the superintendent had found them. After the long period of darkness he felt he had lost his ability to be both conscious and sleeping. In fact, he didn't know if he could still sleep. He waited several days wondering what to do, until finally the train came to take away the rest of the workers and their families. After it left, he went out to survey the empty houses. He pushed in the door of one of them and found Laila and Suad crowded into a corner.

He found Suad crawling on her hands and knees looking for any crust of moldy bread with which to sustain herself.

He brought them food and drink and then left. Then he became afraid that the foreigners would demolish the houses on top of them, so he brought them with him to the station the next day once they had regained some strength. He kept feeding them until enough consciousness returned to them that they burst into tears once again.

After that Laila had decided to go to the City to look for Ali. He was the only person left whom she knew. Suad refused to go along insisting that he would come back. The superintendent kept feeding her, and she grew stronger everyday.

She was becoming a picture of her former self, when suddenly he was surprised to find her transforming back to the opposite extreme. She grew pale and thin once again after only a few days. Her face had always been beautiful, but now it was a face with no body. Her wiry legs that were as wide as fingers seemed to come straight out of her neck, as did her two matchstickthin arms. She shrunk until the superintendent put her in a basket, covered her with a sheer piece of cloth, and invoked God's grace and omnipotence.

The superintendent was silent for a moment during which Ali looked around at his office for the first time. It had a couch upon which he did most of his sleeping, a small desk, and a glass filing cabinet with a lock on it. Some of his clothes were hung in a corner over a kerosene stove with a teapot and some cups on it. There was an old telephone with its receiver left off the hook in one corner. In a third was the basket in which he had placed Suad.

The superintendent noticed the tears welling up in Ali's eyes and said, "It's all over now, isn't it?"

Ali was thinking about Laila in the cutthroat metropolis full of city dwellers, of his family disappearing in the dark streets of the city. The place where dreams began and nightmares ended, or where dreams ended and new nightmares began. He felt a fire burning his insides. It was that oppressive drive to distinguish the truth from the lies that threatened to kill so many. He had never forgotten that in spite of his strength and the maturation of his body that he was still young in terms of age and experience. Now he realized that over the course of the past two days, during the time he had needed it most, he had lost a great deal of his physical strength. What God could solve this puzzle? What hidden force could stand in opposition to this inscrutable talisman?

Ali's train of thought was cut off by the sound of a locomotive coming out of the desert.

It stopped in front of the station's platform. Ali heard the sound of the wheels grinding against the rails and the light collapsing together of the cars. He felt that he was listening to a poignant melody whose absence had strung out time itself. It was exactly midnight when it ground to a halt.

He and the superintendent came out to behold the sight. It bore huge burlap sacks, one of which had been torn during the journey, and its contents were spilling out over the side of the train car near the platform. The sack contained yellow sand.

Ali looked over at the superintendent and found that his eyes were bulging, just as were Ali's. They each knew what the other was thinking. But the old man laughed and sarcastically said, "Perhaps they are trying to move the desert."

The train lurched forward slightly until they found themselves looking into an old passenger car with open windows that seemed deserted. Who, after all, would ride a passenger car connected to the middle of a freight train? But then they noticed a man in thick clothing with a dark blanket wrapped around himself hopping down from the caboose and coming toward them.

As he came into view beneath the pale lights of the station, he took on the appearance of a short tree trunk that had uprooted itself and began to walk.

The strangely formed man greeted them and then asked, "Have you been here long?"

"For more than thirty years."

The superintendent smiled sorrowfully.

"Did you know the railway workers that were living over there?"

He pointed to the place where the houses—whose ruins were blocked by the superintendent's office—had been. Ali's attention was drawn, and he went up on his tiptoes. The superintendent answered as though he spoke of a long-forgotten time.

"Yes. I knew them all."

The stranger said as though he were in a rush, "The train won't stop for long, and I don't have time to go over to them. I just wanted to pass a message on to two people, one named Gaber and the other Hamed, that my name is Masaad and that I said they should come and that I've been waiting for them until I'm about to turn blue."

Ali felt as though he had turned into a railway bumper exposed under the bright sun, while the superintendent said inattentively, "I'll tell them."

"Tell them I'll try to contact them soon, but the main thing is that they shouldn't try to come to me since as you can see, I'm going back. They'll understand completely what you're talking about."

The train began to move again, so he left them there on the platform and jumped into the empty passenger car. The train moved with a painful slowness, as though it didn't want to leave the ground beneath it. The moon hung loftily in the heavens behind the station and gently descended as its glow grew stronger and more brilliant. Both the superintendent and Ali felt the strength of its glow. It drew near to becoming a full moon, then magically became one. They both felt as though it turned into a sun illuminating the dead of night from the excessive glow that inundated that spot. It kept descending until they both thought they could jump up and grab it. The train cars glistened as they passed before them and flashed bits of the incomprehensible, garbled graffiti that children had scrawled in chalk on their side at the stations.

By the time the caboose was passing before them, the moon had turned into streaks of light. Then they both caught sight of a young man on top of the car wrapped in a jet-black cloak to protect against the damp night and the wind of the journey. But his face was exposed and illumi-nated against the blackness of his wrap.

"It's the train guard," the superintendent said. "He's always on the ca-boose."

Ali did not hear him. He focused on the brightly lit face and found himself struggling with an urge to leap onto the train that was rapidly car-rying it away.

As the moon returned to its natural place in the heavens with sadness and remorse, the superintendent looked around for Ali and did not find him. Ali was running with the intensity of a madman between the two rails behind the train. The superintendent watched him and heard him call out in shouts that filled the space around them, "Mursi! Mursi!"

As the moon drew back, the face of the guard remained illuminated, and Ali continued to race after the train and call out. He felt the guard's eyes focused on him as he stared back.

But the guard did not seem to respond to Ali's cries, even with a wave. He continued to sit frozen like a black stone with a small white hole where his face was. Ali watched as his hands brought up to his mouth a thing that Ali could not see, but from the way it was held and the sound he heard it making, he could tell that it was a nay flute. The guard had begun to play it. The passing shadows flickered over his face and hands and flashed all over the caboose and all over the night, which was calm except for the sound of the flute still dancing in Ali's ears.

As he walked back panting, he realized that he had run a great distance. It took him an hour to walk back. He could not believe that he had not tripped while he was running across the grease-covered wood and stones. He remembered Zeinab once telling him about the fine line between the real and the imaginary. But he was sure in his sadness at that moment that what he had seen was completely real. He could never forget the face of Mursi, who had for Samira's sake isolated himself in the caboose where he had hidden away coins and precious metals for her.

For the first time in his life, Ali wished he could become what Suad had become, an ugly thing that no one looked at, shrinking away until he disappeared. The lights of the switch house came into view, and he remembered old Abdel Nur. He felt that even if he exerted himself more he could not bear any more brutal nostalgia. He made it to the station and found the superintendent sitting and crying silently.

The moment he saw Ali he said, "You're the only one left, my son. You must pull yourself together and find a way."

Ali had needed someone to tell him that. The cells in his body felt relaxed as he walked. A sweet sleep pressed his eyes closed for the first time in a long while.

The superintendent pointed to the seller of used goods coming toward them from a distance. Ali looked up to find him riding a cart pulled by a mule, as though he himself had created the universe so that he could ride through it by himself. Ali turned to the superintendent.

"Let me bid you farewell, then," he said to him.

He embraced the superintendent and kissed him on each cheek. The superintendent patted him on the back and said, "I'm no longer afraid for you. You've borne much, and you've become a real man."

Ali walked away struggling against tears. He gently raised the basket in the corner on to his shoulders as he felt his heart in his chest tearing in two. The basket seemed heavy. Before he made it to the seller's cart that stopped at some distance from the station, with the seller silently staring and the old, black, mangy mule kicking at the ground with his right hoof, Ali turned to cast one final look back at the place.

The sun was climbing back up toward the heavens, even more yellow than it should have been. The bulldozers had gone back to work energetically. Dust floated up from every spot to envelop the lake and the cattails and the half-naked bodies. His vision of the spot began to evaporate; he no longer saw anything except an interminable empty space. He only remembered the final word of the superintendent.

He gently set the basket down on the cart and jumped up next to the stone silent driver who seemed to have known beforehand that he was coming just for Ali. He tugged at the mule and spun the cart around. The cart shook as it passed over the uneven ground, and he stretched out his arm to hold down the basket. Underneath this sheer piece of cloth was the most beautiful of women.

He was inundated with feelings that the world had emptied out of everything but the two of them and that it was up to Suad and himself to procreate a new race, as Adam and Eve had in the first days. This beautiful woman had awaited him even before he was born. Yes. She had told him this, when she bid him farewell. And yet. No. He had betrayed her. For the day that she had chosen to open up to him the doors of euphoria was the day he had decided to leave for the City and leave her with the curse of waiting. But it had been the hidden force that had arisen within him and pushed him in that direction. What could a young boy do to resist?

A sense of tragedy closed in on him from all sides, and an oppressive feeling of guilt raged in his heart like the winds of the desert during a sand-storm, and he asked himself sorrowfully of what such a small heart could be so guilty.

He saw the man's dark face, which had grown wrinkled and haggard. The mangy mule seemed to wriggle in its halter more than walk. He said to himself that all the years that had passed were not enough to have de-stroyed all this, and he motioned to the driver to stop.

A lake of perspiration began to gather on his forehead. Searing flames rushed up out of his heart and up to his lips. For the first time—and possi-bly the last—he felt an urge to see Suad's face. To kiss her. The woman who had waited for him since he was still in his mother's womb had never received anything from him. He felt that if he kissed her at that moment she would transform into a woman even more beautiful than before, and the two of them would begin a new era unlike anything that mankind had seen before. They would rise together over all troubles and come back down in the cutthroat City knowing things he had not known before. He would warn the populace of the hidden dangers of which no one had warned them, and she would be at his side, with no one able to catch her or stand in front of her except for him, for he was the boy whose body had matured by a quantum leap that day and who had sought to hurl the stone that would never come down out of space.

Then, like a heartbroken lover, he moved back. He leaned over the sheer piece of cloth. His hands trembled as he took hold of it to raise it off the basket.

He knew that he would need all of his strength to bear such a strange appearance of that most beautiful woman, of the remains of a body that parched with thirst for men long dead, a body full of tempestuous desire and a sensuousness unequalled among women of this world or the next. But surely the sight of her thick, black hair drinking up the sun's light would ward off any sort of fear and spellbind his vision of her beauty, which he would feel take him like a small, warm home. He would not even be able to see whatever ugliness might be beneath that pure visage.

He raised the piece of cloth and saw the sun cast into the basket whose darkness, like the tender night, drank out its heat and then spread its peace onto her face. She was smiling like a specter of the moon plunging into the waters of the lake, or onto the green stems of the cattails on a calm autumn evening. He saw the wide eyes shining and speaking in their own tongue of a longing repressed for millennia, only to be overcome once again by a ceaseless desire and a fear whose source no one knew. The eyelashes flashed, and bright tears like pearls streaked across the soft, quiet cheeks. The lips quivered and formed a smile that beckoned to his eyes. He bent over further until his head was almost inside the basket, but it still did not block the light of the sun reflecting off the illuminated face. His head looked straight over it as though the sun were streaking right through him. Or as though his head and her face became specters of a radiant morning sun in a moment outside of time, in which he felt the entire cosmos crystallized joyfully inside a tattered old basket.

As he came closer, he felt the heat rising up into his face rocking his body and soul. He did not blink as his lips drew near. He remembered this later. As the lips touched, he felt a new, fresh blood rushing through his body. He did not blink. He remembered it later. His opened eyes looked into the most beautiful eyes of any woman, one who had been married to an old man, who had been craved with a passion by men of all ages, on account of whom women had slept afire, who had caused the cosmos to clamor and shower down on her in fragments, unable to maintain itself in her presence. A woman well known by the heavens, to which she exposed her breast at the mere pouring down of drops of rain. She was well known by the sun that disappeared and then came back humbly, shining from the light she cast off, unable to stay away from her any longer. A woman whose eyes said that Laila, who had gone to the City, would be the most beautiful woman there. She had clung to her in the dark for a long time and even drank her tears, and it was up to him now to catch her and rescue her from her predators. His eyes were opened wide before her own. He would remember that always. He would keep remembering until he died watching the stones rain down before him. The people would tell him that these were the stones that people threw when you told them to during an earlier time. The stones were back to see you before dying. They would fly again though one day, for there was no way to stop them. In fact, they are still throwing their beautiful stones, celebrated and known everywhere, from every spot and in all ages. Repeating what you had said to them: that there is a difference between the real and the imaginary, and between the truth and a lie.

Then, he saw the eyes of the most beautiful and intelligent woman blinking in the fire. He felt the two warm lips grow cold, and he kept his face hanging over the face across which a pallor began to spread. The sun was no longer penetrating his head, and his head and her face were no longer specters of the sun on a radiant morning. The basket filled with darkness and shadows. There was no longer anything left in it, that became clear. He raised his face out of the basket with neither tears nor sorrow. She had whispered to him to leave the cart. He would always remember that later. For reasons he did not fully comprehend, the universe became even more radiant, and he began to regain his strength. The tears falling from his eyes still warmed his cheeks. He could now leave this damned coach with its old driver and mange-ridden mule.

He jumped to the ground, and the mule driver sped up as though he had been waiting for him to do so. He watched the basket shaking in front of him atop the rocking cart that appeared very small in the midst of the enormous white universe that swallowed up all things. A stone of unknown source fell before him. Then another. Then a third. He bent over and picked up one of the stones and threw it with all his strength. It flew before him without falling. He followed it with his eyes until it disappeared into space. He threw a second one and followed until it also disappeared. He threw a third, and he felt that he himself was the one flying through space and that his clothes were flapping in the wind. He realized his body had gone back to how it had been before. He kept fingering stones that disappeared until he arrived at the beginning to the modern paved road that led to the City. He asked himself how many stones he would want to fling there. He remembered telling the Coast Guard officer that he was an orphan. Picking up the first stone he found along the paved road, he threw with all his might and it dropped a short distance away. All the old images raced out of his mind, and he screamed from his innermost depths, "Who is left for this wild young man now?" and he knew he had bid farewell forever to the age of dreams and imagining.

Afterword

MICHAEL BEARD

A small community's painful decline as the contemporary economy abandons it is not a new theme in literature. Students of English poetry still run into it as early as Oliver Goldsmith's "Deserted Village," which dates back to 1770, but when we find the same theme in a contemporary novel we are likely to expect a more abrasive point of view, something like socialist realism with a distant observer for a narrator, like the point of view we know from Zola or Abdelrahman Munif or, perhaps, the Steinbeck of *Grapes of Wrath*. We may not expect the lyrical attributes of *Distant Train*.

The individuals who shape the events of *Distant Train*—Suad, Laila, Abdallah, Ali—are appealing creations, but the reader is likely to intuit that down deep the collective is the real focus, and one result is a narrative with a lyrical circling quality. Abdel Meguid establishes that focus early on, in the description of the children playing with tops ("The top spun on his palm and his gaze locked into it until his eyes spun with it, his head spun with it, time itself spun") or in the scene of the women's dance that is the first event of the narrative. Striking as the description of the dance is, the book's beginning is even more compelling as we listen to the women of the community circling the subject in the manner of a chorus:

"It's as though she hasn't had to suffer through the summer."

"As though she weren't bothered when the train didn't come."

"She laughs all day and night."

"She goes to meet Fareed on the roof."

"Her husband defies death."

"Why are you stopping, Suad?"

"She's crying from happiness."

"We play the drum to keep her moving."

The buoyancy of musical repetition balances the prolonged sense of incoming calamity, and it is a narrative rhythm that distinguishes Abdel Meguid's entire presentation.

Abdel Meguid's career is perceived among Egyptian readers as slightly apart from the more visible "Generation of the Sixties." (He was born in 1946, which makes him a little younger than the most prominent among them—Gamal al-Ghitany, Yusuf al-Qaid, Ibrahim Aslan, Edouard al-Kharrat, or Sonallah Ibrahim.) *Al-Masâfât* (literally, just "The Distances") appeared in 1983, Abdel Meguid's third novel. The earlier two, *Lailat al-'ishq wa al-dam* (Night of Love and Blood) and *Al-Sayyâd wa al-yamâm* (The Hunter and the Pigeons), are less socially focused, less "committed" but also explore less lyrical directions.

Recent criticism has suggested that *Distant Train* is at the center of a movement to develop an indigenous magic realism in Arabic culture. If so, it isn't simply a case of influence, since Abdel Meguid has suggested that he read Garcia Marquez (in translation) only after 1983. Meanwhile, *Al-Balda al-ukhra* (The Other Village) was the occasion for his winning the Naguib Mahfouz Award in 1996; in the same year *La Ahad yanam fil Iskandriya* (No One Sleeps in Alexandria) was awarded the "novel of the year" at the Cairo International Book Fair. We will be pleased if our publication of *Distant Trains* allows Abdel Megid's work to be acknowledged in the Anglophone world as well.